Firefighter Jason Merone was severely burned and injured when the building he and his best friend were in collapsed as they were rescuing a young child. Depressed and nearly inconsolable, it's not until his home care nurse, Zoe Calder, spots the telltale signs of severe depression and confronts him that Jason finds the will to live.

A few weeks later, Zoe is sexually assaulted by a man she meets through a dating app, and when he's caught and her transgender identity is revealed, Jason's transphobic mother makes sure she loses her job.

Jason and Zoe stay in touch, as they've built a close friendship, but when Zoe's home is torched, she runs for her life, leaving Jason feeling bereft from the loss of what he knows could be a lasting relationship. Jason learns that Zoe's troubles aren't over, and he must work to identify who's behind it all in time to save her.

THROUGH THE INFERNO

The Inferno, Book One

Jessi Noelle

A NineStar Press Publication

Published by NineStar Press
P.O. Box 91792,
Albuquerque, New Mexico, 87199 USA.
www.ninestarpress.com

Through the Inferno

Printed in the USA
First Edition
September, 2019

Print ISBN: 978-1-951057-42-8

Also available in eBook, ISBN: 978-1-951057-41-1

Warning: This book contains sexually explicit content, which may only be suitable for mature readers, depictions of graphic violence, non-explicit rape, fire tragedy, including death of a child, firefighter funeral, suicide ideation, homophobia, and transphobia.

For Nathan and Daniel and Mom and Bri. I love you!

Chapter One

Jason Merone

JASON MERONE HELD three aces to go along with the two eights on the board. *Dead man's hand,* he thought, pondering the best way to string along the other guys in the pot for the most chips. The game was Texas Hold'em, and he was a great white in a guppy pond.

The Sunday night poker game at Station 7 of the Biloxi Fire Department was winding down. Dinner was devoured and cleaned up, letting the crew relax until the shift's end at 6:30 in the morning. Weekends came with no scheduled duties other than cleaning the surrounding housing area of the fire station. The only call they'd responded to was a fender bender on the exit ramp of the interstate, fortunately with no injuries, making a quick and easy run.

"Too rich for me," Captain Engmeyer said after Jason raised, folding his hand and stepping away from the table with a muttered, "Gonna drain the main vein."

Down to two and time to show. He flipped his cards, showing the nuts.

"Mutha fuck!" The red-faced veteran opposite him yelled as he slapped his beaten flush to the table. Everyone at the table laughed. "Shit, Truffy. I thought for sure I had you beat, the way you were betting."

"Hell, Vince," Jason retorted to the veteran of four years. "You oughta know by now the house always wins." He grinned crookedly, pulling the chips, worth about twenty bucks, over to his side and adding them to his pile.

His phone chirped before the next hand, and he glanced at the screen. Jenna. *Not a good time, love.* He let his girlfriend's call go to voice mail and shook his head at the expectant faces at the table. "What? I'll talk to her later. Deal, deal."

It only took another twenty minutes to finish collecting the rest of the chips from the guys.

THE KLAXON SOUNDED just before three a.m. Jason woke, instantly alert. Around him, the other guys threw off covers and made a mad dash to the restroom. No one wanted to be stuck on a scene for hours while needing to pee. He double-timed to the truck, wiping the crusty sleep out of his eyes.

Jason was almost to the driver's side door before he remembered; Vince, newly certified and soon to be officially promoted to pump engineer, was taking driving duties this shift. His abrupt change of direction caused him to smack into Vince's shoulder.

"Whoops, sorry, dude. Forgot you were driving today."

"Naw, Truffy, you're good." Vince opened the door and slid behind the wheel.

For Jason, putting on turnouts was a ritual, a centering moment of zen and muscle memory before charging into chaos. He threw the Nomex hood over his head as he slid his feet into the boots. In a swift movement, he grabbed the suspender straps to bring the pants up to his waist and shrugged them over his shoulders, then swung his arms into his coat. The faint smell of sweat and old fires wafted around him as he fastened the pants and jacket shut. Helmet, gloves, and air tank would be added while en route. *Inventory: check, check, check. Ready to rock!*

Ritual complete, Jason swung into his seat, back against the driver's compartment. Dave, his best friend, crashed into the seat facing him, grumbling at being woken up. Dave sucked at poker, busting out early and going to bed. Although he only did the bare minimum around the station, no one outworked him at a scene, and there was no one Jason would rather have covering his ass in a fire.

The Engine pulled out of the station within two and a half minutes. Up front, the captain radioed the en route confirmation.

"Copy en route, Engine 7," the dispatcher said over the engine and siren noise. "Responding to River Oakes Manor at 1787 Winding Way Road, between Stanton and Hollyberry Streets, for reports of fire involving multiple apartment units, possible persons still inside."

Faces went grim as the team absorbed the information. "Police unit en route confirms heavy smoke," the dispatcher continued her litany. "Engines 3, 5, and 8 also dispatched with Ladder 2 and Ladder 9. EMS and PD confirmed en route. Time is 02:57."

Captain Engmeyer shifted to face the crew in the back, steel-gray eyes serious, his mouth drawn into a grim line. "Okay, guys, this is gonna be real. We'll be first on scene. Jason and Dave, I want you on the first line in. Get in there, knock it down as you go, clear as many units as you can. Scott, Billy, I want you guys to set up an attack line near their point of entry. I'll direct the incoming engines until the battalion chief arrives on scene. Let's stay safe and get it done!"

Jason looked back over at Dave, whose game face likely mirrored his own, and noticed his focus fixed outside the window. He turned his head in the direction Dave stared and saw the orange glow of flames on the horizon. Dave shifted his attention to Jason, and held up a fist. "Let's kick the tires and fight the fires!" they said in unison as they bumped knuckles, a ritual dating back to when they were freshmen on the high school football team. A few practiced flicks secured the air tanks to their backs, followed by the facemasks and helmets. They pulled the bulky gloves on last. Dave unhitched the Halligan tool, a round metal bar with prongs on one end and flat scoop on the other, and held it vertically between his legs, thrumming a nervous beat against it with his leather-clad fingers.

Final check—Jason did one last inventory—*good to go*. The muscles in his legs began to twitch in anticipation of the looming combat. No matter how many fires he fought, each one set his heart pounding like the first.

Upon arrival at the scene, they were slowed by the sheer number of gawking civilians crowded outside in various degrees of panic. Vince finally maneuvered the engine to the sweet spot, close enough to set up operations, but not too close in case the building collapsed.

Time to go to work.

THE BUILDING DANCED with flames, spewing inky gray-black smoke.

With Dave behind him, Jason held the nozzle and moved into position. Next to them, Scott and Billy did the same. At his signal, Vince pumped water through the line, building pressure. The hose firmed in his hands, and Jason opened the nozzle to vent air and confirm a cone-shaped stream. They approached the entrance of the two-story building, a double door leading to a hallway with four units on each side.

Jason reached back and touched his hand to Dave's leg. *Ready?*

Dave slapped his shoulder twice. *Ready!*

They put their shoulders against the door and heaved it open, ducking to the side as flames roiled bright orange over their heads. On their knees, they crawled into the inferno, the hose trailing them like a lifeline.

The soupy smoke obscured their vision. As they advanced, Jason sprayed water on the flames, changing the shape of the stream to attack any pockets of fire he could reach. Then he switched back to fog to try to clear the smoke and cool down the immediate area. His nerves sang softly, keeping him on his toes.

In the belly of the beast, they moved with a brute grace, sharpened by years of teamwork and training. The hiss of exhaled air from Dave's mask was comforting, an almost subconscious homing beacon, letting Jason know where his partner was, even when they weren't in physical contact. When he came across a door, Jason would call out to Dave, waiting for the reassuring shoulder pat before twisting the knob and using the Halligan tool if he found it locked. Jason fell into the reassurance of the routine. At each unit, Dave stopped at the doorway and pulled slack for the line, feeding it to Jason before following the hose hand over hand until reaching Jason again. Together, they would clear the apartment, then pull the line out, and go to the next one. It was intense work that left them breathing heavily within minutes.

They completed the bottom floor in good time. Getting the hose up the stairs was trickier, but the routine was the same. Clear a unit. Place water on fire. Return to the hall. Go to the next unit.

At the third apartment on the second floor, Jason heard a cry faint enough to be his imagination. He went still, his heart suddenly racing, and tried to hear over the noise of wood crackling merrily away and the thudding of his suddenly racing heart. The scream from the bedroom to his left was unmistakable.

"There's a kid!" he yelled over his shoulder as a new jolt of adrenaline kicked in, wanting to leave everything and get to the kid, before his training kicked in. *Gotta wait for Dave.*

The flames inside the unit illuminated cheap tan carpet melted from the heat. Jason sprayed the room, cursing the immediate darkness as the fire died down and smoke settled in. A smack on his shoulder told him Dave had arrived, and they felt their way to the bedroom area. The small, terrified scream sounded again, as they desperately searched for the source, trying to pinpoint the sound.

Jason swept his arms along the floor for what felt like an eternity, before his hands hit the railing of a bedframe. He reached under, hitting something soft and dense with his gloved hand. The soft mass yielded a cry of pain, and the glow from the outside street lamp penetrated the smoke enough to see dimly. The boy was maybe three years old, body rigid with panic, and wearing pj's with a dinosaur print. Jason's fleeting thought was that all of the toddler's probable night terrors were coming true.

"I got him!" He unceremoniously tugged the child from his hiding spot. The heat was overwhelming. "We gotta cool it down in here!"

Dave took over the nozzle, and they began a careful retreat. Flames rolled and climbed along the wall beyond the door of the bedroom. Dave sprayed it with water, enraging the beast the fire had become. Steam mixed with smoke, and still the fire burned.

Jason keyed his radio to inform dispatch and on scene personnel they had located a victim, and they began to make their way out. Dave was on point now, using the fog setting to reduce the heat around them as much as possible.

A moment later, the line went limp, the stream collapsing to a dribble.

"No water!" Dave closed the nozzle, waiting for the pressure to rebuild.

Jason relayed the information over the radio. The coughing of the child in his arms was getting worse, sending a pang of panic through him. They had to get out now for the kid to have any chance.

The hallway was a flame-filled gauntlet, and the hose was still underpressured. No escape that way. On his back, a bell attached to his air tank chimed, indicating low air supply. *Five minutes or less*, a primal part of his brain chanted, *get out now!*

"The window," Jason called out. He turned back into the bedroom. The heat was all consuming, and over his shoulder the once-panicked child had gone limp and quiet. Oh God, no. Only his training and six years of experience kept his mind calm, as his heart beat double time. It took several moments to reach the dim glow of the street-lit window, long enough for Jason to curse Vince at the engine pump. No time to worry with the window sash. He cocked his elbow and crashed it into the glass. The pane shattered outward from the impact, the cooler air outside rushing in.

The backdraft occurred faster than Jason could realize his mistake.

Fire surrounded him, angry and howling as the outside air gave it new life. The searing intensity of the heat felt like flame against naked skin, driving them to get as low as possible. Jason felt more than saw Dave scramble over to him. Felt rather than saw the floor buckling beneath him as Dave reached him. On his back, the low-air bell implacably chimed.

Get to the window. Get to the window. His brain was on a loop, everything in him yelling to get out. He tried to get to his feet, the child falling away as he clambered for the window. The world seemed to tilt as he turned back, reaching frantically for the kid. Suddenly, the hose in Dave's hand went rigid, kinks popping out audibly as the pressure increased. Taken by surprise, he lost his grip on the nozzle. It smacked Jason near his ear, knocking his helmet sideways and pulling his facemask askew to the right. Dazed, Jason fell back against the wall and heard the hiss of air escaping from his mask as he fumbled to find the boy with the dino pj's again.

Then the floor beneath him crumbled.

Jason tried to grab anything as gravity pulled him down. The weight of heavy wood and plaster around him gave him no purchase, the smoke pushing down to smother him as the hiss of the escaping air grew fainter.

The last thing he heard was the shriek of his personal alarm going off, joining with Dave's.

Chapter Two

Zoe Calder

AS I BUCKLED my seat belt, I regarded the mourning household I was leaving behind. It wasn't easy, but I'd done the best I could for him. It's what I'd want in his position.

He was more sinner than saint, but my hope was that I helped him find some measure of peace before he passed. As a private-duty nurse, I took assignments ministering to those, with grave illnesses and injuries, who have the means to afford medical care at home. Frequently, the care is in place of formal hospice arrangements. This job ended as most did: with lots of paperwork and a mix of sadness, loss, and relief my patient was no longer hurting.

A once-energetic lumber magnate based in Asheville, North Carolina, his well-documented vices had contributed to his terminal disease. My job had been to make his last days as comfortable as possible.

While we were together, I found him to be a thoughtful and deeply wounded man well aware of his flaws. His pugnacious attitude in life and business left him without many fans, even among his own family. The agency assigned me after he'd burned through three other nurses, driven away by his demands and abrasiveness. He warmed to me after some initial fireworks and respected my boundaries.

Most of his days were spent only in my company, and I was delighted to share some of my favorite books out loud with him when boredom set in. He reached out to a few of the people he had wronged or injured in some way, mostly family and once-close friends. The results were a mixed bag. Some forgave; others cursed at him. Everyone was busy, and visitors were sparse.

He was still lucid at the beginning of the final event and knew what the increased *beep-beeps* meant. His look, a bittersweet acceptance of the inevitable, etched grief on my heart. "At least I get to go with a pretty girl watching over me." He smiled weakly. "Read me some of that Poe again, darlin'?"

"Of course." I grabbed the lovingly tattered book from my bag. Watching them go was always the hardest part of the job, but critical. No matter the person, no one deserved to die alone.

Sitting vigil with the lonely rich man, I read "Lenore" aloud, holding his hand to give us both some small comfort as his body spiraled into its shutdown.

Avaunt! tonight my heart is light. No dirge will I upraise,

But waft the angel on her flight with a pæan of old days!

Let no bell toll!—lest her sweet soul, amid its hallowed mirth,

Should catch the note, as it doth float up from the damnéd Earth.

Finally, just as the birds outside began to sing up the sun, he stopped breathing. I unhooked the monitors slowly, tucked the blanket neatly around his body, and noted the time on the chart, calmness settling inside me. The silence after the constant beeps for the last two months was eerie. I waited until 7:30 a.m. to inform his oldest daughter. The home quickly became inundated with mourners who hadn't bothered to come by until he was gone.

It took me until three in the afternoon to complete the paperwork and duties I was responsible for. It took another hour to have all my stuff packed into the car and ready to travel. I was beyond ready for this needed time off. A week, maybe two, to decompress and get ready for the next assignment.

THE EMAIL DING came as I was entering Georgia during my nine-hour trip home. I waited to check it until I stopped for fuel at a Pilot station right before braving Atlanta traffic.

The subject line read: *Could you take another assignment in two days?* It was from the agency director, so whatever it was had to be important. Shit. I smacked the steering wheel in frustration, the car giving a startled beep from the horn. If I didn't read the email body, or didn't respond, I could still have my vacation, right? After a solid minute of creative cursing, I read the email.

> *Hi Zoe,*
>
> *I wanted to take a moment to thank you personally for the hard work and professionalism you have shown while at this agency. All reports from patients and family are full of praise for your work ethic and your ability to care for the clients in your charge.*

I know this is a sudden request and you are scheduled for vacation, but would you be amenable to taking a new assignment within the next couple of days? It would be in your current hometown and would only be for daytime hours, five days a week. You could stay at home, and weekends would be free. Please let me know ASAP?

Thanks,
Thomas Dendrio
Chief Care Coordinator

"Fuck!" I yelled, loud enough to draw a concerned look from the camouflaged redneck pouring gas into a muddy Chevy Silverado across the way. No time off, it seemed. Resolving not to respond until I had topped the tank and used the restroom, I seethed as I pumped the gas.

Back in the car, once all procrastination gambits were exhausted, I reopened the email and downloaded the information. The patient was young, I noted, as I skimmed the info. Not unusual, but this wasn't to be a glorified hospice assignment. He was twenty-eight years old, a burn victim leaving the rehab center for home and private treatment. He would need care and therapy to assist with healing while he continued to recover. His mother was heavily involved in the medical decisions, and family money would pay what insurance wouldn't cover.

So *that* was the reason for this email. I know how to get along with families—even the crusty horrible ones who have agendas that don't always mesh with established goals for the patient. I reread the dossier and caught the words *firefighter, injured during attempted rescue of three-year-old child.*

Holy shit! A real-life hero. In a rush, I felt ashamed for my grouchiness and ill feelings. This man had sacrificed almost everything to try to save a child. The least I could do was help. I closed the pdf and hit reply.

Re: Could you take another assignment in two days?
I'm in.

Decision made, I started the car and headed toward the highway. Before I got back into traffic, I called my best friend and roomie to give her the news. It took another seven hours to get there, arriving at close to two in the morning. The porch light was on, bathing the small clapboard house in comforting orange light, and finally, after two months away, I was home.

Chapter Three

Jason

A WAVE OF agony crashed over him as he woke. Even the morning sunlight through the window hurt where it fell on his skin. He whimpered, the noise itself bringing yet more pain as his raw throat rebelled. Opening his eyes in his own house for the first time in three months, he saw his once-familiar bedroom morphed into an alien landscape of medical devices, the result of his mother's efforts to get him home and out of the burn unit as soon as possible.

He lived in a world of pain. Before this, he'd never given much thought to how many different types of hurt a person could experience. From the extreme eye-watering agony that caused his vision to go black around the edges, to the irritating niggling itches that drove him to distraction, and the almost infinite spectrum in between, Jason had become intimate with the nuances of pain in a way few others ever experienced.

Nothing would be the same. He knew this from the moment he woke in the ICU. His life would forever be divided into "before the fire" and "after the fire."

"Bad dreams?" his mother offered him an insulated cup full of ice chips to help soothe his throat. God, all he wanted was to down gallons of coffee and liters of beer, but the injuries from burns and intubation down his trachea made anything more than ice-chips a herculean task. He could do it, had to for the pills, but it was strictly on an as-needed basis for now.

Martha Merone was a tall, angular woman, with dark hair and a patrician face affirming her New England ancestry. Her schoolmarmish look disguised a steel-trap mind uniquely suited for her business in real estate development. It was a role she'd taken on with aplomb when his father went to jail after a corruption scandal centered on his efforts to bring the Parrot's Cay Casino to town.

"Same as always," Jason croaked.

"Was it the fire monster again?" The way she asked made him feel silly, as if he was five years old again. Maybe, to her, he still *was* five years old.

"Yeah. But a little different this time." He'd described the morphine-fueled fever dreams to her before. Surreal images of smoke and flame and mazelike hallways where he and Dave fled for their life with the child in his arms. The monster made of fire pursued them relentlessly, until they hit a dead-end solid brick wall. The dream always ended with the monster made of fire reaching out to caress and claim him at the end.

"Dave wasn't there this time. When I looked down at the kid in my arms, he was the fire monster too. I had to drop him, leave him." The child had died in reality but now sought revenge in his dreams. Guilt, never far from Jason's thoughts, etched itself into his voice.

Martha didn't answer. Instead she fussed with his pillows and blankets, smoothing and fluffing and helping him to a more comfortable position.

"The new nurse will be here soon." She changed the subject, her discomfort obvious. "I spoke to the agency and stressed who you are and told them to make sure they sent out the best. They assured me the person coming is exemplary."

Jason remained silent while his mother fussed and chattered around his room. The nurse would be here soon, which meant so much more pain. It was necessary, he knew. The care of his burns, the range of motion exercises designed to keep his tendons from shortening, the bandage changes. All necessary, but excruciating. Intense spikes of torment to remind him the daily pain he currently simmered in could always be worse.

Meeting the nurse wasn't something to look forward to. *Let's just cut to the chase and hate her*, he decided.

The hospital had outfitted him with a morphine pump so he could self-administer the liquid that attempted to keep the worst pain at bay. He pushed the button near his left hand, heard the familiar *click-hum* of the IV machine, felt the morphine burn a little on its way in. The heat quickly dissolved throughout his body.

Painkiller my ass, he thought darkly as the numbing solution spread. It helped...maybe...a little.

The cell phone chirped at his bedside.

"I'll get it, sweetie." His mom answered with a soft hello.

Jason waited to see who was calling, staring at his mother expectantly. His mother carefully turned her back to Jason, the tension in her straightened back and drawn shoulders putting him on alert.

"Okay, I am so sorry. I'll let him know. Please extend our condolences."

A buzzing began behind his eyes that he couldn't blame on the morphine.

"Jason, I'm..." she stuttered and wouldn't meet his eyes, locking onto something over Jason's shoulder. "I'm so sorry, sweetie. Dave didn't make it."

He stared at her, watching her lips move but not comprehending the words. Didn't make it? What didn't he make? The buzzing in his head grew louder. She didn't really mean what he thought, did she?

"His family, they...had to take him off life support. He passed during the night." She took a step toward him, and that small movement made the news real, and immediate.

A gaping hole opened in his chest, a bottomless vortex waiting to drag him down. During the night? The night she took him from the hospital, the day he finally gave into her constant nagging? "No."

The denial was a whisper, barely audible and blatantly false. The chasm in his stomach gaped wider. "Fuck! Oh, fuck."

The guilt, his grief at the loss of his best friend, eclipsed all the physical discomfort endured so far, and soul-shuddering sobs racked his damaged body. He'd known things were going badly for Dave who had remained comatose until last night. Jason thought he was prepared to hear Dave had passed, thought it couldn't be much worse than hearing the child they found hadn't made it. Now he knew he had been very wrong. This was complete devastation that left him broken, beyond repair. Beyond forgiveness. Jason deserved everything he'd gotten. Deserved more. Worse.

He was the one who fucked up; he should've been the one to pay for the mistake. But it wasn't the way things worked, was it? Dave was gone, and he was condemned to this existence: a broken, burned shell of what he had once been.

I broke the window. I fed the fire. Should've known better. Should've waited. All my fault.

Dave. Dead. The words didn't feel right together. How could someone so full of life die?

His mother awkwardly tried to comfort him, but she couldn't hug him, the burns hurt too much. He didn't respond to her attempts to shush him. She could only watch him crumble. Watch him sob, curled around his pain and anguish.

Jason retreated into his mind, to a quiet place where David still lived and everything was Pleasantville perfect. It was the only thing he could do to save his sanity.

Hot summer sun blazing overhead. The field of green grass with an earthy-sweet smell after being freshly mown. The crack-clopp *of shoulder pads followed by the shrill coach's whistle to stop play. Sweat-drenched and exhausted, a quick break for water and then back to work.*

Two-a-day football practices in the thick coastal humidity were his and Dave's first real proving grounds. Where they learned to approach their limits, then move beyond, to battle and compete. This was his Pleasantville, even though at the time it had seemed like a version of hell no one would willingly endure.

The sound of his mother tidying his room almost brought his attention back to the real world. Jason ignored it, sinking deeper into his reverie, desperate to escape the grief but unable to think of anything but Dave.

The screech of the whistle, followed by the voice of an exasperated coach.

"Are you kidding me with this?" he yelled at Dave. "You gotta hit that hole hard! The guard is pulling and boxing the tackle to the right, so the only person you

gotta deal with is the linebacker. He's not on the line! So you gotta hit the open hole hard and fast. It's free yardage until he can read and react. Come on! Do it again."

The scrimmage group lines up again, and Jason, the linebacker knowing what was coming, fills the hole. Dave, running hard and fast, obliterates him. Simply lowers his shoulders and drops the boom, leaving Jason on his back with clumps of grass and dirt stuck in his helmet grill, trying to recover his breath as the entire team erupts in howls of glee at the hit.

"That's what I'm talking about!" the coach roars. "That's gonna be our bread 'n' butter play right there! Jason, you okay? Take a break, get some water. Watch from the bleachers until you get your head unscrambled."

He'd known right then he would remember that hit forever.

The doorbell rang and abruptly ripped him from his memories. After a few moments, his mother walked into his tear-blurred line of vision.

"Honey, your new nurse is here. Why don't you take a few minutes to meet with her?"

He didn't respond. From the doorway, he heard a new voice, husky yet feminine, speaking with his mother. He didn't care. The door to his room closed, and the voices went away. Good. He had football practice to get back to.

After ten yards of the playoff game they'd barely won replayed in his mind, the door opened again. His mother strode into the room, and the new nurse trailed behind. Having regained some coherence, he looked up as they entered.

"Jason, this is the nurse who will be helping you. Her name is Zoe Calder. Zoe, this is my son, Jason."

More out of ingrained politeness than any real desire to meet the person who would be dishing out more pain than any human should have to bear in the name of healing, Jason inclined his head slightly. The angry skin at his neck screamed a protest. Zoe stood at the foot of his hospital bed and studied him closely.

He knew what she saw. A duplex's master bedroom converted into a hospital room, the bed taking up most of the space. A charred gargoyle lying in the bed, skin oozing and peeling underneath gauze and pressure coverings, emanating smells with no polite description, covered by the industrial scent of the antiseptics working to keep infections—now the greatest threat to his life—at bay.

"Hi, Jason," Zoe said finally. "I'm here to help you while you recover. It's going to suck, but I imagine you already know that."

Her voice got his attention, and it was his turn to study her. She was tall, about five foot nine, with a slender build, and appeared to be in her mid-to-late-twenties. The blue scrubs she wore were decorated with pink piping, and the long dark-brown hair brushing past her shoulder blades was pulled back into a loose ponytail. Her face was pretty, perhaps not gorgeous, but it was her eyes that caught his attention. Zoe's large, green eyes dominated her face. Those eyes bumped her up from pretty to beautiful, and for the briefest moment, Jason's mind paused.

His mother stepped closer to his bedside. "I'm going to go over your charts with Zoe, sweetie. I know it's time for some meds. We'll get you situated, and maybe you can get a little nap while we cover everything. We'll be in the living room."

After the various tablets were taken, Jason hit the button on his morphine pump in an attempt to soothe the agony from his scream-shattered throat. Soon, his eyelids grew heavy. Before the drug-induced slumber took hold, his gaze trailed Zoe's departure. Almost against his will, his last, guilty thought was *Dat ass...*

IMAGES CAME AT Jason, like debris from a shipwreck, as he drifted in waves of numbness. Fire trucks idling, turnout gear, high school mortarboards, childhood bikes, football helmets. It was as if Salvador Dali had hijacked his memories. Faces began to float up into his vision: his absent father and sister, his mom, his old football coach.

Dave's face was there as well, cockiness writ large in his ever-present smile. He remembered slowly, as if from far away, Dave had died. As he remembered, the dream face began to darken, still floating, yet somehow also burning, looming larger until it filled Jason's whole vision. Dave's smile was gone now, face twisted into a rictus of agony. The face made no sound, yet the scream penetrated Jason's soul. It stared at him, brown eyes full of fear and accusation, until suddenly they glazed over, and all awareness faded. The face froze in mid-grimace, the silent scream dying in Jason's head as Dave's twisted face slowly ebbed away. Somewhere, a coach's whistle screeched.

Jason jerked, body tensed and heart pounding. His cheeks were wet.

The tears were a brutal reminder. The losses, the pain, the grief melded into an inchoate ball of agony. He drummed his arms into the mattress, the resulting flares of pain immediate and intense, yet not enough.

The grief soon began to recede, if only because his body couldn't handle such intensity for too long. He lay in bed with his eyes squeezed shut, yet still leaking tears. Unable to maintain the tension in his body any longer, he went limp.

A light touch on his shoulders startled him. Zoe. The nurse stood there, tissues in hand. His first reaction was to press his eyes closed and wait for her to leave him alone. Childish, yes, but it was embarrassing to have someone he'd only met today witness such a complete meltdown. Then he saw her face.

It wasn't just that she was beautiful, with her vivid eyes set in tan skin, exquisite cheekbones, full lips, with the dark hair swept back. She was remarkable, yes, but it was the empathy on her face that stopped him from retreating from her. Her look conveyed compassion, without pity or judgment. He felt exposed, as if she saw into him and his whole being. It left him off-kilter and vulnerable, unsure of her motives as she delicately wiped at the tears and snot on his face.

"Do you want to talk about it?" she asked.

Jason shook his head no, even as his lip gave a rogue quiver and another tear slipped loose. Zoe nodded her head in understanding and laid a hand on his shoulder. Instead of the comfort she probably intended, the touch ignited anger strong enough to leave him breathless. How fucking dare she? He jerked his shoulder away with vicious intent.

To her credit, she immediately stepped back and apologized. "I'm sorry. That was rude of me."

He glared at her, the unacknowledged rage growing since the news of Dave's death finding a sudden release at the nurse who dared try to comfort him. He let it build, politeness be damned. "Whatever," he gritted through clenched teeth. "I don't need sympathy. Just do your fucking job."

He saw the hurt on her face for a split second before she composed herself, and the part of him that hated himself for causing it was drowned out by the howling glee of his anger when Zoe fled the room. If she was going to hurt him, he might as well enjoy hurting her first.

She came back within a few minutes and took a deep breath after looking at her watch meaningfully. He knew what came next. It was time for range of motion, ROM therapy, to change dressings, and replace the bedsheets. Time for her to hurt him back.

She worked methodically, stripping the soaked and crusty old bandages and next rubbing moisturizer into the burned but unbroken areas of his skin. Then, she would bend the joint, where she was working, through its range of motion. She was as gentle as possible, with an efficiency that underscored her expertise.

Still, it was excruciating. But it was pain he deserved, pain he owed those he'd failed. He turned his head away from her and clenched his jaw as she worked, using his anger to keep the tears at bay.

AFTERWARD, BETWEEN THE opioids and new dressings draped over his body, ridiculous daytime TV, and a relatively comfortable position, Jason found some small relief. Afternoon sunshine streamed through the window of his room, and he closed his eyes and let his anger dissipate. Felt some humanity return if only for these precious, fleeting moments.

He surreptitiously studied Zoe as she moved about the room. Who was she? He wondered idly. What was her story? Was she single? Probably not. Probably has some granola-crunching earnest-type guy totally waiting on her hand and foot. Wait, what? You hate her, remember? Besides, you have a girlfriend, he chastised himself.

He thought of his turbulent relationship with the Helen-of-Troy beauty named Jenna Zambroski. She hadn't texted or called since his arrival home. Strange. Maybe she was waiting for him to call first. Retrieving his phone, he fumbled out a text to her.

Hey. How are you?
Hey bb! Im supr bsy but good. U ok?
Hurting, lots. I miss you.
Imy2.
Coming over tonight?
Yes! Give me couple hours?
K

Jason texted his mom, who had left to attend to some burgeoning building crisis, to confirm Jenna would be staying for the night shift. Zoe's shift was scheduled to end at 7:30 p.m., and it was necessary for a family member or friend to be with him during the evening hours.

His mom texted back to call her if needed. He pushed the morphine button, leaned farther back into his pillow. This time, he slept dreamlessly.

HE AWOKE TO the sound of voices in the living room. Zoe and Jenna. The light in the room indicated late afternoon was slipping into early evening. Pain, always that pain, sank its claws into his body as he awakened. He heard the voices stop and then footsteps in his direction. He hadn't even known he had groaned.

Zoe stepped into his bedroom and began her ministrations. Ice chips. Vitals taken. IV and catheter bags replaced. Meds given with small sips of water. Charts marked.

As she worked, Jenna stood in the doorway of the bedroom, watching. Jason couldn't meet her eyes. Along with his guilt and grief, he was nervous. Being home in this condition was somehow more real than when he was at the burn ward. Also, he knew what was next. He nodded for Zoe to get on with it.

Another bandage change. Oh, joy. Zoe unpeeled the pressure mask, a fabric hood that covered his face, neck, and ears. Exposed the burns festering there. He heard a sharp intake of breath from the doorway.

"Oh my God, baby," Jenna said through hands clasped over her mouth. "My poor baby." She continued to whimper as she took in the injuries. She tentatively stepped to the foot of the bed, looking closer at the carnage. It was her first time seeing his naked face since the fire. *What is she thinking now that she sees what I've become?* He could've made her leave, but he wanted her to see, wanted her to choose him in spite of the damage or end it once and for all.

Zoe finished changing the bandages and gently replaced the mask. It was nearing the end of her shift, and she made the day's final entries in his paperwork. "Okay, Jason," she said when she finished. "I'm going to head out now. I've talked to Jenna about what to watch for and what to do if anything happens. I'll see you at seven thirty in the morning. Are you good?"

Jason nodded, and Zoe left them alone. At Zoe's exit, he gathered enough nerve to look at his girlfriend.

"You heard about Dave?" he asked.

Jenna closed her eyes and nodded, her mouth still downturned. "Yeah. It's terrible. I still can't believe it."

"My fault."

"Jason, no. Don't say that." She tried for earnest, but the change of tone and her shift away from him spoke volumes.

He didn't answer. The lie was obvious, and his throat hurt too much to call her out. Still, it was the last straw, the final nudge off the cliff he had teetered on since learning of Dave's death. He felt a quiet unmooring within himself, a freeing, floaty feeling as the dark abyss claimed him.

As Jenna scrolled through TV channels and made insufferably shallow small talk, Jason began to plan his suicide.

Chapter Four

Zoe

MY FEET ACHED, and the pounding in my head threatened an all-out migraine. I rubbed the sore spots near my shoulders and stretched my arms a little in my car before leaving Jason's. The first day with a patient was always draining. Learning about and meeting the patient and family was like interviewing for a job. Would they like me? Could I prove myself? I knew I was a good nurse. Had proven it through school, in hospitals, and on the burn unit. Neonatal care was my first love, but available shifts were rare, so I had earned my stripes with burn victims. My record quickly got me recruited for private duty nursing. It was a nice promotion, salary-wise, but the hours were frequently hellish.

I glanced at Jason's unit in the rearview mirror as I left the complex of townhomes. He would have it rough as he healed. Several thick folders chronicled his devastating injury and subsequent treatment. One thing was apparent: he should have died. A firefighter with so much thermal injury over his body and in his respiratory system was a dead man walking. Somehow, Jason was beating the odds. The charts, if one knew how to read them and find the narrative thread, told an incredible story.

Mrs. Merone had shown me pictures when we spoke together, from before the fire. He could have been a model. Athletic build, with a strong jaw and light-brown hair that made soft curls when it grew out. His eyes had a magnetic gravity, pools of blue ice.

Even now, with the ravages of the injuries he sustained, it was easy to see how striking he had been. He would never again be the classic Adonis in the photographs. His left ear was missing, along with a fair amount of hair in the temporal area, and the side of his face was burned almost completely, a line showing down his face that marked where the mask he wore had twisted to the right. His wrists were burned all the way around, his right hand broken in numerous places when his hand and arm had been grabbed by the debris slide that shredded his glove and coat sleeve. Tibia/fibula fractures and more burns to his right leg. Left clavicle broken.

How was he still alive? He should have bled out. His organs should have shut down. Infections should have claimed him, but he was still fighting. After a relatively brief three-month stay in the hospital, he'd been deemed stable enough to go home. Simply incredible.

The phone rang, intruding on my thoughts. I answered without taking my eyes off the road. "Hey, it's Zoe," I answered with as much cheer as my tired body could muster.

"I beg your pardon?" A baritone voice many people called both soothing and full of authority filled my ear and sent an instant chill through my heart. "That's not the name I gave you."

My father was on the phone. Fear and adrenaline raced through me, beyond my control. I concentrated on breathing and driving. My hands shook on the wheel.

"What do you want?" I cursed myself for not checking the caller ID. I'd been dodging his calls for at least a week.

"The Lord laid His concern for you on my heart and moved me to call you."

"What?" The word leapt out before thought.

"Repent. Repent before it's too late."

I sputtered, trying to reply, but he talked over me.

"I will pray for you." He launched into the skin-crawling preacher's cadence I knew from years of fire-and-brimstone sermons. "Pray that everything and everyone around you rots and withers and falls away until you know the full extent of your sin, and you cry out to me and the Lord for forgiveness of your wretched—"

I smashed the disconnect button on the steering wheel. "Fuck you, asshole!" Talking to my father always left me feeling like the scared kid I'd once been, the private bravado my only way to rebel.

Tears welled in my eyes, and my hands were shaking on the steering wheel as I put on my hazards and pulled over. It had been years since we had spoken. Why had he called now? What was he doing? Along with the questions came memories; of his face, red with rage, as his thickly muscled arm swung a belt—buckle first—into my back, of his contempt when he truly saw me the first time, of his glee whenever I messed up enough to give him an excuse to "correct" me.

Next, came thoughts of my mom and brother. Beautiful people who were broken like me, and I missed them more than I could express. Those memories hurt more than the ones starring my father.

I gathered myself together enough to get back on the road, though my stomach still roiled like I wanted to vomit. It took another ten minutes to get home. I parked in my spot in the yard and sat alone, numbed and drained by the day and the call.

"Hey, girl! Wake up, cheri. Come inside!" My reverie was interrupted by the creole-drenched shout of my roommate, Delphine Roulet. I looked through the windshield and waved off-handedly as she stepped out onto the wraparound porch. Her outfit was colorful as usual; today her dress was a riot of lime greens, pinks, and oranges, cinched at her waist with a royal purple sash that made her café-au-lait skin glow, along with a sash-matching scarf that failed to tame the thick dreadlocks she had spent years growing. What might have been a fashion fail on anyone else was, on her, a beautiful self-expression. I constantly marveled at her ability to be so very different, yet so very regal.

I took a deep breath, opened the car door, and made my way to the house. It was a recently rebuilt shotgun-style home outside city limits, close to town but far enough away to be considered rural. This place was my sanctuary.

The smell from the kitchen was everything good and lovely in life distilled into an olfactory blanket one could almost snuggle up with on the couch. I dropped my purse and keys at the table near the door and inhaled the spicy, nutty, multi-textured aromas. My stress faded with each exhale as I walked into the kitchen.

"Coffee? I made some fresh," Delphine said. My best friend's Creole accent never failed to calm me. Between her friendship and her cooking, it was a no-brainer to keep living together after school. Her vivacious joy had helped me through countless dark places.

"Oh my god, Del, yes, please." I learned during nursing school there was never a bad time for coffee.

Delphine handed me a chicory-blended brew in my favorite mug, a heavy green crockery piece with Minnie Mouse on the side.

A slight smile tilted the corner of Del's burnt-umber mouth as she stirred the pot bubbling on the stove. She double-tapped the spoon against the edge of the pot and lay it down. "First days are always pretty tough for you."

I sighed at her. "Especially with such a quick turnaround. I gotta say, this guy has a lot of healing to do. It's staggering he's even alive."

"Is he what had you zoned out in the car?"

"My father called me on the way home." My voice clenched around the word "father."

"Ah." From her, the short sound communicated volumes. A gifted artist with a fellowship at our local university, she could convey worlds of information with a simple brushstroke or a meaningful sigh. Her bohemian exterior belied a sharp, caring mind.

Delphine was more than a roommate—she was a mentor and my best friend. She knew my history, and all about my father.

"He started a rant that would've made Fred Phelps proud. I finally hung up on him." The words slid out easier than I expected them to, a note of pride at the end. Years of trying to build boundaries, so he couldn't hurt me, and the best I could manage was hanging up mid-call. Still, it was better than I could have done five years ago, and I was proud of the progress.

"Atta girl," she purred. She hustled around the kitchen, stirring pots, chopping things, and checking the oven.

"Jesus. I haven't been under his roof in fifteen years. What's his deal this time?" Being rejected by my family was a wound that never seemed to heal, the price paid for being different. "Every time he pulls a stunt like this..."

Before I knew it, a sob escaped, the tears in my eyes a surprise attack I didn't see coming. Delphine closed the oven door and spun toward me, the brown skirt of her kaftan dress flaring. I tilted my head up as if I could keep the tears in my eyes by sheer force of will and defiance of gravity. Del came over and hugged me protectively.

"Oh, child. Shh, hush now. He is shit, and you mustn't let him get to you like this." Her hug enveloped me, making me feel safe. "Fuck this coffee, cher. We switch to wine."

"I'll get the glasses," I sniffled.

"Non, cheri. You pick the bottle."

I chose an elegant pinot noir, the label from Portland featuring three mischievous otters.

"Excellent choice, mon amie," Delphine said. "This will go perfectly with the gumbo."

"I thought that's what I smelled," I confessed with a mischievous grin and gave her a thank-you hug.

Delphine tossed her head back and laughed while she returned the hug. "Ah, my dear, you are priceless. Never forget it."

Delphine opened the wine and poured me a glass. She took her own in hand and raised it to me. "To the vine..." she began.

I smiled, falling into the rhythm of our private ritual. "To the vineyard..."

"To the vintage..."

"To the vino," we finished together and clinked the thin wineglasses .

"And happy thirtieth to the friend who endlessly inspires me with her courage and heart," Delphine added before saluting and sipping. Those stupid tears welled again, the emotional whiplash of the day threatening to completely overwhelm me. I preferred to ignore my birthday whenever possible. It brought too many feelings to the surface, feelings I was otherwise better at ignoring. It was a momentous thing, however, turning thirty. I hadn't expected to make it to this milestone.

We ate seafood gumbo and drank wine. Then, for dessert, a key lime pie and the coffee we had set aside.

"Holy God, Del, this was amazing! Thank you. Thank you, thank you, thank you!" The words ran together as I gushed, leaning back to let my stomach escape the elastic waistband of my scrubs.

"You're welcome. It was good to get in the kitchen. I wanted to at least show you some love for your birthday. I'm sorry you missed your vacation. Maybe we can make up for it next year."

"Gah, stop it. You are getting me way too emotional."

"It's true. You are a lovely girl, and a beautiful human."

At that, I did tear up. Again. She handed me a napkin and squeezed my arm.

"You know, I've been thinking. Maybe I should try something online, see what's out there, you know? I'm not getting any younger." I jokingly tried to change the subject.

"You could use some love in your life." She tilted her head toward me, raised her eyebrow, and gave an excited shimmy.

"I'm talking about boys," I clarified with a grin, knowing exactly what she was thinking with her little wiggle.

"Yes, I know," her smile was innocent. "If you were into girls, I could introduce you to some lovely dearies, but, my child, the heart wants what it wants." She sighed theatrically. Delphine was unapologetically gay, and some of the "lovely dearies" she brought home from time to time had certainly been exquisite. "I think you should get online, see what is out there for you. Carefully, of course."

"So maybe OkCupid or Tinder?"

"Indeed. I don't think Grindr will work for you."

I laughed. Delphine stared at me with her dark-brown eyes glimmering, completely still. It was her way of forcing attention to the present, a way of waiting that gave space while simultaneously demanding a response. I felt my cheeks and face slowly getting red.

"Okay. Okay!" I said. "Yes, let's do it. But first, I'm going to need more wine."

IT WAS A lot later than I intended before I got ready for bed. Slightly buzzed from the wine and heady from the process of publishing a dating profile online, it was after midnight before I managed to get into the shower.

For me, the ability to have a shower every night is still the height of luxury, second only to bubble baths. Taking my time in the heated waterfall, the soap and heat sluiced the day away as I fantasized best possible outcomes for the online dating, even as doubt crept in. Who would want to be with me like this? My thoughts turned dark. I'm plenty fine for one-night stands, but who wants to grow old with a carnival freak?

I shook my head against the thoughts. So many hours had been logged with a therapist deconstructing and eliminating the sabotaging thoughts and self-loathing underpinning my self-image for so long. As a result, my life blossomed into something good, and worthy. Still, when it came to the thought of sharing my life with someone, the old doubts and dark narrative were never far away.

The steam and heat worked magic on my knotted muscles as I rinsed away the soap, leaving my skin silky in its wake. I ducked my head under the water, my gaze trailing past my breasts and falling on my penis as the water rinsed through my hair.

My penis. Ugh.

Transgender. Yep, that's me. Designated a boy at birth, I was born into a conservative family with an abusive father who ruled with rigidity and narcissism and couldn't stand me because I was "a queer-acting faggot." He felt it reflected badly on him as a preacher and head of the household. Every time I thought about childhood, the scars by my shoulder blade and kidney from that belt buckle itched—the permanent, personal brand that served to remind me I'd always be seen by some people as different, ugly, and worthless. No matter what I changed, part of me would always carry those scars.

But I survived, I thought as I turned the shower off. Now I have friends and a great job. I'd carved out a life I could be pretty proud of. Worked my ass off for it too. I dried off and smiled at myself in the mirror. "Plus, I'm really cute!" I said out loud. The reflection grinned back at me, and I threw a sexy wink over a bare shoulder as I turned away.

Snuggling into bed, I forced my thoughts back to a happy medium. *Happy thirtieth, you beautiful wreck.* I allowed myself one last fantasy of a Dwayne Johnson doppelgänger who was gobsmacked after one look and swept me off my feet. *And we lived happily ever after*, I sighed as I drifted to sleep.

Chapter Five

Jason

THE NEXT MORNING, Zoe arrived a little early, relieving Jenna from her duties and releasing her back into the wild. Jason was happy to see her go. The evening had been strained and awkward, as she made uncomfortable small talk while he stayed obstinately quiet.

He'd spent the night plotting his death. First, he considered the morphine pump. Was it hackable? Could he rig it to where the entire amount in the pump would dispense at one time? Could he hide the tampering? Furtive searching online when Jenna left the room—*thank god,* he thought each time her nattering left him alone—led him to realize that option was beyond his skill set. There were lots of other opioids in the house, for when his throat was up to swallowing pills, and caching a few here and there until he had a lethal dose shouldn't be too hard or take too long. Option B, then.

A part of him idly wondered if it was only a night thing: the yearning to return to the dark, blank unawareness he'd occupied from the time the walls collapsed until being brought out of his coma. Wondered if the seduction of the idea would lose its luster in the daylight.

It didn't.

As morning ended the listless night, he settled on a plan and found, paradoxically perhaps, some peace. If all the hurt and grief and guilt were ending soon, he could handle the pain until then, right?

All he had to do was make it through Dave's funeral.

"Good morning!" Zoe called out as she entered the room.

Jason groaned in response. "The mistress of pain has arrived."

"Hey, mister, it's for your own good. If I happen to derive some small pleasure from your suffering, well, that's just a bonus, isn't it?" Her smile softened the sadistic words.

"Never thought I'd be the kind of guy who paid a woman to hurt him," he shot back, startled at the banter. Even if he hated her, he could cut her some slack for now. After all, it would soon be over.

"Yet here we are." She grabbed the bandages, ointments, medicines, and assorted items she needed. She went to work on him, gently, starting at his legs this time and working her way up to his head before changing the sheets soaked by his seeping wounds.

THE NEXT DAYS were dedicated to finding a rhythm and workable schedule for them both. The negotiations were fractious, with Zoe setting firm boundaries around what she would do as a nurse and caretaker and what she would not do, because she wasn't a maid. Jason set expectations as to meal times, bandage change times, and ROM therapy times.

Therapy sucked without exception. He summoned every ounce of grit developed through those football two-a-days and the fire academy as he progressed through the exercises, clenching his teeth and grunting through the pain as she pushed him for just a bit more range. The only thing that got him through each session was the thought it would all be over soon.

Instead of taking all of his usual pain medication, he began to palm any he thought they wouldn't notice, secreting them in his nightstand whenever Zoe or the late shift left the room.

MORNING DAWNED, WITH fog and low clouds, and a chill in the air that signaled an approaching autumn. It was Friday, and today his friend and partner would be laid to rest with full honors. Later tonight, Jason would atone for his mistake. Tonight, he would finally stop hurting.

His mom arrived early to help Zoe get him ready for the funeral. Jason retreated into himself, the blinding pain as he was dressed and moved to the wheelchair welcomed as penance. When he was situated in the chair, his dress uniform jacket was draped over his shoulders, the only part of the uniform he was able to wear. The rest of him was dressed in oversized black dress clothes to accommodate all the bandages and to avoid chafing his skin. He felt frumpy, but there was no help for it.

Jenna was out of town again, so Jason rode with his mother in her BMW, and Zoe followed behind in her car. They arrived at the moss-covered stone cathedral about forty-five minutes ahead of the scheduled start of service. After Zoe helped him out of the car and into the wheelchair, his mom took command of it, wheeling him slowly through the back, accessible entrance.

"Okay, Jason," Zoe said, "I'll stay as close as I can in case you need me. Just tell your mother, and she'll wave me over. I'll come running."

He'd be damned before he asked for his nurse to help him here.

The century-old cathedral was standing room only as David Fontaine was mourned and honored.

Rites and rituals for the fallen were never easy. The department's chaplain gave a short message, his eulogy for Dave given with grace and hints of humor. But when he began to recite the fireman's prayer, the raw emotions overwhelmed him at the pulpit.

"*When I am called to du—*" he started, then stopped and wiped his eyes. The chaplain cleared his throat and looked around the room in a silent plea for help.

Two, three, and then ten firefighters stood, until the entire department, except Jason, rose and, as one person, they began:

> "*When I am called to duty, God,*
> *Wherever flames may rage.*
> *Give me strength to save a life*
> *Whatever be its age.*
> *Help me to embrace a little child*
> *Before it is too late,*
> *Or save an older person from*
> *The horror of that fate.*
> *Enable me to be alert*
> *And hear the weakest shout*
> *And quickly and efficiently*
> *To put the fire out.*
> *I want to fill my calling*
> *And give the best in me,*
> *To guard my neighbor*

And protect his property.
And if, according to my fate,
I am to lose my life.
Please bless with your protecting hand
My children and my wife."

Silence reigned in the chapel as the chaplain bade everyone else in attendance to stand. The silver ceremonial bell stationed near the flag-draped casket glinted from the sun beaming through the oval stained-glass window above the pulpit. Two men approached it. Jason knew what part of the ritual was next, wasn't sure how much longer he could maintain his dignity as his heart was further shredded with each ceremonial gesture. He clenched his jaw against the grief and focused on a spot on the dais directly above the bell station, the tensing of his muscles bringing physical pain he could distract himself with.

The first officer, Captain Engmeyer, the man who had commanded Engine 7 that fateful night, unfolded a sheet of paper.

His voice trembling, he read: "Throughout most of history, the lives of firefighters have been closely associated with the ringing of a bell. As they began their hours of duty, it was the bell that started it off. Through the day and night, each alarm was sounded by a bell that called them to fight fire and to place their lives in jeopardy for the good of their fellow man. And when the fire was out, and the alarm had come to an end, the bell rang three times to signal its completion." Captain Engmeyer bowed his head, wiping at his eyes, the sound of his hitching sniffs barely audible. Unable to continue, he waved the chaplain over. The chaplain took the paper from Engmeyer, cleared his throat with difficulty, and found the place where the captain left off.

"And now our brother, David Fontaine, has completed his task, his duties well done, and the bell rings three times in memory of, and in tribute to, his life and service." As the chaplain finished reading, he nodded toward the second officer, the light and movement causing the tears to glint in his eyes.

The officer stationed at the bell pulled the lanyard three times, his gloved hand silencing the bell after the third ring. A second time, the officer rang the bell three times, again his gloved hand silencing the ring. A third time the bell rang, the final peal left to fade away to mournful silence. Jason realized belatedly the man was his own uncle Billy, himself a highly decorated officer.

The casket, preceded by an honor guard, was carried out of the church as a bagpiper played "Amazing Grace" in a mournful dirge. Once outside, the pallbearers placed Dave on the top hosebed of the waiting firetruck, now a bunting-shrouded caisson. With help from the other firefighters, Jason took the seat he had occupied that fateful night and fully faced the emptiness across from him. Blinking fast to fight tears, just for a second he swore he could see the outline of Dave there, still in his turnouts with the Halligan tool between his legs. *I'm sorry, Dave*; his shame was a mantra. *I'm so goddamn sorry.*

After a call and response from dispatch, Engine 7 went en route for Firefighter David Fontaine's final alarm.

Fire engines, pumpers, and rescue trucks lined the way to the cemetery, police and ambulance units arrayed amongst the large number of civilian cars and trucks who had turned out to pay respect as the convoy snaked through town.

Jason sat in silence, unable to meet anyone's eyes, the random tear streaking down his cheek the only betrayal of the volcano of emotion within. Dave deserved every bit of this hero's farewell, but Jason deserved none of it. He needed to make sure they didn't give him the same treatment after he'd carried out his plan. His thoughts were darkly taunting, but he didn't mind. It wouldn't be proper atonement if he were given the same honors.

At the entrance to the cemetery, two trucks had extended their ladders, touched together with a large flag fastened under the arch where they met. The procession slowly passed beneath and into the hallowed grounds.

Marked by fewer ceremonial flourishes, the graveside service was still emotional. At its conclusion, the honor guard fired three volleys from rifles, followed by a lone bugler playing taps. The cemetery was on a hill, and fog had settled in the low area, muting the notes from the bugle as they echoed away from the rise. Then, the flag draping the casket was folded and presented to his widow. Her primal wails lashed Jason's heart with yet more guilt.

After the funeral, most of the mourners made their way to express condolences to the crew of Engine 7 and to Dave's widow. Quickly tiring from the social niceties, he asked his mom to move him to the outskirts of the crowd.

He turned his attention away from the people, needing solitude. The fog had almost disappeared as the sun beamed down, and the trees down the hill rustled in a slight breeze. After a time, he noticed a young boy watching him, a freckled, towheaded tot with sadness crowding the edges of his eyes. His godson was the spitting image of Dave at that age.

The child stepped closer and asked, "Uncle Jason, were you with Daddy in the fire?"

Jason nodded. "Yeah, Noah, I was."

"That mask makes you look like a superhero. Is it because of the fire?"

He forced his lips into a smile he didn't feel. "I guess it does, huh?"

"Mommy said it was a really bad fire. She said you were helping a boy stuck in his room, and you were lucky to be alive."

"It was really bad," Jason closed his eyes against the sudden image of a toddler in dinosaur pajamas, a gut-punching shadow of the child he'd failed to save. He clenched his fist, the sharp pain helping to banish the image before he could trust himself to speak. "I'm sorry about what happened to your dad."

"Yeah. I wish he didn't die. I wish it was you instead." His tone was innocent, direct.

Jason's head snapped back as if he had been slapped. To hear his thoughts so closely mirrored by Dave's spitting image took his breath as surely as a fist to his stomach. It was as if Dave himself were speaking directly to him.

"Me too, buddy," he said. "Me too."

Jason glanced up to see Zoe kneeling to meet the child's eyes. "Hi there. I'm Zoe, and I'm helping Mr. Jason get better. Was Mr. Dave your dad?"

The boy shifted his attention to her. "Yeah. Everyone says he was a hero. But they only say that because he's dead." There was no bitterness in the tone like there would be if an adult said the words, only resigned sadness.

"Well, he was a firefighter. So I definitely think he was a hero, even before he died. I'm sorry about what happened."

"Yeah. He was a hero. Now he's dead."

"It's not fair, is it?" Zoe said. The kindness she'd shown him on their first meeting radiated. For a moment, Jason wondered what magic made her so empathetic, without pity or scorn.

"No. I miss my daddy."

Jason finally lost all his composure at the simple, honest declaration followed by the large tears and strangled cries of the boy who'd lost his hero.

"Oh, sweetie." Zoe gathered the child to her for a hug as Jason struggled to breathe against the sorrow sweeping through him. "I'm so sorry. Your dad was a brave man. And I think your mom is going to need for you to be brave now, like he was."

He pulled away from her embrace. "I know. I have to be very mature now and help get her through this." There was strength in his voice again, along with a wistful weariness that belied his age.

"What's your name, love?"

"I'm Noah. I-I have to go. Mom is calling me." Noah turned and left. Jason watched him run to his mother, who hugged him before returning to the funeral limousine.

Still kneeling, Zoe turned to Jason, her eyes going to full alert when she noted his distress. He watched as she reached out to touch him before freezing when she remembered his response to her previous attempts to comfort him. Instead, she placed her hands on her knees and stood. "Should we go?" she asked quietly.

He nodded, refusing to acknowledge the pang felt when she stopped reaching out to him. His mother, having been expressing condolences, joined them as they made their way back to the vehicles. Her mascara was smeared, a sign she had been emotional throughout the funeral as well.

"Jason," she said, "would you mind terribly riding back with Zoe? I have some matters to attend to on the Riverview project."

He glanced at Zoe, who nodded. "Yeah, it's fine." So that's why she insisted on two cars. Maybe it was for the best. He could be as grouchy with Zoe as he wanted. Wasn't that what his mom paid her for?

Martha gave him a perfunctory shoulder pat before turning toward her vehicle, phone already rising to her ear.

After Zoe got him situated in her car and stowed his wheelchair, with some careful shifting around of things from the trunk to the backseat, they headed back toward his house in silence. The weight of what he planned for tonight bore down on him, and the evening seemed to speed up as it grew closer.

"Hey," he said, voice raspy from overuse at the funeral. "I could really use a milkshake or something. Don't really want to go home just yet. You wanna?" *Although Dave didn't get a last milkshake, did he?* No one could taunt him better than himself.

She drove quietly for a moment, and he could see the calculations occurring in her head. Time until the next dose of medication, pain and energy level, risk of exposure. There were likely a hundred more calculations she was weighing he wasn't even aware of.

"Sure. I think we can take a little detour. Whataburger?"

Jason nodded, and she shifted lanes and headed for the burger joint.

At the drive-thru, he ordered a chocolate malt, while Zoe ordered a burger and small fries to go with her own vanilla shake. The smell of the food made his stomach growl loudly, drawing a laugh from them both.

"I wish I could've gotten a burger," he lamented, "but my throat couldn't handle it right now."

"I'm sorry!" Zoe said. "I didn't even think that might be why you were sticking to a milkshake."

"That's okay. Do we have time to stop for a bit and drink this?"

Zoe furrowed her brows, and Jason could see the calculations happening again. "Did you have a place in mind?"

He did.

A WARM BREEZE and the caw of nearby seagulls came through the open windows. The cold milkshake felt good going down his throat. He watched through the front windshield as a regional jet came in for a landing on the tarmac a small distance away. Jason had directed Zoe to a small lot overlooking the airport.

Jason hadn't been here in a while, but he loved this spot on the south end of the Bruce Campbell Field. In times past, whenever he needed to make a decision, he would go there and watch the planes land and take off. There was something profound about watching a mass of metal and humanity defy gravity with power and physics, then return and become earthbound again.

Zoe studied him as he sucked at his straw and followed the jet's taxi toward the airport buildings.

"That's what I wanted to do," Jason broke the silence, pointing his straw toward the plane. "Fly. My first real dream was to be a pilot. Was gonna go Air Force, then be a helo pilot for a city or a hospital."

"Really?" Zoe cocked her head. "I guess I can understand the draw. No way I could do it though. I've only been on a plane a few times, and it was all terrifying from start to finish. I kept expecting each flight to end in a massive fireball." She dipped a fry into her shake. "What made you decide against it?"

"Didn't decide. Turned out I'm color-blind."

"Aw, babe. That must've hurt, having your dream snatched away for something not even your fault," she said, then paused with the french fry in midflight and stared back at him. "What?"

"Babe?"

Zoe's face turned deep red as she realized the endearment she used. "Oh, shit! I didn't even realize I said it. No offense. Just being Southern, you know?" Her eyes pleaded for understanding as she wiped the hair out of her face. This was the first time he had seen her with her hair down, he realized.

"It's okay," Jason said. Her discomfort at the social faux pas left him amused.

He reached slowly and cadged a single fry from the center console, causing her to smile a little.

"Hey, we're not that comfortable, you thief!" she responded in mock rage. "You, sir, now owe me one french fry."

"Ha! You'd better start a tab now," he said with a grin. "'Cause if we'd kept score, I'd probably owe Dave at least a fifty-pound bag of potatoes."

Reality rushed back in, leaving him hating the moment of levity he'd allowed himself. "Owed, I mean. Shit." He sighed heavily. They were both quiet as a two-engine propeller plane lined up on the runway and took off.

"The funeral was a hard thing to witness," Zoe said, after the plane became a dot on the horizon. "It was so emotional. I can't imagine what you were—are—going through."

Jason didn't respond for a while, but his lips trembled, and he sucked on the shake to swallow the lump in his throat. "Yeah. It was tough. He deserved the honor though. I was able to hold it together, barely, until Noah—" His voice seized at the mention of Dave's son.

"Yeah. Noah, wow. He's working with such a shitty deal."

"You know he's my godson? Like, for real Catholic-stamp-of-approval godson. Was there for his baptism and everything. Now...shit. I killed his dad. And we couldn't even save the kid in his bedroom. Just an utter clusterfuck. Damn it. He's not even seven, and his childhood is over." Jason's throat threatened to slam completely shut as he forced himself to talk over the grief and anger he wrestled with. "Over," he repeated, softer.

Zoe didn't say anything. She reached out and squeezed his hand. That she didn't stop herself this time made Jason's heart go swoopy in a way he didn't want to examine too closely.

"He was right, you know," Jason said as he swiped at his wet cheeks. "It should have been me. Dave... He had a family. He loved Noah, and his wife loved him like Meg Ryan loved Goose in *Top Gun*."

His throat was on fire from talking so much. He took another slurp from the milkshake. Zoe remained quiet, but her attention never wavered as he composed himself. She seemed expectant, and suddenly Jason wanted— needed—to tell someone about the Dave he knew. Declining an invitation to speak at the funeral, fearing his throat wouldn't allow it and fearing the emotions it would bring was something he regretted now.

He steeled himself against the pain and started talking again. "He was my first friend. We met in kindergarten and clicked, you know? Mom called us 'Mutt and Jeff,' after the old cartoon-strip characters." He studied the horizon, searching for the next airplane. "We'd been best friends ever since.

"You know what I couldn't stop thinking about during the funeral? The time he went out on workers' comp after hurting himself at the station during a dead shift. He was always so damn competitive, and one of the guys decided to proclaim himself the fastest pole slider. You know, the pole you can slide down to skip the stairs? Well, Dave couldn't let that sit without a challenge. So they started racing down the pole, trying different methods. Trash talking each other the whole damn time.

"They were fast, but neither one was really faster. Suddenly, David gets this look on his face and yells, 'Scott, lemme borrow your hoodie.' Mind you, they were already wearing their own hoodies, to help reduce friction from the pole and get more speed. They would wrap their arms around the pole and then use their feet to slow down just before the floor. This dummy wrapped the hoodie around the pole and held it with his feet, then dropped. Damn pole might as well have been greased, he fell so fast. Hit the cushion at the bottom, and we all heard the crack from his ankle when he landed. Dumbass. He jumped up on one foot and said, 'Yeah! Beat that, bitch!' Then he fell back down and asked for some medical attention. I thought about that the whole damn service."

Jason had to stop and slurp the last of his shake.

Zoe blotted her eyes with a napkin. "God. This sucks so much. I wish I could say something that didn't sound shallow or laughably inadequate."

She turned more directly to him, and he caught a puzzled expression on her face. "What?"

She hesitated. "Can I ask you something?"

Jason nodded and waited.

"Meg Ryan in *Top Gun*? Really?"

The burn-coarsened laugh was a bark. "We fucking lived for that movie," Jason said. "We had all the lines down pat. 'I feel the need...'"

"'The need for speed,'" Zoe finished the line with him. "It's always been a favorite of mine too."

"Dave thought of himself as more of a Goose than a Maverick," Jason mused. "Said he knew Adriana was the girl for him on their first date. Evidently they ended up in a karaoke bar, and on a drunken dare, he sang 'Great Balls of Fire' onstage. When he got back to the table, Adriana said, 'Hey, Dave, you big stud...' Dave said he looked at her, decided to go with it, said, 'That's me, honey. Take me to bed or lose me forever!' He swore that's how it happened. They were inseparable after the first date."

With a subdued chuckle, Zoe started the car. "Let's get you home."

His dark thoughts taunted him. This was his last ride; he'd better make it good, because he'd never see the sunshine again.

As she steered into traffic, Jason left his window down. He wanted to feel the salty wind in his hair, even though it hurt. Wanted to smell the gas fumes and the pavement and the faint whiffs of food from the eateries they passed. Wanted to absorb the sights and smells and sounds of the city he'd helped protect one last time. He wanted to, but as the ride progressed, one thing kept bothering him.

He couldn't stop looking over at Zoe.

Back home, Zoe helped Jason out of the car and into the wheelchair when he heard someone clearing their throat behind them. Zoe turned him toward the visitor.

Vince, the driver of Engine 7 the night disaster struck, stood there in street clothes, instead of the uniform he'd been wearing at the funeral. His tightly curled hair was frizzy and stuck out in every direction, his face was shadowed, and his eyes were puffy and bloodshot. He swiped at them with the heel of his hands, and hung his head as his shoulders slumped.

"Vince. Hey," Jason said to break the awkward silence.

"Hey." He seemed much less substantial than before the fire, as if hollowed out by misery. "Hey," he said again. A sob escaped. "Goddammit, Truffy. I'm so fucking sorry. This is all my fault, and I know you hate me, and I know I'm the last person you want to see. But I just wanted to tell you I'm sorry for getting you hurt and Hammerhead killed."

Vince slurred his apology, the scent of sour mash carrying the distance to Jason.

Vince stumbled before catching his balance. "I also wanted to tell you, in person, I wrote my resignation to the department. I know it's too late for you guys, but I won't be hurting anyone else."

Jason leaned forward in his chair, alarm bells starting to ring. "Not your fault, dude. It's not on you."

"I had too much pressure on the outside line, and when they radioed me to throttle it down, I did yours because I got them switched up." Vince seemed to have a need to confess. The words spilled out, almost tripping over one another. "It was my first fire on the pump, and I FUBAR'd it to hell."

"Vince, no, man. Don't do that to yourself."

Vince wasn't listening, just talking and swaying and grinding his hands into his eyes. He dropped his arms and faced Jason again. "I need you to know that it's okay to hate me. I deserve it. But I won't let anyone else down again, since, you know, not gonna be a firefighter anymore."

His face was calm now, his lips pursed and slightly upturned in a facsimile of a smile. Something about the look, and the way he squared his shoulders, bumped the alarm bells to klaxons in Jason's mind.

Zoe stepped into the conversation. "Hey, guys, why don't we go inside? I could put some coffee on." She'd probably caught the smell of whiskey from the bereft firefighter as well.

Jason didn't respond. He measured the face of the man who had sat across from him so many nights during those evening poker games at the station. *He's not bluffing.*

"I-I need to go," Vince mumbled and stalked toward the truck parked under an oak tree down the street.

Zoe took a step toward the retreating man, then glanced back at Jason. "Should I call someone?"

"No," Jason said, mouth dry and heart beating faster as Vince got closer to his truck. "No. You need to stop him from leaving. He's about to do something permanent. I'll call."

He watched comprehension flare across her face. She pivoted and raced after Vince. When she reached him, she placed her body between him and his beat-up red truck, as Jason called an ambulance for the brother whose shame and guilt so eerily matched his own.

"TIME FOR PHARMACEUTICALS," Zoe said.

She placed the pills in his hand and gave him the water glass. Jason washed them down, grimacing at the pain. He left the TV off, staring into space while Zoe updated records and cleaned. He was wrung out, though he suspected less from the physical exertions than the emotional ones.

She was marking his file when she looked up, head cocked at an angle and pen poised over the paper. "Can I ask you a silly question?"

Jason waited a moment before nodding.

"All those firefighters at the funeral. Who was guarding the city?"

"Atlanta." Her confused expression told him she didn't understand. "Well, a person who knows the city at each station, and volunteers and equipment from Atlanta and Gulfport. They covered the shift so everyone could go to the funeral."

"Wow. Y'all really do look after each other."

"We try. Hard to see so much happening because of a mistake I made though."

"Don't do that to yourself, please. What happened sucks. But this wasn't your fault. It's a dangerous job, and you did what you could in a bad situation. And you're obviously not the only one carrying guilt from this." She marked the chart and turned her attention to him again. "He called you Truffy. Odd nickname. How'd you get it?"

She wasn't going to leave this alone, was she? Jason crunched an ice chip while she waited. "When I was a rookie, the class found out my father was the main person to get Parrot's Cay Casino here on the coast. He'd gone to jail by then, but he'd squirreled away some money in an untouchable fund to support Mom and me. Paired with the fact my uncle is a captain in the department, there was some...resentment. They started calling me Trust Fund to get under my skin. After I proved myself in a few fires, they shortened it to Truffy, and it stuck. Vince is pretty much the only one who calls me that now, but he calls everybody by their nicknames." He shrugged. "It's who he is. He's a good guy, though."

"That was a good catch earlier. You know you saved his life, right?"

Jason had watched her intercept Vince in the parking lot. Watched her guide him firmly, but with compassion, to sit against his driver's side door. Watched as she sat next to a man she didn't know, letting him talk, and finally, cry. Watched her keep Vince occupied until police, fire, and an ambulance arrived. Her actions, more than Jason's, had saved his life.

"I just made a call," Jason said. "You kept him here."

"But you knew he was suicidal," she replied. "He had a pistol in his truck, and he was headed out to the marsh at Beauman's Bridge with a suicide note. That was what he meant when he talked about the resignation letter."

She was going somewhere with this. Jason fixed his eyes on the wall over her head and waited.

"Jason, how did you know?" Her tone was soft, but firm. There would be no easy way of dodging this.

Decision time.

Jason didn't answer for a long time. She waited, the silence between them demanding a response.

He wrestled with his thoughts. His mouth was a desert, his tongue impossibly thick. He shouldn't tell her, shouldn't weigh her down with his problems. If she knew, she'd stop him, and he'd let Dave down. It was only fair, his life for the life he took with his stupid decision. The decision was made. He couldn't go back on it now.

But then he thought of the horde of firefighters who showed up when the call went out for Vince, the haunted looks in their eyes when they realized how close they'd come to losing another brother, to ringing another bell. Was he willing to add to their baggage, simply because he was hurting? Was this a card he could play, knowing he was all in?

She waited for him to respond, debating life and death as he struggled to remain calm on the outside. Penance leading to absolution, or selfish abandonment of responsibilities?

And that was the thing, wasn't it? He'd sworn to protect the community, sworn to give his life, if necessary, in the line of duty. If he didn't blame Vince for his mistake, how could he blame himself?

If he couldn't shoulder all the blame for Dave's death, didn't that strip the grandeur from this plan? Turn it into a selfish act taken only to end the hurt and guilt he felt, and let's be brutally honest here, the grief of wrecking his pretty face? Was it worth hurting everyone who loved him?

Death penalty or life sentence?

Zoe still waited, but her poker face was for shit.

Finally, Jason sighed and laboriously tugged the drawer in his nightstand open. Nestled innocuously among the detritus inside was the red-and-white Altoids tin holding his escape ticket. He gave the tin one last, longing glance, then turned back to Zoe as the taunting thoughts howled in impotent rage.

"Do you want to save two lives today?"

Chapter Six

Zoe

MY FEET WERE heavy on the front porch steps as I dragged myself home. Between the funeral and the anguish of those two firefighters laid bare, I felt wrung out, like a sponge squeezed dry. I'd never met Dave, but the stories Jason told me, coupled with meeting Noah, painted a picture of a man who was loved, loving, and special. That he was gone, forever lost to his wife and child and friends, and to the world at large, left an emptiness in me. I grieved the loss of a man I'd only known through Jason's eyes and Noah's heart.

It was obvious Vince was in a bad place when he approached Jason, apologetic and inebriated, but I hadn't recognized him as suicidal. Maybe I should have. I obsessed over how Jason had known so confidently and quickly as Vince was leaving. Was it a firefighter thing? He'd changed out of his uniform. Was that what tipped him off? He was drunk and talked about his resignation letter. Was that it? The questions swirled in my head.

The light bulb went off as I was marking his chart for the end of shift. He recognized there was a plan because he had his own. The realization had left me cold, in a near panic.

Understanding Vince and Jason each blamed themselves and wanted to 'fix' it through self-sacrifice left me fighting panic and hurting fiercely for them.

Maybe Jason didn't like me much, but his decision to open up had me even more invested in his healing. I hadn't known that was possible.

However, I was left with a dilemma. Should I call an ambulance for a seventy-two hour hold like Vince? I shuddered to think of the care of Jason's injuries in the psych ward, not to mention the risk of exposure. Could I guarantee he would be sent to the burn ward an hour away? There were counselors there, but was there a bed open?

Unable to control what would happen once I made the call, my worry was that anywhere he went for an extended period could neglect his physical issues while focusing on his mental situation. This couldn't be up to me.

I called Mrs. Merone.

She fussed and tutted, but I emphasized the seriousness of the matter, and she came over, bringing back-up in the form of a tall, sturdy man wearing a flannel shirt and Red Wing boots. It took me a moment to recognize him.

Captain William Merone was Jason's uncle, and the officer who rang the bell at the funeral. He shared Jason's dark complexion and wavy hair. Grief weighed on his frame, but his face showed compassion and resolve. He would take the night watch.

When I left, well past my normal shift's end, I knew Jason was in good hands.

Not that I needed an excuse, but times like this required wine. I'd certainly earned it.

I stripped down, took a shower, and pulled on my comfy flannel pajama pants and a white cotton boyfriend T-shirt. Post-funeral ponytail undone, I curled up on the couch—free.

My weekend started now, and since Delphine was at a retreat with a lady friend for the next couple days, I was alone. I worked twelve-hour shifts at Jason's Monday through Friday, and although I hadn't pulled a full week due to starting on Tuesday, I was utterly drained and needed to decompress.

I poured a glass of dark-red, surprisingly nuanced Cabernet, and fired up the Chromecast. A Netflix binge was just what I needed. I scrolled through the homepage, skipping down through the categories: Spotlight, Popular on Netflix, Trending Now. Nothing grabbed me as I perused the catalog. I scrolled through My List, TV Dramas, and still nothing seemed right. I arrived at the Watch It Again category, and there it was, three spaces to the right.

Top Gun.

I took a gulp of wine and pressed play.

It wasn't my second time watching the movie, nor even the fifth. It's a classic for the simple fact it kicks all kinds of ass. Still, watching it today was like seeing it for the first time. I watched Maverick's copilot, Goose, love on his wife, only to die a short time later in a tragic accident. Alone and wrecked, I sobbed through tissues, wondering why I was doing this to myself, but unable to stop the movie or look away. Strangely, when the movie finished, I felt better. It was surprisingly cathartic, a bittersweet memorial both to the man who first seduced his wife with lines from the movie, and the friend he left behind.

After a refill of the glass, I needed something lighter. I needed fun, fantasy, and...maybe a bit of time travel? Yes. *Doctor Who* it was.

As the iconic theme music *doo-wee-oooo*ed and the blue police box traveled through the time vortex, I opened my laptop to check my dating profile. Sure enough, there were a couple of guys who had expressed interest. Well, alright. I sipped wine and saluted myself.

The first guy expressed his interest in vulgar fashion, letting me know he wanted to check "get with a tranny" off his bucket list. Ew. No. Unfortunately, the responses I'd received since posting my profile were frequently peppered with "admirers" along those lines. Immature guys with a fetish. Or seemingly nice guys who didn't spark my interest. It was getting disheartening.

The second guy was kind of cute, and his note to me was short and sweet.

> *Hi. I saw your profile and wanted to say I think you are beautiful, and you seem really cool. Maybe we could chat? I am intrigued and would like to know more about you.*

His name was Arthur, and the profile pic showed a handsome face with sandy-blond hair framing a generous nose and strong chin. He was tall, his body lean, with a rangy build that made me think of cowboys and those vintage "hunk of the month" calendars.

I clicked on his bio to learn more. Self-employed. Was that a euphemism for unemployed? Loves kids and animals. *What kind of monster doesn't?* Enjoys biking. *Hello!* The kind with motors. Oh! So close! He listed his full name as Arthur Dent. *Wait. That can't be his real name.* "My parents adored all things 'Brit-lit' when I was conceived, and their last name gave them the perfect excuse to pay tribute to Douglas Adams. I still haven't forgiven them."

A cute guy with wacky parents, named after the main character in the "Hitchhiker's Guide to the Galaxy" series? Okay. Definitely some potential there. *Please, please don't spoil it with a dick pic.*

I replied to his note.

> *Hey you. Yes, would definitely love to chat. Hit me up sometime.*

Closing the laptop, I lost myself in the last Gallifreyan's adventures in the TARDIS. I loved all the Doctors, but David Tennant? He was *my* doctor, the one who'd turned me into a hardcore Whovian. I could recite his "wibbly-wobbly" monologue word for word, rooted for him and Rose, the bad-wolf girl, and got unseemly emotional when he had to leave her behind in Darlig Ulv-Stranden—Bad Wolf Bay.

Okay, so I am a pop-culture princess with moderate geek tendencies. Don't judge me.

Finishing my wine, I slid into bed determined to sleep for however long my body felt like being horizontal.

Drifting off, I thought about Jason; remembering him at the graveside, stoic yet vulnerable, and then recalling the events immediately after. Today changed my impression of him. Before, he was a broken patient, needing so much from so many around him to heal. Now, I could more clearly see the substance that made him who he'd been and what he'd lost. I would probably never know how close he came to carrying out his final plan if Vincent hadn't stopped to apologize.

My thoughts were slow and drowsy as I wondered how much in him would change from this, what would stay the same, and what the combination would be. At the end of this wrenching day, he—and Vince—were still alive. That was enough for now.

I WOKE UP to midmorning sun in my window, terrible post-wine halitosis, and a driving need to pee. It was up and at 'em time, and a day with no itinerary stretched out before me. The best kind. After sprucing up in the bathroom, cleaning my room and making the bed, to imagined kudos from Delphine, I changed into some spandex. It was time for a bike ride. Three hours at least, usually more, of pushing pedals and climbing hills and zooming back down like an excited child. Since receiving a blue BMX bike for my sixth birthday, bicycles meant freedom. I loved their style, what they represented. With a bike and enough time, you could get anywhere in the world. In a life that saw its share of shit, the absolute worst times were those when I didn't have a bike. It was my escape, my therapy, my happy.

The sun was high and the day was humid by the time I got on the road. My legs were tentative at first, and it took a couple of miles for them to loosen. Finally they warmed up, and the ride became fun. Blasting Taylor Swift, P!nk, Halestorm, and Lana Del Rey through my earbuds, I glided over country back roads, greenways converted from old railroad lines, and enticing random turns. The only fly in the ointment was the asshole behind me in a red Corvette who matched my pace for a quarter mile before accelerating past me close enough to force me off the shoulder and into the grass. I valiantly resisted the urge to flip him off, for which I promised myself an extra glass of wine tonight.

When I returned home, I was sweaty, smelly, pleasantly fatigued, and ravenously hungry. I cleaned up and threw on some jeans and a tank top. I grabbed one of Delphine's ever-present Luna bars for some quick calories and then popped into town to get the makings for grilled steak and stuffed potato.

Afternoon deepened into early evening by the time I had steaks sizzling on the grill and potatoes baking in tinfoil armor. I promised Delphine there'd be leftovers when she got back tomorrow. For now, there was wine, Andrea Bocelli and Rob Thomas coming from the speaker, and I was content.

I checked on the social media world while waiting for the grill's heat to transform its contents into an edible nirvana. Waiting for me was a response from the perhaps-soon-to-be-suitor Mr. Dent.

As I cooked, and later as I ate, the back and forth with Arthur added to the enchantment of the day. As the conversation continued and became more flirtatious, I found myself dangerously drawn to the beautiful Mr. Dent. The wine had me buzzed, the steaks had me fat, and everything together had me primed for romance.

After a polite query, he sent his cell number to me. The conversation, in this more intimate virtual setting, quickly became more suggestive, more sensual, more promising. I looked again at his profile pictures, appreciating his style and his, well, everything. He sent a tightly cropped picture of his abs, showing a lean six-pack with jutting hip-bones suggestively leading my glance downward.

You like? He texted.

So very much, yes. I said, still swooning over the picture. *You purrrrty.*

Your turn, beautiful.

The request left me panicked. The years of doubt and self-loathing screamed against reciprocating. Shushing the fearful thoughts, I snapped a picture of my cleavage, pressing send before I could overthink it.

He responded with six heart emojis and an exclamation mark. Then a few seconds later, a text that said, *Hanging out at Turk's Landing. Good band playing. You should come.*

Aaaaah. Can't drive, already drinking. Alone (boo). Sounds fun though. Have a drink for me.

Five minutes went by without a response. I was about to call it a night when the phone dinged.

Can I call you?

I gulped half a glass of the Cabernet for courage.

Yes.

The phone rang, and my heart galloped.

"Hello?" I tried for seductive. Miserably failed.

"Is this the beautiful and unbearably sexy Zoe Calder?" His voice was lava, flowing through my ear and filling me with heat.

"It is. Is this the ever so lovely Arthur Dent?" I cringed. This siren stuff was so far beyond me.

Delphine had been right to gently force this when I joked about it, though. I needed to get out into the dating world, and this online stuff had some promising points.

"So I only have one question: What's a girl beautiful enough for armies of men to start wars over doing single? And how did I get lucky enough to catch your attention? Dammit, that was two questions, wasn't it? Shit, there's three. Ugh, I'm the worst. Sorry about the cussin'."

Jesus, this guy's personality was as sexy as his pictures.

"Ah...ah...I wouldn't say you catching my attention was lucky. Don't you own a mirror?" I stammered my way through another flirt fail.

"Damn, girl," he drawled in a way that threatened to completely melt me. "I wish you could come out. It's a crime against humanity you're drinking alone. What's up with that?"

"No, no, no. I've got the whole weekend to myself, which is a luxury I don't have too often. Plus, it means I don't have to fight with anyone over the steaks I've grilled."

"Naw. Don't tease me like this. You had a steak cookout all by yourself? That's so sexy. Like, right now I'm imagining you flipping steaks over the charcoal wearing nothing but an apron and a smile. Oh, shit! I just spilled my beer thinking about it." His voice faded for a moment. "Dammit. Now my pants are wet, and I smell like beer."

I laughed at the mental image. Maybe I wasn't the only awkward one.

"Seriously though," he said. "I would love to see you soon. See if this could go somewhere."

Me too, you sexy man. Me too. "Well, if you weren't too far gone, you could see me tonight. I still have some steak, and the wine here don't play."

He was quiet for a moment. "I would love to. Where are you?"

Giving him the address left me hyperventilating and anxious, and needing to sit down and count breaths when I got lightheaded. Once my breathing returned to normal, I slathered on some fresh makeup, changed into shorts and a cute, collared green shirt paired with my sexiest sandals, and grabbed another bottle of wine for when he arrived. Waiting, I sternly laid ground rules for myself. Mind your manners. Be funny but not too bawdy. Don't geek out too much about stuff you like. Nothing physical without full disclosure about yourself. Definitely no sex on the first date.

Within half an hour, Arthur pulled into the driveway in a well-worn pickup truck with the windows down. He stepped out, taller than I thought, maybe four inches over six feet and looking even better in person than his pictures suggested. He wore khakis with a white T-shirt and broken-in Doc Marten boots, blond hair slightly ruffled from the ride. His aquiline nose centered an angular face chiseled from marble, his sharp jawline slightly scruffy and leading down to a dimpled chin. The lips above his dimple were full, and oh my god, I had to stop with this thirsty shit. *Ground rules.*

He stepped onto the porch as I opened the front door. "Hey, you."

"Hey, yourself, beautiful," he said. "I'm Arthur. It's so nice to meet you."

"Yes." His semi-formal tone left me charmed. "Hello, Mr. Arthur. I'm Zoe. Lovely to meet you, as well."

"Call me Art." His hug was warm, and I invited him in. I ushered him to the back deck and placed a nicely warmed steak with baked potato still in the foil jacket on a plate in front of him while he sat. I poured some wine and cued up the jazz. Citronella candles around the perimeter of the porch helped keep the mosquitoes at bay, and the chirp of crickets in the dark beyond added to the ambiance of the evening.

He made appreciative sounds as he ate, raising his eyebrows at the wine after a sip. I grinned. "Told you our wine don't play."

He finished the plate and leaned back with a satisfied sigh. Regarding his near empty glass, he glanced back over to me meaningfully.

"So, Mr. Sexy-man Art, what do you do to pay the bills?" I asked as I grabbed the bottle and poured us both a new round.

"Well," he said, as he wiped his lips with a napkin. "I guess you could call me a handyman. I fix things for people. Make sure everything is working properly for them, you know? Proper maintenance is important for a happy house, a happy car..." A suggestive waggle of his eyebrows, and then he said, "How long has it been since your last tune-up?"

He wasn't talking about my car, and I felt the heat rising in my face. I waved the question off with an embarrassed silence that probably told him more than he needed to know.

As the evening progressed, we talked. About nothing, anything, everything. Small get-to-know-you talk, big what-do-want-to-do-with-your-life talk, and things political and personal. He was charming, roguish, and impossibly pretty after the second bottle of wine was polished off. As much as I liked wine, I don't often over-imbibe. But tonight, with Arthur Dent at my table and another day off tomorrow, it was easy to keep going.

A worry began to tinge my thoughts. He might not know. If he didn't read my bio, or if he'd somehow forgotten... I pushed it to the back of my mind. We would have to clear that up before anything physical happened, but it wasn't a conversation to have tonight. For now, I simply wanted to enjoy being a girl flirted with and flattered by this lovely man.

Still, when he asked the question, it was harder to say no than I expected.

"Hey, you wanna go inside? To the bedroom?"

Did I ever. Especially after the way he purred the question. My body yearned to be touched, tingled, caressed, and fulfilled. But I'd set my ground rules. "I'm sorry, Art. Yeah, I really want to, but…I mean, we just met, and I want to get to know you better before we, you know…"

A shadow ghosted across his face before he smoothed it over and pasted on a smile. I knew that look. Knew I wouldn't be seeing Art again.

"Okay, sure, yeah. I should probably head home then. It's getting pretty late." He glanced at his watch. "Or rather, early."

I struggled to keep a smile on my face as the tentative flame of hope flickered out like a snuffed candle leaving only wisps of dreamlike smoke behind. We stood from the table, and he opened his arms for a hug before leaving. I stepped toward his embrace.

Flashes exploded in my skull, and I fell to my knees. I lay there for a moment, not understanding for a split second that Arthur had belted me behind my left ear, leaving me hurt and disoriented.

"Bitch, I wasn't asking, and I didn't come over here for blue balls," he growled as he grabbed a fistful of my hair, wrenched me up, and bounced my head off the table.

Blood spurted from my nose, and I fell in a heap, blindly scrambling to get up. I needed to run, needed to fight back, something. He was on me before I could get my knees under me, calloused hands around my throat, knees on my left shoulder and back, pinning me down. His hands squeezed tighter on my throat, and dark spots swam in my eyes as Sia's song about swinging from chandeliers blasted over the deck speakers.

"I am going to fuck your ass, bitch," his sinister voice in my ear, close enough to smell the steak still on his breath. "That's what you want, right? A real man to fuck you and make you feel like a woman? Yeah, fucking faggot. I got your number. Act like you don't want my stuff, but I know you been giving it up to any hard leg looks at you twice. Sissy-ass bitch."

Another squeeze, and the world swam out of focus.

He dragged me to my bedroom by my neck as I choked and gasped, flailing for air. The knife he produced was large, and he made sure I got a terrified look at it before he dragged the point across my jaw, leaving it stinging and sticky. Then he clenched his fingers around the hilt and swung at me. The punch from his hilt-reinforced fist exploded through my brain, shutting off coherent thought.

When awareness returned, I was facedown with half my body on the bed and knees on the floor. My hands were tied behind my back with stockings, and I was naked from the waist down, unable to move. Arthur was on top of me, putting on a condom. I screamed and tried to squirm away.

"Shut the fuck up!" He punched me in the back of my head. I gasped, and he stuffed a wad of socks and panties in my mouth. He put his legs between mine and forced me open. "Figured you'd wake up for the show. Fucking tease me, cocksucker. I'll show you. Fucking slut don't want to give it up, the hell sense does that make? Lemme finish getting my rubber on, betcha have all kinds of diseases from the whoring you do; gotta be careful."

He raped me. There was no other way to put it, and I won't fancy it up with more than that.

After, he tied a ripped length of bed sheet around my neck, and secured it to the head of the bed. A gentle movement drew the slipknot tighter around my neck. My legs were secured to the bottom feet of the bed with more of the ripped sheet. Unable to escape, all I could do was wait for what was next. Arthur went into the bathroom. I heard him piss loudly and then flush the toilet.

He came back into the room.

After the second time, he left the house. I listened for the sound of a truck cranking, desperate for this nightmare to be over. My wrists chafed from the constant struggle to free my hands. The gag muffled my scream when I heard the rattle of silverware and a dragging sound across the floor in the kitchen. This wasn't over yet. He came into the bedroom with a black garbage bag containing the dishes and silverware from outside. In his other hand, he held a roll of additional garbage bags and a length of stained and oily rope that must have come from his truck. He saw my panic, and his face seemed regretful.

"Yeah, I'm afraid this doesn't end well for you. Hell, you're lucky I didn't take you out on your bike earlier. This works out better for both of us, don't you think? You got a steak dinner and all the cock you could handle. There are worse ways to go, wouldn't you say?" He smiled sadly as he watched me realize I had been stalked. That I was about to die.

He began to fill the garbage bags with things he'd touched or used in the bedroom. He had my phone and held it up to me. "5-5-5-5 as a security code? *Tsk, Tsk. Tsk.*"

He was in my phone. His thoroughness fueled my desperation, crowding out rational thought as my increasing movements caused the noose to squeeze my neck ever tighter, leaving me struggling for each short whistling breath.

Stepping in the hall for a moment, he came back with a folded tarpaulin and spread it out on the floor near me. *Oh, fuck,* I thought. *I'm dead. Just another statistic. Oh, shit. Oh, shit. Oh, shit.*

He took another garbage bag off the roll, shook it out. He untied the noose from the head of the bed, took it off my neck, and I gasped the sweet air hungrily. He draped the bag over my head, working it down my body until it reached almost to my belly. I couldn't see anything, and my gasping breaths made the plastic stick to my mouth and nose. This was it. No chance to say goodbye to anyone, no way to fight back.

"Bye, slut," he said casually.

I felt the sheet go around my neck again, then begin to tighten. My attempts to move, to fight, were easily overcome. My chest heaved, and fireballs of light exploded in the darkness behind my eyelids, the reptilian part of my brain screeching for air at any cost. Then, with the suddenness of a light switch being turned off, the deep dark calm claimed me.

JUMBLED MEMORIES. LIGHTS and sirens. Paramedics and nurses. Doctors waving penlights in my eyes. Needle pricks and IVs. Beeps and alarms.

The world slammed back into painful, bright immediacy. I flailed blindly, trying to sit up, the alerts and monitors going crazy as I lashed out.

"Shh, shh, no, cheri. Be gentle. It's okay. You're safe."

Delphine. Safe. I was in a hospital, but I didn't know how.

I took a ragged breath, arching my back. She came into my line of sight, brushing the hair out of my eyes. Seeing her helped calm the panic.

"Lord, child. It's okay now. You're still with us, love. Shh."

I tried to speak, could only croak.

As if by magic, a nurse appeared. She stabbed something into the IV, and reality dissolved into blankness again.

The next time I woke I was calmer. I winced against the headache and the light streaming through the windows of the room. Delphine stood and began to caress my face with a wet washcloth. Everything hurt.

"What?" I croaked. "How...how am I here?"

"Oh, cheri, I will tell you the story soon, I promise. But for now, please, let's be still and rest."

I squinted at Delphine, still waiting for my eyes to adjust to the brightness. Worry etched lines in her face, and a disheveled, stained blouse betrayed how long she'd stayed by my side. Her dark eyes were full of concern, her body radiating an intensity I'd never witnessed before.

There was a knock at the door, and a white-coated doctor came into the room.

"Ms. Calder, hi. I'm Doctor Whittaker. Glad to see you're still with us." He stepped closer and flashed the penlight in my eyes. He slipped the stethoscope from around his neck with practiced ease and listened to my heart and lungs. He made some notes on the chart in his hands and placed it back in its spot at the end of the bed. "Quite remarkable, really. We almost lost you. Your friend here saved your life. If you'd been in that position even a minute longer..." he trailed off, but his meaning was clear.

I wouldn't be here. I shouldn't be here. What happened? How did I survive? "How...how long?" I said slowly.

"Have you been here? Well, you got here last night around two a.m. It's now Sunday afternoon, shortly after three p.m. So it's been about thirteen hours."

Jesus. Thirteen hours? I'd lost half a day. Delphine's nod confirmed the doctor's information. Panic. *Jason.* I was scheduled to be at work tomorrow at 7:30 in the morning.

"Jason...work."

Delphine laid a calming hand on my shoulder. "I've already let the agency know you won't be able to work for a bit. They are making changes to the schedule as we speak. No need to worry, mon amie."

I lay back against the pillow, closing my eyes against the headache. Dr. Whittaker finished his checks and stated he would send a nurse in with something for pain and sleep.

"If all goes well, we'll try to send you home tomorrow. I want you to rest and get some strength back tonight. Now, before I send the nurse in with the meds, I do have to ask: would you be willing to talk with a couple of detectives about what happened?"

My heart beat faster, the metallic taste of terror in my mouth at the thought of reliving the memory of what happened. I nodded weakly.

"It is important to help them find the person who did this, and the sooner they can speak with you, the better. But I am going to limit them to a ten-minute visit, and I *will* put a clock on them," Dr. Whittaker said.

I wasn't looking forward to the interaction, but was relieved Dr. Whittaker was drawing a line at how long I had to endure the meeting.

I carefully nodded again, and Dr. Whittaker went to retrieve the detectives.

They were a male-female pair, who introduced themselves with no nonsense, and asked Delphine to leave. She left, grudgingly, and let me know she would return in ten minutes.

I spoke in short sentences recounting the events as I remembered. After, they were kind enough to ask mostly yes-or-no questions so I could shake my head.

"So, you asked this guy—whom you've never met—over to your residence? Is this correct?" The male detective was almost a stereotype: heavyset, with florid cheeks that spoke to an intimate acquaintance with booze and disappointment. His navy blazer was rumpled, and the mint in his mouth did little to offset his coffee-scented breath.

I nodded, shame heating my face.

"Is it possible this was some kind of roleplay? A fantasy-type thing that went a little too far?"

Jesus. Did this guy really ask me that? I shook my head no, hard enough to make me dizzy.

"Okay, okay. I have to ask these questions, you understand." He tried for a placating tone.

No, no, I don't understand.

The female detective laid her hand on the guy so she could take a turn. She was lithe, with chin-length frizzy brown hair in a no-maintenance hairdo and blunt-shaped hands holding a small notebook.

"Ms. Calder." Weird emphasis on the "Ms." as she spoke. "Are you sure this is an accurate depiction of what occurred?"

My eyes widened, and I gave her a quizzical stare.

"You are transgender, yes?" The word transgender seemed foreign to her, and she said it haltingly.

I nodded slowly, the question opening a pit of unease in my stomach.

"Do you engage in sex work? I mean, that's a pretty standard thing for you types, right? Was that what happened? You had a trick who went a little far? Or is it possible this person didn't realize you were actually a guy and felt...slighted?"

Fuck. I should've known better. These detectives weren't going to be any help. I shook my head weakly. The events of the previous evening being dismissed in such a cavalier fashion by those supposed to help was yet another betrayal I should be used to by now. Gritting my teeth against the frustration, I pointed to the door. "Leave."

"Let's go, John," the frizzy-haired detective said, snapping her notebook shut. "Told you he was trapping. Sir—ma'am—ah, if we find out anything we'll let you know."

John ponderously rose from his chair, exhaling more coffee breath. "You called it before we got here," he said to his shrewish partner. "Bet us taxpayers will be on the hook for his hospital bill too."

I evil-eyed their stupid asses until they left the room. *I do have insurance, you fucking assholes, thank you very much. And no, I don't do sex-work, but why should it matter? Would I deserve it then?* The hurt lanced through me.

After their exit, I slowly turned on my side and curled into myself as much as possible. The tears that waited until I was alone couldn't be dammed any longer. I shook, seethed, and cried. Everything hurt, especially my lower region.

Delphine returned, took one look, and called for the nurse. Her tone had someone at my bed within seconds. She held my hand, as the nurse assessed me, asking what was wrong. I ignored her until she left for the medications Dr. Whittaker promised.

"Oh, cher, was it bad with the cops?"

I opened my eyes to her concern and wiped at my nose. Without another word, she bent in for a hug. I grabbed her and held on as the fear and anger and helplessness overwhelmed me again. Within a few moments, the nurse returned with medication, injecting it into the IV. Soon, the physical pain faded into a lower volume, and sleep began to creep in around the edges.

Haltingly, I told Delphine what happened with the detectives. The medication dulled the pain in my throat enough to let me talk in a low tone. Her face darkened as I spoke, gaze going flat, the intensity within her seeming to thrum harder as she listened.

Against my will, the medicine took me under.

AFTER ALL THE scans and tests and the incessant parade of medical professionals were complete, I went home the next afternoon with multiple prescriptions for antibiotics, pain, sleep, and a stool softener. I gingerly walked into the house, stopping short when I reached the hallway to my bedroom. I couldn't go in there. But it was where my clean clothes were and I wanted—needed—a shower. Steeling myself against the onslaught of terror, I forced myself step by agonizing step down the corridor. Delphine hovered close without touching or speaking, matching my slow progress. Reaching the bedroom, I leaned on the doorjamb, unable to move as the images of my last time here assaulted me.

Finally, I opened the door, fear like a banshee's wail screaming against it.

The room was messier than I'd expected, probably from the police investigation. The mattress was bare, and every hard surface was covered with powder. Small pieces of broken glass from the window glinted on the floor, and damp spots from recent rain darkened the carpet. Seeing the state of the room, I realized Delphine hadn't been home since the events of that night. She'd stayed close to me. Overwhelmed, I turned and buried my head in her shoulder, the wrenching fear mixed with the gratitude of her support leaving me a gibbering wreck.

She led me back to the living room, and made me sit before my legs completely gave way from exhaustion. She retrieved a spare set of her own sheets, and placed them on the couch. After helping me lay down, she turned the TV on and set my meds nearby with a tumbler of water. Once I was settled, she marched into my room and began to clean. As I absently watched the crew of the *Serenity* stumble through a job that didn't go as planned, Delphine cleaned and scrubbed and cursed in a low voice until my chemically induced sleep finally turned off the lights.

I slept fitfully, haunted by visions of Arthur and the events of that night. Whenever I clawed my way to reality, hands at my throat and fighting to take a breath, Delphine was in the chair nearby, wide awake and on guard. She would look at me and say, "It's okay, cheri. Nothing can harm you tonight." Reassured, I would sink back into the world of nightmares.

At morning's light, I woke to see Delphine asleep in the chair. She'd finally succumbed to exhaustion. God, I didn't deserve her. Even the bathroom sparkled from her efforts, I realized when I staggered in for the delayed shower. I stayed in long after the hot water was gone, scrubbing myself raw but still unable to get clean. Afterward, I looked in the mirror for the first time since waking in the hospital.

The battered image staring back shocked me. Inflamed nose under two black and swollen eyes. Cuts and bruises on my face, a prominent scrape straight across my upper right cheek from where my head was bounced off the outside table, and a nasty gash down my right jaw from the knife. My throat was a mass of angry red marks and soreness.

Suddenly, with an intensity that swept through me like a wildfire in a drought-stricken forest, I became angry. Angry at rapists, and at unsympathetic cops, and at myself most of all for the mistake that had put me in this position. It was energizing, that anger. I survived and I would learn from this. Fuck that guy. Fuck those cops.

I drew strength from the rage, finding a clarity of thought that allowed me to engage with the world again. I brushed my teeth with purpose, staring at myself in the mirror as I vowed *never again.*

Never again would I allow this to happen. Never again would I be seen as a victim. Never again would I be vulnerable.

On my way to the kitchen, I passed my ferocious protector who still slept. Coffee and breakfast for her, I decided, spooning grounds into the filter and pre-heating the oven. I was adding sausage from a sizzling pan into white gravy when she glided into the kitchen. Cocking her head at me, she watched for a moment as I cooked, her face still sleep-starved. She poured a steaming mug as I pulled the biscuits out of the oven and began to scramble eggs in the sausage skillet.

"Feel better, I see," she said as she sipped the coffee. A smile curved her lips, unspoken approval in her eyes.

I set the spatula down, turned and faced her. "Del, Jesus, I owe you everything. Thank you."

"Of course, cher. Welcome to the club no one wants to be in." Her smile tightened into something more sympathetic. "Better catch those eggs before they stick to the pan."

We ate breakfast at the dining table in near silence. Delphine called in to the university to let them know she would be taking another personal day.

Finishing the meal, she drained her coffee. "We should talk."

"Yes, please." Whatever the story, I needed to know why I was still alive.

We moved into the living room, clearing the sheets before sitting together on the couch. Delphine tucked her legs under herself and angled her body toward me.

"I found you," she started, then took a shaky breath. "Found you in the bedroom, tied up and stuck in a garbage bag, with a noose around your neck. And I wasn't even supposed to come home that night. But I starting feeling icky up there in the woods and didn't want to hang around any longer. You know me, if I'm sick, I want to be in my house, in my bed. My apologies were extended to everyone and I headed home. It was a two-and-a-half hour trip, and I got to you within a couple of minutes of you dying."

I hugged my knees to my chest, my arms trembling. The earlier anger faded, and I sat numbly as she talked.

"When I got home, there was an older pickup truck in the driveway behind your car. I thought, 'Aw, she has a visitor. Hope he's cute!' But when I walked in, everything just felt...wrong. Call it intuition, bad juju, whatever. It felt dark. Heavy. Ugly. I yelled out to let you know I was home. There was some jangling back in your room, and the sound of glass shattering. I grabbed my purse pistol and headed toward your room, turning on lights as I went. Your door was open when I got there." Delphine glanced down and away from me, her body tensed against the memories. "I saw you... Lord, Zo. I saw you and I will never get that sight out of my mind. You were limp, covered in a garbage bag, and dead. Truly, I thought you were dead. I heard the old truck crank up as I got to you, but I couldn't leave you. I got you untied and breathing again and then called the ambulance." A tear rolled down her face as she finished talking, still unable to look at me.

The trembling in my arms had deepened into full body shivers by the end of Del's recounting. I was here only because Delphine felt ill enough to leave the retreat early and had headed back before anything occurred. The silence spun out, and I glanced over in time to catch her quizzical look. Naturally, Delphine wanted to know what happened before she arrived but didn't want to push. She deserved the story, but my mind balked at recounting what happened, yet again. The weight of shame and embarrassment at putting myself in that position bore down on me, along with the fear of her disappointment in me when she heard how everything had occurred. Then, thankfully, the anger flared up again, burning off enough of the shame and fear for me to start talking. Gripping my knees and staring into the distance, I told her the story in a detached monotone.

Delphine remained silent and listened intently. When I finished, she was the one trembling. A closer look, and I read the emotion on her face. Unbridled fury.

"Fuck. Fuck that fucking fucker," she spat venom. "And fuck those cops for being fucking shits who didn't give a damn about you. Fuck him and fuck them and fuck every fucking asshole that fucks with women like they're a personal playground."

Angrily, she stood and retrieved her phone. After taking a few moments to calm herself, she said, "I have a friend who is a therapist. You need to talk to someone who can help you through this because, love, this is gonna be a rough journey. She is incredibly kind and has some experience with this. Not just the rape, but with transgender people as well. Let me call her. I don't want you going back to work until she signs off on it." Her tone brooked no objections, as she held the phone to her ear.

"Okay," she said after the call. "Dr. Jones will see you tomorrow at eleven. She's skipping lunch as a favor. Do not be late."

"Thank you again. For everything."

"No thanks necessary, mon amie. Had I gotten home sooner, the tarp and garbage bags would have still been used, trust and believe. No one would've ever heard from fuckhead rapist Arthur again." She was deadly serious. Her eyes narrowed as she remembered something. "He took your phone, you said?"

"Yes."

"But he didn't get your laptop. I borrowed it for the retreat, remember?"

"Oh, yeah, sure. Hadn't exactly thought about it." Where was she going with this? "Why's that important?"

"Maybe we can use it to trace the phone. There's an app for that, yeah?"

She retrieved the laptop, and we went to work. After several minutes, it became apparent we wouldn't be able to track the Android phone. It was most likely dead or destroyed.

Shifting gears, we went to the dating site where I'd met Arthur. He wasn't there. As well, probably because he'd taken the phone, my profile and interactions had been scrubbed away. It was as if he'd never reached out to me. As if we hadn't existed on the site at all.

Arthur had been very thorough.

I was discouraged, exhausted, and hurting.

After some time, I noticed Delphine was in my bedroom. I went as far as the doorway and peered inside. She was going to all four corners of the room holding a bundle of smoking sage, smudging the room, a practice used for healing and clearing an area of negative energy. The warm yet astringent smoke was underpinned with a vanilla scent that told me sweetgrass had been woven into the bundle.

I didn't recognize this room. The setup was changed entirely. My bed sat against a different wall, and the other furniture was rearranged. Delphine had placed a fresh set of sheets on the bed and cleaned and organized everything. The only evidence left of what happened here was the missing windowpane covered with precisely cut cardboard.

As exhausted and ill as she was, she'd spent a massive amount of time and energy doing her best to reclaim this bedroom from the evil that happened here. Yet again, I was moved to speechlessness at the way Delphine showed her love. Now, with the changes and the smudge smoke hanging lazily in the air, the room felt somehow lighter, cleaner. I found myself inside the room, only realizing after I hadn't had to fight with myself to walk in.

Delphine smiled at me as she waved her arms in a *ta-da!* motion.

"What magic have you done?" I asked. "This is my room, but it feels completely different. Not...unsafe anymore. Is that the right word? I don't know. It feels better."

"The window will be repaired later this afternoon. This is your space, and I will be damned if some psychotic cuntwaffle comes in and takes that from you." She waved her arm again, smudge stick trailing white smoke. "What do you think?"

"I like the changes. Still not super excited about this room, but I really, really appreciate everything you've done."

"Welcome, mon amie. No rush getting back in here. I imagine it might take some time to feel comfortable in here again." She snuffed the sage out in a clay bowl on the nightstand. "I'm going to leave this in here. I think it might be helpful if you did some smudging every day for a bit."

"Promise." It was the least I could do. Something had been bugging me, so I decided to ask, "Del? What happened to you?"

"What do you mean, child? What are you asking?"

"You said earlier, 'Welcome to the club.' Were you raped?"

"Bluntly, cher, yes. And I will tell you the story someday, but I don't think telling you right now helps anything. Let's say, I have a very good idea of what you are feeling right now, and what you are about to go through."

"I'm sorry that happened to you."

"Hush, child. It's in the past, much farther away than what happened to you. It's a shitty milestone in womanhood that happens far too often to far, far too many."

She took both of my hands in hers, face charged with the intensity I had noted before. "You will change because of this, ma cheri. I can't tell you what that change will look and feel like because it is different for everyone. Some allow it to consume them, to hollow them out and leave them empty. Some become rigid, brittle. Some become strong, incredibly strong. Fire destroys wood, makes iron weak, but tempers steel. I think you have steel in you, cheri, and for your sake, I hope so."

ELEVEN A.M. FOUND me in Hattiesburg, seventy miles north of Biloxi seated in the stereotypical waiting room of the therapist Delphine had contacted. There were tasteful furnishings and ancient magazines, low-pile carpeting and a noise machine creating an auditory curtain as I filled out the intake paperwork. The innocuous ritual never seemed to change. Bored with life? Fill out this paperwork. Husband cheating on you? Fill out this paperwork. Raped and almost killed by a psychopath? Fill out this fucking paperwork. It had been years since I saw a therapist, although I usually appreciated the sessions. There is something to be said for the concept of talking exclusively about yourself and your problems for an hour to a willing ear, even if you have to pay for the privilege. This was different though, and I dreaded what was coming. The fact Dr. Jones was skipping lunch to shoehorn me into her day spoke to the gravity of the situation, and I was grateful Delphine arranged this. The clipboard of papers in my lap still left me irritated, though.

There was one other person in the waiting room with me; a stylishly dressed bottled-brunette with expensive red-soled high heels and Hermes bag, gorgeous purple silk scarf accenting her muted camel-colored yoke dress. She was polished and coiffed, and simply looking at her made me feel frumpy. Her movements were choppy, absently flipping pages back and forth in the magazine on her lap. I recognized that jumpy, distracted dread because it mirrored my own. The soul-deep sigh she gave when she was called back after a few moments left me silently wishing her strength as I was left alone with my trite paperwork.

I finished the forms and returned them to the receptionist.

After several minutes, the reception door opened, and a mature woman with observant hazel eyes and silver hair stepped into the room. "Zoe? Hi, I'm Dr. Jones. Let's go to my office."

Dr. Jones led us down the hall to a tastefully appointed room. Large windows opened to the south with a view of a compact wooded area with a small stream and wildflowers. A desk fronted the window, and the room held a leather couch, a couple of straight-backed chairs, and a bean bag. It seemed cozy, if a bit formal, aside from the bean bag. She invited me to have a seat. I chose one side of the couch. Dr. Jones adjusted one of the chairs to face me and took a seat. She folded her arms into her lap and studied me frankly. "So, how are you today?"

Such an open, loaded question.

Here we go. To get help, I had to pull the metaphorical bandage off first. I had to tell her what happened, and I wasn't completely sure I could get through it again.

Taking a deep breath, I haltingly told her my story of being raped and almost murdered. She stayed quiet but with absolute attention, handing me the tissue box when the tears shimmered and escaped. Her eyes darkened when I recounted the interaction with the detectives, and she made emphatic marks in her notepad.

"You have been through something incredibly painful and traumatic," her enunciation was Ivy League precise. "I'm glad you reached out for help so quickly."

"I'm glad I'm not dead," I said flippantly.

"That too. It's incredible that you were saved at literally the last moment. How are you doing with that?"

I caught myself absentmindedly stroking the injured part of my neck. "Haven't really let myself think about it too much. I mean, it kinda skitters around the edges of my mind, but...I don't know. It hasn't really sunk in yet, I guess. That I should be dead. Just another statistic."

"Statistic. Such an impersonal word to describe a life. I've always found it so cold. Every life leaves an imprint on those around it, in ways big and small. Including yours. Why would you say 'just another statistic'?"

"Because I'm transgender, and it's a hazard of the job." I shrugged.

"And the detectives who spoke with you offered confirmation of that, didn't they? It's expected that you are a sex worker, and even more, that you aren't deserving of basic justice because of who you are?" She leaned toward me, her words suffused with compassion. "Zoe, being transgender is part of what makes you unique, beautiful, and human. I can only imagine the many forms of fear being transgender brings, and you have faced the primal nightmare of being raped and almost murdered because of who you are. Beyond the evil that psychopath did to you, what I want you to realize is those cops were wrong and horrible at their jobs. You absolutely deserve justice."

Her earnestness had tears threatening again. Swallowing hard, I managed to stutter out, "I— Yes, thank you. I agree."

"How is your support network?"

"Delphine has been my everything since this happened. I have a few friends, some trans, some LGB, but I haven't been brave enough to tell them what happened yet. I worry about triggering some of them, and, I mean, I don't really want to intrude on anyone, you know?"

Her expression was puzzled. "What about your family?"

Abruptly, I realized I hadn't even told my family what happened.

"Why not?" Dr. Jones asked.

I related the story of my latest interaction with my father on the phone a few days earlier. At her request, I delved into the history with my father.

"It's one of those cliché things, really. I was always 'less than' to my father. I was the 'sissy faggot' who made him look bad. He's a preacher, in an 'old school' type of church where the pastor has all the power. There isn't a board of deacons or anything. He is it; he speaks for God, and anything that crossed him or upset him was upsetting to God. And a big thing with them is that family is a direct reflection of the parents, especially of the father as head of the house. I guess I wasn't a very good reflection.

"So, yeah, he threw me out when I was sixteen because I wouldn't 'man up.' And I tried. I really tried. I was so scared back then of going to hell, yet everything I did just seemed to be...wrong. So, now I'm persona non grata. With the church and the family. Have been for almost fifteen years. Fuck 'em. Their loss, right?" I offered a smile and a chuckle.

She saw the hurt through my bravado and shook her head slowly. "Zoe, it sounds like what you've recently been through isn't the only trauma in your life. It had to be incredibly difficult to survive being rejected from your family at such an early age. And you didn't just survive, you thrived. You found a way to go to school, became a highly-skilled nurse. That says so much about you. You went into a field to help others heal. That's an incredible response. I know that wasn't easy. Getting through this won't be easy, either, but knowing what you went through before, and how you responded, gives me great hope for your future."

The hour ended with Dr. Jones giving me some visualization and breathing exercises. She wanted me to come once a week for the next month at least. I agreed, but with trepidation. How the fuck did I get roped into exploring the worst parts of my life when I already felt so broken?

Chapter Seven

Jason

JASON WOULD NEVER have admitted it aloud to anyone, but he happily anticipated Zoe's return. She was an intriguing woman who had disappeared with little explanation from the nursing agency. The nurses who filled in had been competent, and he had no actual complaints. But it was clearly just a job to them, and he was just a patient. He hadn't realized how much emotional support Zoe offered during that short week, even as he'd denied and raged against it.

After five weeks of absence, she was back.

She was different when she arrived, that vibrancy he remembered muted. What could have happened to her? Completing her tasks with clinical efficiency, she was gentle as ever. Still, she was distant, distracted.

After the morning medications were administered and coffee placed on the hospital tray that hovered over his bed, she opened the curtains and blinds to let in the morning sun. Golden light streamed in, illuminating the room and Zoe. At his gasp, she flinched and turned away.

It still hurt Jason to talk before the morning meds kicked in, so he only raised a questioning eyebrow. He wasn't prepared for the embarrassment that spread across her face. Embarrassment and shame. What could she be embarrassed about? At his stare, Zoe waved her hands as if to dismiss the marks revealed by the bright sunlight.

He studied the scrapes and scabs on her face skillfully camouflaged with makeup, the darker marks that looped around her throat as if...she'd been strangled. Those weren't marks from a fall or car accident. Someone had grabbed her throat. She was attacked. It made sense suddenly. The limp. The emotional distance. The time away from work. Anger and a fierce protectiveness rose up. While the fire department didn't see as many battered women as the EMTs and police did, he'd seen enough to recognize the signs.

Zoe mumbled an excuse and left the room. He heard her in the restroom, caught a sob that wasn't quite covered by the running faucet. He watched TV blankly, mind running feverishly. Soon, Zoe came back with freshly applied makeup, and set about cleaning the area. Jason took a sip of coffee to lubricate his throat. "I'm sorry. Don't have to tell. Just...glad you're okay." He didn't want to pry, but the injuries, coupled with her distance, plucked at his heart.

Zoe gave a crooked smile, face blooming red, and nodded an awkward acceptance to Jason.

It touched him, that smile. But he wouldn't have admitted that to anyone either.

ZOE USED THE day to settle back into the routine of his care.

"You're making good progress physically." Her voice was warm as she completed her assessment, the earlier distance fading. It made him oddly proud of his body's skill in healing, that it could give her a tiny bit of happiness. "And you're still here. I'm *really* happy about that. How are you doing? How is Vince?"

He had fielded a lot of questions about Vince since the afternoon after the funeral. But no one knew about his own plans, and his mother took great pains to keep that fact quiet. After Zoe called her to inform her of the situation, she nixed the idea of a therapist, swore Uncle Billy to silence, and badgered him into taking the night shifts she couldn't. She stressed the need to "keep a close eye on him" to each nurse who rotated through, while reminding them of the expectation of "medical privacy." He hadn't told anyone anything, either, as ashamed of his weakness as she was. Except for Vince. They had bonded over their guilt, grief still raw but easier to bear together.

He came to loathe those questions about Vince, but Zoe got a pass. She was there, the one who saw them at their worst and threw the lifelines that saved them.

He cleared his throat gently, remembering how much worse it had hurt talking to her before. "He's doing better. Not super great, but he's still here, like me. We text a lot now, whenever one of us is down or going to a dark place. We promised to reach out if we are getting close to doing something. It's our little private club." He fussed with his blanket, not wanting to see her face at his confession.

After a prolonged silence filled with worry, he raised his eyes back to her. He wasn't prepared for the look on her face as she stared into the distance, sadness and horror stamped on her frozen features. She shook her head privately, noticed his attention, and abruptly left the room again. As she fled, he heard her mumble, "These fucking clubs are the worst."

What the hell had happened to her?

AMONG THE GUESTS that came and went, there was one who showed up less and less frequently. His girlfriend, Jenna. She always apologized for her absences when she showed, claiming busyness and work-related travel. But he noticed she avoided his eyes when she visited, the distance between them when they were together was too hard to ignore.

It hurt and puzzled him. Was he different now? Was he too grouchy around her? Too loopy from pain meds? He tried to bring it up in text messages or the occasional call that taxed his throat. She always insisted nothing was wrong. He knew better. He just didn't know how to fix it. She was his first love, the one he always came back to. He loved her. That was all he knew, all he could cling to.

About two weeks after Zoe came back, Jenna stopped by as morning was slipping into afternoon.

He was awakened by their voices in the living room coming through his open door. Zoe had probably knocked and noticed he was napping.

"Hey Jenna. Jason's asleep right now, but you can hang out in the living room if you want to wait for him to wake up."

"Yeah, I kinda need to talk to him. I'll wait. Can we make some coffee?"

"Sure. Give me a sec. I'll get it going while I finish up in the kitchen."

"Okay. Thanks."

"Hey, um, can I talk to you for a sec?" she asked Zoe.

"What's up?"

It was quiet for a few seconds. He heard a mug set on the coffee table with a thunk.

"Did Jason ever tell you how we met?" Jenna said.

"Ah, no."

"Makes sense, I guess. Since it's really hard on his throat. The talking, I mean."

"Right."

"Well, when I was seven years old, I met Jason. It was my first year here. My parents had moved from Las Vegas to work at one of the casinos that had just opened. Parrot's Cay. There was a bit of culture shock, as you can imagine. I made friends with his sister because we were in the same class in second grade."

"Culture shock, for sure. I didn't know Jason has a sister."

"Had. Christie. Well, Christina, but we all called her Christie. She left us sophomore year. Leukemia."

"Oh, no! I'm so sorry."

"Yeah, thanks. It was tough. Especially for Jason."

Understatement of the century. Her death was the hardest thing he'd ever experienced, at least until the fire and everything after.

"I apologize for interrupting."

"Oh, right, um, so Christie and I were fast friends at school, and eventually we made plans to go to her house to hang out. I brought my dolls and princess clothes, so we could have a tea party. She had this adorable playhouse we played pretend in. We even put out a cute little sign that said 'no boys allowed.' Ha! Boys were so icky then. Right?" She laughed at the absurdity of it. Jason snorted. There was no doubt she had gotten over the ickyness.

"At some point, I got up and opened the cabinet on the side wall to see what all the buzzing I heard was. Evidently, it had been some time since Christie had been in the playhouse, and I opened the cabinet to the largest wasps' nest anyone could imagine. There were hundreds, possibly thousands. And they...were...pissed. Christie made it out with only a couple of stings, but I got tangled in the play table and fell. Christie ran, screaming, outside, and all I could do was curl up and wish I was somewhere else as I got stung over and over. Suddenly, I felt someone grabbing my arms and dragging me out. Jason. He had been doing loops on his bike in the driveway when he heard us screaming and charged into the playhouse to drag me out of there. He got stung about a dozen times, including a nasty one on his right nipple. Poor guy. I always give that nipple extra love when we're together. And he always wonders why."

Jason smiled, the old mystery finally revealed. Maybe someday he'd be up to that again. Not yet, not soon, but someday. It was a tantalizing lure.

"But that's how I met Jason. He was the first boy who wasn't icky to me."

"Wow. Quite an introduction," Zoe observed.

"Yeah. I started crushing on him pretty hard after that. But he was two years, two grades ahead of me. I was pretty much invisible to him. But when we were freshmen, Christie got sick. And then she died, first part of sophomore year, and it fucked us both up. We bonded over her and got friendlier and friendlier. He invited me to his senior prom, and we've been off and on ever since. We were a pretty stormy couple. Big breakups and lots of time dating other people, then torrid affairs with each other, and we'd get back together officially. We've always circled toward and away from each other. It's been quite the roller coaster."

"Been?" Zoe interjected.

Jenna paused an extra beat. "I've been given an opportunity I've got to take. I've signed with an acting agent who can get me work in New York. I'm going to be moving there in a week. I'm here to tell Jason."

"Wait, are you breaking up with him?"

"Well, yeah, I guess so. He's kind of stuck here while he heals, and I'm close to aging out of the modeling world. God, I'm going to hurt him so much, aren't I?"

"Yes. Yes, you are." Zoe was direct. "But I don't think he would try to stand in your way."

"No, I don't suppose he would. But I feel like absolute shit. Here he is, injured and stuck, and I have this once-in-a-lifetime opportunity. I mean, I just have to take it, but..." she trailed off.

"Congratulations. See you on the big screen." The words sounded sincere, but Jason could hear the tension in them.

"Thanks. God, I don't want to do this."

Jason remained still as the conversation ended. *I don't want you to do this either.* He had known something wasn't right between them, and now she had an out that could be forgiven. This way, she's not the cold bitch that dumped the crispy critter because he's broken. Just a woman going after her dreams. Convenient. Could've saved her all this trouble if Vince hadn't shown up the other day. His thoughts were dark and ugly, until he reminded himself that it was Jenna, and that he loved her.

Even if she needed to break up with him.

He raised the head of his bed to indicate he was awake, preparing himself to meet what was coming.

Jenna knocked on the open the door, peering in. "Hey," she said, voice straining for normal. Her nose wrinkled for a moment, though he couldn't tell whether it was from the smell or what she was about to do.

He waved her in. Took a sip of water for the conversation.

She closed the door behind her, and he prepared for what came next. She sat in the recliner and fussed with her clothes. "I was telling the nurse about the first time we met. Do you remember that?"

He nodded, stretching his lips in an obligatory smile as she laughed.

She seemed to be working up to the real reason she was here. "Jason," she said slowly.

"Yeah, I know." He wanted to avoid the script. Wanted her to pursue a life without him in it, and leave him alone. The relief he felt was unexpected, different this time. As she talked, he compared his life with Jenna to Dave's life with Adriana and Noah. Dave had built something good, while he had ridden the roller coaster with this vapid person. Until Jenna had mentioned them bonding over Christie, he had never fully faced the fact his sister was the only thing they had in common, and the reason he had clung so tightly to her.

"I guess we've done this a few times, haven't we?" she said. "It's just, I have an agent now who can get me auditions and work in New York. I'm not getting as much model work as I used to, and I—"

"It's fine, Jenna. Really," he interrupted. "Good luck."

"Is that all you have to say? 'Good luck'?" her voice rose.

Fuck, he realized. Guess we're going to do the script anyway.

"Jenna, this has been coming for a while now. I've made peace with it."

"What does that mean? You think this is because of what happened? How you look now?"

"You brought it up, not me."

"Oh, fuck you! That's not fair. And it's not even close. You want to get honest? Real honest? Because yeah, it's not just the agent and moving to New York. Do you want to know the real reason? Are you sure?"

He waved his hand toward her. Please, do continue.

Her body was rigid with emotion as she spoke. "Okay, then. You killed the only man I've ever truly loved, and I can't see you without thinking of Dave, and I can't be around you anymore."

Wait, this wasn't part of the script.

"Dave?" he asked with confusion.

"Yeah, Dave. You remember your best friend, right?" Her tone was full of spite. "I've been in love with him since the senior prom you took me to. I would ask him out every time we broke up and he was single. But he had his stupid, asinine 'bro code' and wouldn't give me the time of day because I was 'yours,' like you fucking pissed on me and marked your territory. What is it with you guys?" She was huffing angrily, body rigid. "You want to know why I kept getting back with you? It was the only real excuse I had to be around him. Especially after he married that bi—, that girl."

The anger seemed to leave her, and she slumped as her body went soft. "Noah should've been my son. It's not fair." Her tears were real this time.

There it was, the bald truth. He had played second fiddle this whole time to a guy who'd always been just a bit better than him. "Bullshit," he hissed, needing to twist the knife. "You didn't even come to his funeral. Don't tell me you loved him when you couldn't be bothered to say goodbye. Fuck outta here with that."

Exasperation along with weary long-suffering showed on her face. "You really don't get it, do you?" She shook her head, her tone low and clipped. "I said my goodbyes the night he died. I was there with the family in *your* place."

Stung, he darted his eyes at her. Her face was guileless.

"Shit, I was in his room way more than yours. The only time I spent with you was when Adriana was visiting." A dark chuckle. "I don't think she likes me much. Like I give a shit what some frumpy hausfrau thinks of me."

Rage tunneled his vision, every muscle in his body wanting to explode. He didn't know this vindictive, petty person. The fact she had been there with Dave in his stead wrenched at his chest.

She narrowed her eyes, sadistic glee lighting her grin. "Oh, you didn't know? Mom wanted to protect her poor baby's feelings." She drew the word out in a baby-talk taunt. "Made them wait until you were discharged to pull the plug. You killed him, bub. He'd still be in that bed if you'd stayed."

Fuck every goddamn cell in this bitch's body.

As Jenna's departure was marked with squeals of burnt rubber in his driveway, he trembled with anger. Anger at her words, at her using him, at her being able to be by Dave's side when he died.

Then he called his mother. She didn't like what he had to say.

WHEN ZOE BROUGHT evening medications, long past her usual end of shift time, Jason broke his melancholy enough to send her a quizzical glance.

"Your mom was scheduled to stay over tonight," she said in explanation. "Captain Merone is on shift."

No way his mom could be around him tonight. "Ah. Well. Sorry you got stuck." After today, he did hate that she would have to deal with him. Strangely, he couldn't think of anyone he would've preferred to stay.

"'S okay. I've done worse for less."

The blank stare he threw at her made her smile.

"The extra money's good; the company's not too terrible either. You definitely aren't the worst patient I've ever had."

What kind of people had she been taking care of? Jason gave a slight nod of acceptance at the sideways compliment. Suddenly, he realized he didn't want to be alone with the raging maelstrom of his thoughts. They left him exhausted and needing a break. He fired up Netflix on his TV and held up his hand as Zoe turned to leave. "Wanna watch with me?"

"What are we watching?" Zoe said, as if weighing her options.

"You pick." He held up the remote to her.

"Oh, I don't know. What if I picked some chick-flicky kind of thing that tortured you? And then you hated me and got insomnia from all the seething rage I caused," she said with a grin, pushing the remote back to him. "I couldn't have that on my conscience."

Jason considered her for a moment, giving serious thought to what she might like. He made a selection, and in a moment, the sound of Regina Spektor singing the theme to *Orange is the New Black* blasted in the room. Zoe beamed in delight.

"Great choice! How did you know I like this show?"

Jason grinned and pointed to himself, then gave a thumbs-up, because he liked it too.

She settled into the plush armchair his uncle had dragged into the bedroom one night, and together they watched the hijinks of the residents of Litchfield Penitentiary.

As the episode ended, Jason realized he hadn't watched most of it, focused instead on Zoe. The way her hands kept absently rubbing at her neck, the way a slammed hand on the table in the show made her tense up.

"What? Did I spill something?" she asked studying her scrubs and brushing at them with her hands.

When she looked back at him, he waved his hands over his face to indicate her fading injuries. "Want to tell?"

He wanted to take the question back as soon as he asked. It wasn't his place to pry. Jason forced himself to be patient as she grappled with her decision, the same as she had done for him once upon a time. Her jaw shifted as if to speak twice, stopping herself each time.

When she did start talking, it was with a detached flippancy. He could see the tension in the lines of her body, the stiffness of her neck, and he ached to be able to help. "Oh, it's no big thing, just your usual boy meets dumb-dumb girl who invites him over to her house because she is an idiot. You know the story: dumb-dumb girl feeds boy steak and wine and gets tipsy and talks all night, and everyone is happy and peachy until dumb-dumb turns down the bedroom offer. But boy insists and dumb-dumb ends up tied to the bed while boy enjoys her *hospitality*, then tries to strangle dumb-dumb to death and comes within a minute or so of succeeding. Tale as old as time, really."

Jason's heart pounded as she spoke, and he gulped past a lump in his throat. Was she fucking kidding? Not if her expression was anything to go by.

"Jesus," was the most he could mutter as the horrifying images of what she had gone through ran through his mind.

"Yeah. Not the most pleasant of times." She shook her head slowly.

Understatement of the century. His dry mouth struggled to find words at all, much less adequate ones. "Glad you're not dead."

"Aw, thanks. Me too." Her shrug was awkward.

"Police?" Hopefully, they threw the motherfucker under the jail, never to be seen again until archaeologists in the far future stumbled across a corpse with its skull jammed into its pelvic cavity.

"Less than helpful."

His gaze sharpened at her dry answer. She returned his look, but stayed silent. It was clear she didn't want to talk about this anymore. He didn't blame her.

Eventually, his attention switched back to the TV screen, hand on the remote. They both needed a break from all this misery. He glanced back at her, inclined his head toward the screen. *Unbreakable Kimmy Schmidt* was queued up. He waggled his eyebrows at her. They both needed a laugh. She grinned, and her heaviness seemed to evaporate, her movements lighter somehow, and the furrows in her brow smoothed away. His heart gave a stupid lurch he willfully ignored.

She took a bathroom break after the first episode to get into comfy sweats and remove her makeup. As memories weighed heavy in the silence, he reached into his dresser drawer and retrieved a small, two-sided picture frame.

Swamped in nostalgia, he didn't notice Zoe's return until she cleared her throat. Blinking tears away quickly and hoping she didn't notice, he tilted the frame in her direction so she could see the picture: two young girls, blonde and brunette. It was easy to recognize Jenna as the blonde, the beauty she would become already evident at that young age. The brunette shared his features, his forever-young sister, Christie.

Zoe pointed. "Your sister." It was a statement instead of a question.

Jason nodded, the ache sitting heavy in his chest.

"Jenna told me a little about her. I'm sorry about what happened to her. That had to be really hard to get through. She was so young and beautiful." When he met Zoe's green eyes, the bottomless empathy she always seemed to have warmed his heart.

"Sucked," he agreed. "Wish it could have been me instead." His eyes took in the picture frame again, at those young faces frozen in eternal smiles. "I miss her." In that moment, he wasn't sure which "her" he meant, sadly realizing it didn't matter. They were both gone, weren't they?

When he finally fell asleep for the night, the fire monsters and maze were joined by Zoe's battered face.

Chapter Eight

Zoe

THE THIRTY-SIX-hour shift at Jason's left me with bone-deep weariness. Catching catnaps the evening before, I'd slept lightly, waking at every shift and noise as he slept fitfully. It wasn't anything I hadn't done before, but it was always a relief when the shifts were over, and I could get home and shut down.

Shrugging the bag off my slumping shoulders, I beelined to the shower. I made it hot and thought about Jason as I let the previous days melt away. Thought about his hands as he held the gold-edged frame with his sister's photo. Thought about the heart that absorbed the grief of his sister's death, his best friend's death, and the dramatic departure of his girlfriend. Thought about the way he looked at me, and the way he laughed in spite of his pain. He was truly something—someone—special. It was the first time I could remember laughing since the attack. It was a gift to laugh again.

I guess he's single now.

The unbidden thought caused my eyes to fly open. *Whoa!* Where did that came from? Unprofessional at best, possibly unethical, and illegal at worst. My thoughts were a jumbled mess now, exhaustion letting emotions off their leash. Not that it mattered. If he really knew who—

what—I am, it wouldn't matter. He wouldn't want me. Besides, the last guy who seemed to like me—

I jerked back to reality before the thought could finish, almost slipping in the tub from the sudden movement. Still, the cynical echoes of the notion tortured me as it faded into the back of my mind. Exhaustion. That's all it was. Yet, even as I tried to convince myself, I knew it for a lie.

After the hot water faded, I toweled dry and slid into fresh pajamas. Clean sheets and cozy times waited for me. While double-checking the doors and windows—a recent obsession when I was home—I waved a passing hello to Delphine, geared for a full night of painting canvas in the room that served as her studio. I walked into my room, noticing there was less hesitation before entering each time I went in.

Delphine had been in here.

A large painting hung over my bed. It was a warrior angel, rendered in exquisite detail. Large wings swept across a nude, athletically built woman, her gaze fierce as she wielded a blade, eyes narrowed and staring straight ahead. She stood on a rock as ocean spray rose behind her from crashing waves. Her muscles were tensed, tendons in sharp relief as if preparing to leap from the canvas and do battle. Windswept hair streamed across her faintly Polynesian face, the effect highlighting rather than obscuring her features. It was a picture of power, primal yet ethereal. Enraptured, I drank in every detail as a tingle ran down my spine. A title card had been tucked into the left bottom corner of the painting, and I reverently plucked it from the frame, holding it to the light. Delphine named this one *Zoe's Guardian*.

Making my way to her studio, I gave her a fervent hug. "Thank you, Del."

"Do you like it, then?" She gave me a side hug, holding the wet brush away from us, her smile warm.

"God, yes. It's so beautiful. So strong. I don't deserve it. You could make so much money from that painting."

"Bah. I can make other paintings if I need money." She dabbed paint onto the canvas as she spoke, "It was made for you. I wanted to give you something to help you take your power back."

"Dear God, it's gorgeous."

"I'm glad you like it, cheri." Del paused, studying my face. "You're tired."

"Yeah, freaking wiped. I'm going to bed." I didn't manage to suppress the yawn that reinforced the statement.

Delphine squeezed my hand. "Sleep well."

"I will with that fierceness standing guard."

Greeting the bed with a groan of relief, I snuggled into the sheets. As the guardian over my head kept watch, I slept soundly, and for the first time since the attack, dreamlessly.

THE INSISTENT CHIRPING alarm of my cell phone woke me the next morning. Cursing, I reached out to smack the snooze button. I was off today, dammit! My sleep-fogged mind finally registered the noise as a phone call.

"Hello?" I answered in a sleep-thick voice.

"Yes, hi, Ms. Calder?" The voice on the other end was faintly familiar. A guy I couldn't quite place. "Ms. Calder, this is Detective John Overstreet with the Biloxi Police Department." Ah, the asshole.

I stayed silent.

The detective stumbled on. "Ah...yes...well...ah...it's been brought to our attention that perhaps we were a bit hasty in our assumptions. We heard from a couple of sources that you don't...um...behave the way we may have...ah...assumed. We wanted to know if there was any way you could come down to headquarters and speak with us again about what happened to you? Perhaps there are some details you may have remembered after getting some, shall we say, distance from the event."

Maybe this wasn't making sense because I was still foggy. "Wait a minute. Are you saying that all these weeks later, now you believe me? Really?"

"Ms. Calder, it's certainly understandable if you're upset. I apologize for the way my partner and I may have dealt with you at the hospital. It was an...ah...unusual situation we may not have handled as delicately as would have been preferred."

"As delicately?" anger blazed, hot and undeniable, burning off the dregs of sleep. "Delicately? Detective, you and your partner fucking accused me of both making it up and engaging in sex work as I lay in a hospital bed recovering from shit I literally would not wish on my worst damn enemy."

"Ms. Calder, I understand you're angry—"

"Goddamn right, I'm fucking angry!" It felt good to curse, to yell at the detective.

"Okay." His voice had changed, become more straightforward. "Then can we expect you in about an hour or so? Will you help us get this guy, Ms. Calder?"

"Fine," I said, ending the call. It took a couple of seconds to realize he had played me, Columboing around in conversation until I was livid and ready to punch him in his face, then smoothly setting a meeting time, knowing

I would be there steaming. It was a pretty good piece of work, I had to admit. A glimmer of hope flickered that they might find the guy, but I viciously quashed it before it could catch hold and hurt me again.

THE BILOXI POLICE Headquarters was on the western side of the central part of town in a large concrete and stone structure that also housed the Fire Department Headquarters. The front desk officer escorted me back to the detective's area, and Detective Overstreet stood and walked over when he saw me. He pointed me to where the female detective with the horrible haircut sat.

"Ms. Calder, thank you for coming in. Again, this is Detective Roxanne Brandly." After handshakes all around, we went into an interview room and I repeated the story of Arthur. As we spoke, I suddenly remembered the red Corvette that had almost run me over while biking earlier the day I was attacked.

Sitting up straight, I interrupted Overstreet midsentence. "I think he stalked me," I said. "I mean, more than just on the dating site."

"Stalked you?" Roxanne asked. At least this time she had the courtesy of keeping her face fairly neutral.

"Yeah. He said—right before he put the trash bag over my head." The images assailed me, red cars and red wine and my red, red blood. Taking a shaky breath, I continued. "He said something about almost taking me out on my ride. I just thought it was an asshole at the time, but there was a red Corvette behind me for a second, then it flew past me close enough that I dove off the road to keep from getting hit."

They scribbled furiously in their notebooks and then turned the desktop monitor toward me, and we image searched Corvettes until I found the type that had passed me that day. It made my gut cramp, but I knew it was right.

Detective Overstreet shuffled through the case file. "We made inquiries at the dating site where this Mr. Dent connected with you. We hit a wall there. The accounts were deleted, as you mentioned, but those sites generally hang on to a lot of personal information. The problem is that it seems he was using a VPN service—a virtual private network—to obscure his identifiable information. So there are no ISP addresses. The VPN sent his traffic through a server in Hungary after several other bounces. We will keep working that angle, so maybe we can find something, but it's not promising right now. I'm assuming you don't have any pictures of him?"

"Only on the phone he took."

"Would you be willing to meet with a sketch artist to help us?"

Arthur's face haunted me every night. The last thing I wanted to do was recall it in the daytime. Still, it might help end this nightmare. "Fuck it. Sure." If it'd take him down, I'd hula dance in the middle of the town.

After a couple of hours, we'd nailed a pretty close approximation of Arthur for the police to distribute. His eyes seemed to stare at me from the page, giving me chills.

As I grabbed my purse and went to leave the police headquarters, I turned back to Overstreet and Brandly. "Why do you believe me now?"

Both detectives looked chastened, and Overstreet spoke. "Well, your roommate, a Ms. Roulet, has been quite persistent with the higher-ups, and we were already getting some pushback from that. Then a certain injured firefighter made some inquiries, and now this has become our top priority. Again, Ms. Calder, our apologies for the way our first meeting went."

Delphine and Jason. They both went to bat for me.

"Alright, well, please find him. Quickly."

"It's our top priority, ma'am."

That stupid glimmer of hope tried to flicker again, a persistent ember still struggling to catch flame. It was harder to extinguish this time.

Back in the car, a new worry took form in my mind. What if he was caught? I'd have to attend his trial to testify. I wouldn't have any secrets. The defense would harp on the fact that I'm transgender. Could I handle the stares, the circus, the comments, and the hatred? How would the nursing agency react? How would Jason react? Or any other patient?

A trial presented the real possibility of destroying this part of my life. Still, I would do whatever necessary to make sure that psychopath was removed from society. The next person might not be as lucky as I was. *Please catch him quickly, detectives.* I'd handle whatever happened, just get him before he raped or killed someone else.

I couldn't—wouldn't—dwell on the what-ifs anymore. Whatever happened next was out of my hands.

It was a beautiful day on the Mississippi Gulf Coast. With fall approaching, the summer's humidity faded to a pleasant level. The sky was a vibrant azure blue, with a couple of small puffy clouds adding a touch of whimsy to the tableaux. Windows down and blasting Fall Out Boy, I took the beachfront highway west. I needed coffee and a view of the water.

The coffee shop situated near the beach was called Java Jane's. It was popular because they roasted their own beans and the wooden deck, festooned with rainbow flags at the corner, was elevated over the sandy beach and gave an unobstructed view of the Gulf waters. Getting there during the midmorning slump, I ordered a cappuccino and took it outside. Choosing a spot on the nearly empty deck, I retrieved the ever-present Moleskine journal from my bag. It had been a spur-of-the-moment decision to come here and journal, and I hesitated a moment before I touched pen to paper. Then, as the breeze ruffled my hair and caught at the pages, I transcribed what had occurred that night with Arthur.

As the sun marched first higher, then lower, I drank coffee and wrote. After finishing a clinical recounting of the event, similar to the statement I had given the cops, I turned the page and wrote about my visceral responses to the event. The more ink I placed on the page, the better I began to feel. Delphine had called it "getting your power back," and I started to understand what she meant. I felt lighter, as if the psychic residue from that night was being shed like a snakeskin. Hope, always a dangerous thing, blazed brighter within me. The future, in that sun-drenched setting, beckoned without as much fear.

Was contacted by a certain detective. I texted Jason. *Seems my case is top priority now. Thank you.*

After a moment, the phone dinged.

;)

Smiling, I put the phone away. The waves lapped at the beach, and I watched them roll into the sand as I sipped coffee.

AS FALL ARRIVED with its cooler weather, I began to reengage with the world. Autumn had always been my favorite season, the time of year when the best personal milestones occurred. Tentatively, I began to go out, meeting with people like me in spaces for people like me. Reconnecting with my tribe, their affection at my return was overwhelming. It was humbling and healing to realize so much support was available, and had been all along.

Working with Jason also brought satisfaction as his healing progressed. Jason now approached therapy with an intensity I hadn't seen before. He gritted through the misery, always reaching for more range and determined to build his strength, not stopping until he was completely exhausted and drenched in sweat. Now, instead of pushing him to work harder, I frequently had to dial him back, cheering inwardly when he took his frustration out on me.

He wanted back on the line with his brothers.

The laptop dominated his nontherapy time. Parked on the hospital tray, he pounded away at the keys when he wasn't doing therapy or joking with the guys who dropped by for visits and updates.

He was learning to code, delving into programming languages and app-building with the same singular focus he brought to physical therapy. Sometimes he would show me the results of efforts he was particularly proud of.

"Because," he said when I asked about it, "it's better than any medication for getting away from this constant pain."

Vince visited more than nearly anyone else. There was a camaraderie between the three of us I hadn't anticipated, a bond forged by our proximity to each other's hardest battles. I understood a little better now why professions like the one Jason and Vince shared were referred to as a "brotherhood."

It was also getting harder and harder to maintain professional boundaries around Jason as he became more open.

He took to jokingly flirting with me, especially when Vince was around. I could handle and easily deflect that. It was in the quieter times, when he opened up about his hopes to get back on the fire department roster and told stories about Dave, my heart screamed to cross lines set in stone.

WEDNESDAY AFTERNOON, I opened the door to a blonde woman it took me a moment to place, with a child in tow I had no trouble placing. Recognizing Noah, I knew this had to be his mom. *Trouble.*

"See, Mama, I told you she was pretty," Noah patted his mom's leg to get her attention, smiling shyly up at me.

"Yep, you were right, chipster." She smiled at Noah, then turned back to me. "Hey there. I'm Adriana. Can Jason have a couple of visitors?"

"Yes, of course. Come in. I'm Zoe." Turning my attention to Noah, I extended my hand, stooping to his level. "Hi, Noah. It's nice to see you again." He took my hand solemnly, nodding as he pumped it twice.

I led them back to Jason's room before excusing myself to give them some privacy. The tightness around his eyes was the only clue to his mental state as I left them alone.

Strangely, the bubbly laughter of Noah and chuckles from Adriana and Jason soon escaped from behind the closed door. Ten minutes later, Adriana exited the bedroom.

"Zoe," she said as she came into the living room. "Jason's been talking about you in there, and I thought it might be rude to leave you out here."

Not trouble, then. But why were they talking about me?

Adriana caught my puzzled expression and laughed, "Nothing bad, I promise. You can come back if you like. I don't want to leave Noah alone too long in there because he likes to climb, and if he gets on the bed, I don't know that Jason would ever recover."

Following her toward the room, she hesitated in the hallway as I got close to her.

"Thank you," she said in a low tone that wouldn't carry into the bedroom.

"Sure. For what?" I matched her hushed voice.

"For making sure he didn't die. Vince told me about what happened after the funeral." She squeezed my shoulders in a gentle hug. "Thank you for both of them." She turned back toward the bedroom.

I followed behind, stopping at the doorway as she pulled up short. Over her shoulder, I could see Noah had climbed onto the bed as predicted and latched his arms around Jason's neck. Jason returned the fierce hug fully, and they both lay with their heads on the pillow looking at each other. I cringed at the pain this must be putting him in as Noah traced a chubby finger down Jason's face mask. Adrianna held up her open hand behind the doorframe, a silent plea to wait before barging in farther.

"If you're a superhero, you have to have a crime-fighting name. Can you tell me what it is?" Noah asked in a conspiratorial whisper.

"Well, buddy, I hadn't thought about it. Maybe you can help me think one up after I get my first bad guys and put them on ice." Jason gave no indication of the pain that must be close to wringing tears out of him, his attention focused only on his godson.

"Hmmm, yeah. Maybe something from *Top Gun*, since that was Daddy's favorite movie. Oh, maybe we could call you the Flaming Maverick, since you got hurt in the fire?" His eyebrows were raised and chin tucked, an excited yet tentative hope for Jason's stamp of approval.

A shimmer of tears glinted in his eyes, but Jason blinked them away before Noah noticed. "What about the Flying Goose? I feel goofy enough to be a goose sometimes, and it would be cool to fly." Jason's attempt to joke was betrayed by the tremor in his voice.

"No, silly. That's Daddy's superhero name. Because he had to fly to heaven after trying to help the boy who died. I think maybe he took the kid with him, instead of me." He snuggled his head into Jason's shoulder, staring at the ceiling. "Can you be my daddy now?" Noah said in the heavy silence of the room.

"As long as you need me to be," Jason answered, giving Noah a fist bump.

My heart was complete mush watching this child reach out to Jason, and hearing his perfect response.

Jesus, I could fall for this man. The thought caught in my throat, nearly prompting my own tears.

Too late.

Achingly, I realized I would have to request a transfer from his case soon.

Trouble indeed.

THAT EVENING AT home, I reluctantly sat at my laptop and began to compose a formal request for transfer. It was more difficult than expected, putting words together to sever the relationship with Jason. I stopped and started frequently, going back and making changes midsentence. Everything in me screamed against leaving Jason's care to anyone else. Everything in me screamed for more time to be around Jason, ethics be damned.

When the phone rang, I quickly answered, grateful for the distraction.

"Yes, hi, Ms. Calder. Detective Overstreet here. Just wanted to inform you we have arrested a suspect in connection with your rape and attempted murder. Would you be able to come down to the station to confirm we have the right person?"

"Holy shit!" My head spun with the idea. "Really? Yes. Yes. I'll be there in about twenty minutes."

I ran to the studio where Delphine was engrossed in her latest project. "They got him! Arthur! They got him. I'm on my way to the station to confirm."

Delphine placed her brush down. "I'll go with you."

We got there in eighteen minutes.

We were met by Detective Brandly. The rumpled state of her clothes attested to the long day she had put in. Her manner was oddly formal, as she held a file folder against her chest with folded arms. "Ms. Calder, Ms. Roulet. Hi. Thank you for coming in. At this time, we are requesting confirmation the suspect we have in custody is the person who assaulted you."

Anxiety mixed with hope in a gut-churning brew. If it was actually Arthur, the machinery of justice would go into action. Maybe I could put him behind me forever, knowing he could never again hurt anyone like he hurt me. But I would also have no control over what happened to my life once it began, no idea what the fallout would be. Pensive, I looked to Del for help.

She read the panic in my face and touched my shoulder. "Be strong, cher," she said simply. *You have no choice,* her eyes added.

Taking a steadying breath, I went alone into a cramped room on the backside of a one-way mirrored window. There were several people already in there, but no introductions were made. Instructions were given as to what was about to happen, and I nodded that I understood, unable to trust my voice. A door on the right side of the room beyond the mirror opened, and six men trooped inside in single file.

Arthur Dent was lined up in the number two slot. I knew that face, that build, the eyes, the arrogance. Struggling to keep my composure, inside I was screaming. *They nailed the motherfucking cuntwaffle!* Shaky, but without doubt, I confirmed that number two was the man who had raped me. I left the room quickly, when finally allowed, trembling as I walked out.

Strangely, no other information was forthcoming from the police. It was if they closed ranks. My questions of who he was, how he was caught were deflected with "We can't comment" and "It's an ongoing investigation, so we can't really say right now." Rather than continue to beat my head against the wall, I found Delphine. I nodded a confirmation to her questioning look. *Yes, it was him.*

She gathered me in an embrace. "My warrior," she whispered, as I let myself sob into her hug. "My goddamn Amazon."

Fighting dry heaves in the aftermath and leaning weakly on Delphine as we left the building, we went home.

TWO DAYS LATER, on a Friday morning in early October, I woke to a circus. I could hear Delphine speaking at the front door, in tones that brooked no argument. I jerked awake. My phone was ringing incessantly, and I had twelve missed calls. I sent the current caller to voicemail and put the phone on *do not disturb* as I got up to investigate.

Delphine had closed the front door and all the black curtains on the visitors when I got into the living room. I risked a peek out the front window. Multiple TV vans were parked outside, and people buzzed about on the front lawn. It was chaos. I gave Delphine a grouchy face.

"So it begins," she murmured. "Coffee?"

I huffed a surprised laugh. Nothing got between us and coffee. "I have a feeling I'm gonna need it today."

We clinked full mugs and sipped for a moment, each to our own thoughts. I broke the silence first. "I suppose this ruckus is my fault?"

"Indeed, mon amie. It would seem the press have gotten wind of a story. As I haven't scandalized anyone lately, and my work, lucrative as it can be, has never caused quite this much fondness, I must lay this 'ruckus' at your door."

"Gah. I'm sorry, Delphine. Can we make them leave soon?"

"I'm not sure. I imagine we will need to know what they want first."

"Good point. I thought they may have told you when they were on the porch."

"I didn't give them the chance, cheri."

Retrieving my phone, I saw another eight missed calls. I wouldn't be able to use this one without significant distraction. "Del, can I use your cell?"

Rolling her eyes at the corny poetry, she handed me her phone. I called Detective Overstreet.

He picked up on the second ring. "Detective Overstreet."

"Detective, it's Zoe Calder. Can you tell me why my house looks like it's being sieged by hypercaffeinated Capuchins with cameras?"

"Ms. Calder. Are you referring to the media?"

"Yes I am. Why are they here? Couldn't you have given me some warning?"

"Ah, well, we are being scrutinized pretty closely here in regards to this investigation. It took a rather unexpected turn. The identity of the suspect, coupled with the nature of the charges, has set off a buzz."

"Who is he? You guys clammed up three days ago when I picked him in the lineup."

"Yes, ma'am, sorry it had to be like that. But, well, he is a cop."

"A cop! What? From here?"

"He's employed with the City of Dantzler. Legal name is Randall Bogen. He showed up to the arraignment with a pretty high-caliber defense attorney. The attorney successfully argued for bail, which caught us all off guard, given the charges. Three hundred twenty-five thousand. His attorney produced the cash, and he walked out yesterday afternoon."

My blood froze, the optimism I had allowed myself to feel folding into itself. "He was arraigned and got out on bail, and you didn't think to inform me?"

"It was our understanding the District Attorney's office would make contact with you to inform you. Ms. Calder, this matter has been turned over to them. They have the case now." His tone was apologetic, defensive but final.

"Wait, how the hell did a cop come up with three hundred twenty-five thousand for bail?" Fucking fuckity fuck.

"You'll have to direct your questions to the DA's office. I really can't say," he hedged.

"Fine. What is the number? Who should I ask for?"

Overstreet reeled off the number, informed me the case was currently being handled by an assistant DA named Malcolm Hutto.

Shaken, I ended the call. Delphine, who had been intently following my side of the conversation, stepped closer. I caught her up to speed, fear gnawing at me.

My shift with Jason waited, and I was perilously close to late. Couldn't call the ADA right now. I quickly dressed and gathered everything I would be taking with me for the day. I threw my laptop in its carry case, as I still needed to finish the email about Jason. Time to get on the road.

I surveyed the crowd outside. It was a gauntlet out there. I tossed my hair at Delphine, jutted my hip in a model pose. "I'm ready for my close-up now," I said in a deep, breathy voice.

Delphine snorted at the image I presented. "Stay behind me. I'll get you to the car. Don't leave Jason's house without me. Never be alone. Keep your mace close." Her words were sober, intense. A commander's last instructions before battle. I squared my shoulders, nodded my readiness. Delphine stood still, waiting for something.

"What are we waiting for?"

"Keys, love. Where are your keys?"

"Oh! Crap! Here in my bag..." I started rummaging through the large bag that held most of my essentials and lots of my junk. It took half a minute to find them. "Here they are. Whew. Glad I didn't have to do that out there. Good looking out."

Delphine nodded, and this time we moved. She opened the door quickly, grabbed my wrist firmly, and waded into the crowd of reporters who erupted into a cacophony of yells, camera whirs, and flash pops. The surge forward was instant, the hurled questions almost a physical assault.

"Zoe can you com—"

"Calder, what was the nature—"

"Comment—"

"Who is—"

"What—"

Words bombarded me in nonsensical chunks, making my head spin.

Delphine waded through the melee without breaking stride, pulling me along as she pushed against the throng. Finally, I was at my car, quickly entering it as the cameras continued to flash. Delphine caught my glance, motioned her hand down at me. *Lock your door.* I locked the doors. At the click, Delphine turned her back to me, facing part of the crowd. The questions still came, and I began to pick voices out of the din.

"You Noah—"

"Noah—"

"Is Noah—"

Noah. Noah. Noah. My birth name, the one I shared with Dave's son. I finally realized what should have been stupidly obvious before now. They were here because of who I was as much as for who Arthur—Randall—was.

Delphine held her arms out to the crowd. "There will be no comment," she said loudly. "Now move so the lady can leave. Now! Move!"

I cranked the car, put it in reverse and slowly began to back out, terrified I would hear the crunch of crushed bones at any moment. The crowd parted, still taking pictures and recording the scene. Finally, I was on the street and had open road before me. Multiple cars raced behind me as I gained speed. They were going to follow me.

I couldn't allow this to come to Jason's doorstep.

Driving carefully and following all the rules of the road, I watched the following cars in the rearview. I stopped at a red light, mind racing as I waited for green. *Timing, Zoe. Patience.*

I studied the phone in my lap seemingly engrossed. The light turned green, and the three cars in front of me began to move as I sat. The cars behind me began to honk impatiently, and I looked up as the light turned yellow. I slowly pulled up to the white line to wait for the next light. The light turned red.

I floored the fuck out of my car. The jackrabbit start got me through the intersection before the other traffic went across, but prevented the media hounds from following. I picked up speed, turning off the road a half mile later, smoothly drifting the rear a bit as I made the right hand turn without touching the brakes. I dove and juked through twists and turns on side roads, eventually getting to Jason's neighborhood on the opposite side of my usual commute. There was a covered parking area near Jason's home, but not directly in front of it. I backed in, a precaution against nosy reporters identifying the car by its license plate. Gathering my things with a deep breath, I went to work. I was shaken, and I was late, but I had made it.

Chapter Nine

Jason

ZOE ARRIVED FOR her shift almost a full hour late. He was reading on his laptop when she walked in, as haunted and harried as he would have expected given the stories spreading online like wildfire.

"Hey!" he said. "What's up? Big morning or crazy night?" He wiggled his eyebrows suggestively.

"It was a little hard to leave the house this morning," she deadpanned. Given how harried she appeared, he knew he couldn't keep it light for long.

"I heard some things," he said, dropping the joking tone. "Want to tell me about it?" He patted his hand on the side of the bed, inviting her to talk.

Instead, she held up the charts in front of her face and sat in the recliner. "I need to go over these," she deflected, refusing to look at him directly. "Have you had your morning meds yet?"

"I have, courtesy of Captain Merone."

"Gotcha. I'm so sorry I'm late. It couldn't be helped, but I know that everyone depends on me doing my job properly and being on time."

"Well, we asked you to pull an overnight with no warning, and you did. I imagine we can overlook a little tardiness."

"Thank you." Zoe continued to chart, eyes down. "How are you feeling today?"

This distance was breaking his heart. He didn't respond until she glanced up as the silence lengthened. "I'm hurting like hell, and everything feels raw. But I imagine I'm in better mental shape than you are right now."

"Yeah. Well, good news, they caught the guy who tried to kill me," she smiled tightly through clenched teeth in a forced cheerful tone.

"I heard. Then the press came after you, which is strange. Isn't there a rape shield law here? Do you know why they're hounding you?"

"I...I...no, I don't. Haven't had time to think about that." Her brows furrowed in thought and confusion.

Jason had seen that face before. It was part of what made her adorable. But not today. Today, she simply looked lost and alone. Jason stared at his keyboard and clicked a few keys.

"There's an article here, top headline of the *Biloxi Ledger*, that claims to have received an email from you about the case. Seems you identified yourself and then made remarks about a cop who was arrested for rape and attempted murder. I'm not sure this will help your case."

"What email? What are you talking about?" She sprang up and stalked over to the laptop, her movements sharp and agitated. "Let me see that."

He watched her read, watched the hurt and anger war on her face as she gnawed at her bottom lip. Her eyes narrowed on the screen, jaw dropping as she read. He knew what the article said, had gone over it twice already in disbelief.

My name is Noah Calder, and I was raped by a cop. His name is Randall Bogen, and he is absolute scum. I met him at a bar, and I thought he might be up for something different. You see, I am a transsexual, and I mostly wear women's clothing. I go by the name Zoe, and I prefer to pick up straight men. Sometimes they pay me because I am very discrete. I thought Randall was looking for the type of service I provide. We hit it off in a bar and then went to his vehicle. I thought he knew the deal, but as we began to make out he noticed I was a guy. He got very angry at me for "trying to fool him," he said. Then he kicked me out of the car and left.

Later that night, I woke up blindfolded and someone was on top of me, and I couldn't get away. I knew immediately it could have only been him. And then he raped me and said he was going to kill me because "no one could know he was a faggot." With all my strength, I managed to get away just before I passed out from being strangled by him. I don't know how I did it. I'm so lucky I didn't die. I am writing this to you to make sure his blue brothers cannot sweep this under the rug or come after me.

Zoe covered her mouth as if to stifle a scream. Then she grabbed her phone and checked her email. Her eyes went wide. She must have confirmed the message was in her sent folder.

"There are more emails," she said, scrolling. "I never sent any of these. I never responded to them. I don't talk like this!"

He watched Zoe crumble before his eyes, head hanging and shoulders dropping as she absorbed what was happening. It jabbed him in the heart. He wanted to hug her, but as jumpy as she seemed, he resisted trying.

She met his gaze for a moment, before her eyes skittered away to a spot on the wall above him. "I'm not a whore, and I didn't meet him at a bar," she said slowly. She didn't need to convince him. He knew enough about her to know how much bullshit was spun there. "Every person there would swear on a stack of Bibles I was lying. And if they thought I was lying about that, wouldn't they think I was lying about everything? Fuck!" She slapped the recliner armrest, her anger finally lashing out. "Jason, I did *not* write this email. Who the hell would? I didn't even know his real name until this morning. He told me his name was Arthur Dent. Like the Hitchhiker's books."

She rubbed at her eyes, as if willing away what they had seen.

"He took my phone," she said in a distracted monotone. "I thought he got rid of it, but he must have held onto it. If I had used the app more than the one time, maybe we could have tracked him down faster."

"App? The find-my-device app?" he asked.

"Yeah. We tried to use it when it first happened and after the cops were shitty to me. It didn't do anything. It was like the phone was turned off. I figured he'd gotten rid of it."

"Well, it's not the best app in the world, but good instincts," he said flipping open the lid on his laptop. "You should probably change any and all passwords he might have accessed with your phone, like bank accounts and any social media. It's too late for the email, but you could start with that one." As much as he wanted to, he couldn't go charging after the guy with retribution in mind, but maybe he could help her another way.

Zoe nodded her agreement. "I can't believe I didn't think to do that already." She flushed a deep red as she thought of something.

"Jason—" she started. Then went silent, shaking her head.

He waited for a beat. "Yes?" he asked in a drawn-out response, watching the blush bloom on her face.

"Obviously, you know now I wasn't born female. It's— it's a long story but—"

"You were born male, but always felt female. You took steps to align your body to better match your brain and internal identity? Something like that?"

Zoe pinned him with a look, mouth gaping wide.

Jason met her eyes and shrugged. "When I made calls, I got the story from the detectives. They used it as a defense for why they had it on the back burner." He tensed at the excuses they'd used, remembering the hell he had raised. "I had a friend who went through something similar. It didn't turn out so well for her."

Her face was equal parts horrified, embarrassed, and puzzled. "What?"

He really didn't want to talk about it. Still felt embarrassed at how he'd responded. "Well, I mean, there was a firefighter my rookie year who needed to change, you know, transition? Her name was Chastity, although that wasn't her name when I met her, but I know you aren't supposed to talk about, you know, the dead name." He took a deep breath both to stop himself from rambling and to focus. "Anyway, she came out as trans. Jesus, the way she got treated..." He shook his head, shamed at the memory of how he had responded with the other guys.

"She basically got run out of the department. Although nothing was outright illegal or actionable. And, full disclosure, I wasn't sure how to respond. To her, or the situation. So I laughed at the jokes in the station. Never really stuck up for her. And I hate myself for that now. Swore I would never let it happen again in front of me. And now here you are, karma making me put my money where my mouth is."

She stared at him, cocking her head and waiting for him to continue. He cleared his throat. "After I talked to the detectives, I started googling transgender stuff again, similar to when my friend came out. That leads down a rabbit hole, let me tell you. But what I took away from it was you definitely aren't crazy, just a bit outside the norm. Which is okay. I'm kind of outside the norm as well." He moved his hand down to indicate his body. "Knowing you're different, and what you have been through to get to this point in your life...it...gives me hope."

"Hope?" she asked guardedly. He could see the questions in her eyes.

"That I can one day go through life with confidence again, in spite of how I look. That maybe one day, a girl can see me for who I am inside, not just this crispy body." He shrugged. It was true. After finding out about her assault when she had returned, he started observing her more closely than before. He considered the strength it took to become the person she was. Not only to transition, but to also become a nurse, and a damned good one.

"Does this mean you believe me? That I didn't write the email?" she asked.

"Yeah, of course. I knew it wasn't you as soon as I read it."

"What? Why? I mean, thanks. But...how?"

"One word," he shrugged. "Transsexual."

"What?" she tilted her head in puzzlement.

"The email writer used the word transsexual. After the research I did, I knew it wasn't a term you would ever use in reference to yourself. It's...antiquated." He gave a slight chuckle, oddly embarrassed that this knowledge was the reason he believed her so completely.

"Thank you, Jason. For believing me." She gave him a brave grin that squeezed tears out of her eyes.

"Yeah, of course," he said, returning the smile. "Maybe I can help you make sure he doesn't have any more access to your personal stuff. Perhaps there is something we can trace. Did I mention I was pretty handy with a computer?" He positioned his hands over the keyboard and fluttered his eyes at her.

Zoe gave a small snort. "You may have mentioned it once or twice."

"Did you ever use your laptop when interacting with him?"

"Maybe a couple of times? My phone was mostly what I used when we were messaging. But he completely wiped the messages and stuff from my phone. Off the site, I mean."

"Well, maybe there's something on the hard drive we can dig up. Can't hurt, and might help, right? Can you bring your laptop next shift?"

Zoe gave a slight smile and stood. She left the room and returned with the laptop. "Ta-da!" she said triumphantly. "Something told me to bring it to work today."

He laughed, happy to see the hope blooming in her. "Just set it here." He motioned to his tray, and she removed his own laptop. "Do you mind me poking around in your computer? Perhaps some light cyberstalking?"

"No, of course not. Especially if it helps nail the bastard."

Jason booted the laptop, and went to work. Zoe gave him the pertinent passwords, then sat and watched TV as he delved into the inner workings of her system.

After a bit of silence, she glanced at her phone and spoke to Jason. "Hey, I need to make a call. Are you okay for a bit?"

Jason waved in response but didn't look up. Zoe went into the kitchen.

"Ms. Calder," Jason heard from the kitchen. His mother had arrived. *Oh, shit.* "Ms. Calder, I am distressed at some recent information that has come to my attention. I believe we need to revisit our choice for you to work here as Jason's private nurse."

"Mrs. Merone," Zoe began, but his mother's sharp tones cut her off.

"No, I don't wish to hear anything from you. I am endeavoring to have a replacement sent here as we speak. I shall remain here until they arrive. Please do not attend to Jason without my presence."

"Yes, ma'am." Her answer, devoid of any of the emotions he knew she was feeling, raised every protective instinct he possessed and left his blood boiling.

His mother was here throwing her weight around. Trust her to go into dictator mode when anything scandalous threatened to touch her.

"Mother," he said, but his voice didn't carry over the sound of the motor as he raised the bed.

"Oh, come now," his mother said. "You know I pay for all of this, right? The home nursing and the treatments and therapy that insurance won't cover? So I have a good idea of how much you make, and I know it isn't peanuts.

Why on earth would you need to work a side job? It can't be because you need more money. " Her voice rose as she began to get more heated.

"Mother"—anger made his voice louder this time—"Stop. Leave her alone. Come in here."

With a huff, Martha walked into Jason's room, closing the door behind her firmly.

"The agency will be hearing from me, and they won't be happy when I'm finished," she said without preamble. "Did you see the news about that--" She pointed toward the living room with disgust.

"Mother, you have to stop."

"It should be illegal for one of those types to work with patients," she raged, chin thrust forward with lips tight in a prim snarl.

"One of those?" he said slowly, and his icy tone finally caught her full attention.

"You know, a whore. " She sneered disdain into each word.

"Stop...it...now!" he said as loudly as his throat would allow. "She is not a whore. She is my nurse. Also, she is a fucking human being."

"A human being who admitted trading money for sex while accusing a cop of an unspeakable act." She adjusted her blazer, smoothing out nonexistent wrinkles and refusing to meet his stare.

"She didn't write that email. I'm sure of it. She stays, and you will be civil while you are here." He stared until she locked eyes with him.

Martha stood mute for moments, gauging his resolve. Finally, she turned and stalked out.

"It seems my son wishes for you to stay on as his nurse," she said to Zoe in clipped tones in the living room. "I will abide by his decision, for now."

He heard her gathering her things, almost unable to believe she was actually going. "But I think it would be better for everyone, especially those in this family, if you found other employment as soon as possible."

Her heels clacked toward the front door. "Perhaps if we aren't paying you enough, you should try the world's oldest profession on a more full-time basis."

"Mother. Enough!" The woman was positively insufferable, and his throat shrieked in agony at the sustained shouting.

The front door opened and slammed shut without another word.

ZOE CONTINUED HER duties while Jason labored over her laptop. She was quiet and tentative again, in the same way she had been when coming back to work. The helpless feeling, the desire and need to help her, gnawed at him. His mother was so far out of line, she was painting her own new ones. In her spare moments, he would guide her through setting up a new email account and changing passwords on the various apps and services she had used on her phone. While she worked, he scoured her digital imprint to make sure her stolen identity wasn't being used, especially financially. It took several hours before he was satisfied he had done all he could, at least for now.

Finally, he lay back against the pillows and let his arms drop onto the mattress.

"Okay," he said, "so far we've made sure you are in control of most of the services you use. I'm sure we didn't get them all, and I can't guarantee you won't get any more nasty surprises." He delicately rubbed at his eyes. "I'm sorry."

"Why? My gosh, you've worked at this all day. I really appreciate it. You didn't have to do that."

"I meant I'm sorry for my mom's response. It was wrong and cruel." He was still livid about it. There would certainly be more conversations about this with his mom in the future.

"Oh, that. Again, no need to apologize." Zoe waved it off, trying for flippant again. "I'm used to it."

Jason thought about it for a moment. How horrible that she had to be used to it. "I'm sorry for that too."

He saw her face scrunching up before she fled the room. He wondered if it was something he said. Probably, dumbass, he concluded.

He gave her a sideways look when she came back. "Are you okay?"

"I am now, yes. Thank you for being nice." Her face was blotchy, but her eyes had a gleam that wasn't there before.

"I'm sorry I made you cry." He made a goofy face, pursing his lips and crossing his eyes in an effort to get Zoe to laugh.

It worked. "It's okay. You didn't make me cry. Well...I mean you did. But not really. Not your fault, except kinda. I mean, I didn't expect you to be so understanding, but— Oh, hell. Anyway, I think I'm better now. Thank you." She seemed closer to her old self, which thrilled him.

Jason grew serious again. "Yeah, of course. You're a good person. You have a great big heart, and you are an amazing nurse. This fucker wants to play games with you, wiggle out of these charges by violating you all over again. I'm not gonna let that happen. I'll be making some calls. So just stay safe, but try not to worry too much. I know people, and I've got your back."

Zoe stayed silent, crooked smile blooming on her face at his compliments. Jason felt his heart go just a bit gooier for her. They heard the front door open, indicating her relief was here.

"Hey," Jason said as she got ready to wrap up her day, "I know you have the next couple of days off, and I'll understand if you need it, but if you leave your laptop, I could check it some more. Maybe find something that helps nail the bastard. If you like."

He waited while she mulled it over, hoping he could help her get through this shit.

"I think I'm going to need all the help I can get. If you think you can find something, I'll leave it here." She watched him, eyes glimmering with determination.

He nodded. "You know, they say true beauty is on the inside. And I really hope they're right, given my current position. But you know what I find most beautiful about you?"

"Aw, Jason, you're so sweet. Tell me, what do you find most beautiful about me?" She batted her eyelashes at him, blatantly.

"Dat ass." He grinned impishly at her shocked expression, laughing as she left the room.

Chapter Ten

Zoe

AFTER BRIEFING THE weekend nurse on Jason's care, I walked into a rainy twilight. I jumped when I heard a car start up near me, but an alarmed glance confirmed Delphine had arrived, as promised, to escort me home. Shit, I had completely forgotten about that. She rolled her window down at my approach. "I'm here, cheri. Let's go. Quickly now."

I followed her into the rain-slicked evening, dreading the crush of the press and the taunts and questions they would hurl when I got home. After a time, I realized she wasn't taking a convoluted way home, but headed toward a different part of town. Following Delphine's taillights, the events of the day wore a circular worry track in my mind. Working with Jason had proven to be a pleasant respite from personal problems, at least after Mrs. Merone left in a huff. Now, though, the issues outside his care bore down on me.

After almost twenty minutes of driving, she pulled into the driveway of a cookie-cutter house in one of the suburbs situated outside the city. The lights from our cars shone on a two-level brick home with two garage doors, one of which was open. No lights came from inside the house, and the streetlamp only cast a soft glow here.

Delphine exited her car and walked over to me, as I was parking behind her.

"Mon amie," she said softly at my window, "we park the cars inside the garage." She inclined her head toward the open garage bay currently occupied by some sort of large vehicle.

Delphine turned and walked into the darkness. In a moment, the garage lit up and the second bay door began to roll up. As I pulled my car into the empty bay, wondering whose house this was and what the hell we were doing, Delphine eased the vehicle parked in the first bay out to the driveway. It had been backed in when parked, front facing the street. She left the SUV running, a Chevy Trailblazer I realized, now that I could see it better. She crossed over to her car, pulled it into the first bay.

"Back the Trailblazer up close," she said to me as she finished pulling hers in.

I reversed the Trailblazer, bringing it close to her vehicle as her trunk popped open. I stepped out to help, and we transferred suitcases, three cardboard boxes, and a handful of grocery bags into the cargo area of the SUV. She closed the hatch with a thump.

"Let's go," she said, sliding into the driver's seat without explaining the baggage. She pushed the buttons on the garage door openers latched to the sun visor, and the doors trundled down behind us. She asked for my phone and took the battery out, then put the truck in drive and pulled away from the house. She'd saved me in my darkest moments, so I knew I was safe, but I was sure as hell curious.

Windshield wipers slapping a staccato beat, we rode together into the night.

DELPHINE WASN'T DISPOSED to conversation, which was fine with me. I slowly relaxed into the rhythm of the road, the darkness and rain wrapping us like a protective cocoon. The miles spooled out and the landscape grew swampier, the air heavier, danker, with Cypress trees illuminated more frequently by the headlights.

After driving for about twenty-five minutes, Delphine broke the silence. "How was your day?"

She wasn't asking a rhetorical question, and I knew she wasn't expecting a small-talk response. By now, she knew about the news articles, and the email that had touched off the firestorm. I told her about Jason's efforts to find something within my hard drive, and about his confrontation with his mom. She nodded at Jason's actions, an approving smile softening her face in the dashboard's glow.

We were out of Mississippi, somewhere in Louisiana, if I had to guess. Delphine's shoulders lowered, and she seemed to relax slightly, which served to reduce my anxiety some too.

"So, here's what is happening," said Delphine. "We, well, you, ma cheri—but I am along for this ride—we are hiding. Because the press at the house is insufferable and not altogether very nice. They are out for blood, and I will not have you exposed and vilified and victimized again at our home."

"I could've handled it," I said bravely, although the thought of swimming through that crowd again gave me palpitations.

"I know," Delphine said. "But I cannot. There will be a time when you will have to face them. There will be a time when they must know the truth. But for now, it seems the defense of Officer Randall has kicked into gear and poisoned the perception of who did what to whom. And for now, you do not need to be exposed to this. Also, the fact he is out on bail makes this a prudent option." Her lips thinned, and if I didn't know and love her so well, I'd be scared of that look. She watched out for her own.

"At least for this weekend, likely longer, we hide. Leave the battery out of your phone. Do not log in to any social media. There will be a computer with a satellite link where we are going, and I have purchased two throwaway phones. Obviously, none of it is traceable to you, unless you do something foolish online."

It made sense now. The hiding of the cars, the disabling of the phone. To truly hide, we needed to be able to move without being traced. I hadn't realized how on edge and anxious I was about Randall being out after his arrest. Delphine was right, as usual. Bitterness washed over me, mixing with exhaustion and anxiety that felt like a permanent part of me now. "He's going to get away with this, isn't he?"

"Non, mon amie. I swear this to you. We shall give the system its chance, give them the opportunity to put this evil away where we cannot reach him. But if the system fails, I swear to haunt him until one of us is dead by the other."

One thing I knew about Delphine Roulet: she did not make idle threats. I almost pitied Randall the choices he had available to him. Almost.

THE BAYOU CAMP we pulled into after almost two hours of driving was the definition of isolated. We had left civilization behind a while ago, driving down roads becoming ever more potholed and neglected, until turning onto a dirt trail. That had led us another few miles farther from civilization, the swampy overgrowth and fetid, heavy air closing in on us as we progressed. It had stopped raining, but the skies were still heavy with clouds, and the only light came from our truck. The weeds on the trail were high and thwacked against the undercarriage as Delphine drove with white-knuckled concentration. Finally, the headlights illuminated a clearing and the roof of a houseboat sitting low in the water and attached to a pier. Delphine maneuvered the Trailblazer in a tight circle, until the nose of the truck was facing the way we had come. She backed up close to the edge of the pier and shut the engine off.

The sudden silence and darkness had an almost physical weight. I didn't know how Delphine knew of this place, or even the house where we picked up the truck, but I felt...safe. No one could find us here; no one could *hurt* us here.

From God knew where, Delphine produced a flashlight, and together, we began to tote our clothing and supplies from the cargo area of the truck, down the pier, and into the surprisingly roomy houseboat. It was dusty inside, telling us no one had visited for some time, but clean and orderly otherwise. There was a queen-sized bed in a walled-off area toward the bow of the boat, and a small restroom toward the stern. In the middle was a tiny galley, a couch, a foldable table, and an entertainment center with TV and a desktop computer tower. Everything was brilliantly arranged to maximize space.

It took a couple of trips to retrieve everything from the truck. Once done, Delphine shooed me toward the bedroom. "Get changed. You are here to relax and forget about the world. I will get everything put up in due time."

I took my suitcase into the bedroom and changed into soft, purple pajamas. When I came out to the couch, Delphine had placed a glass of red wine on the table.

"Oh my god, Del, the wine looks amazing. I haven't had wine in, well, I don't know how long."

"You haven't had wine since Randall."

I froze for a second with the realization. "I didn't notice. But you're right. Feels like he took that away from me too."

"No more. He took so much. He will not take this. Not any longer."

I took the glass in hand, raising it in salute to the friend who would murder for me. She walked over with her own glass of red and clinked glasses with me. "To the vine..." she said.

"To the vineyard." Relaxing into the ritual felt like a rebellion.

"To the vintage."

"To the vino!" we said together. Triumph flushed through me.

A sip, a tingling of taste buds. It was a Malbec, and suddenly, it was girl's night in, and the real world could go fuck itself for an evening. I found the remote and pointed it at the TV. The houseboat had a satellite dish, but there wasn't much on. I searched the on-demand menu. "What do you want to watch, Del?"

Delphine cleared her throat meaningfully, but didn't say anything. She kept her back to me, and I heard the small microwave door shut. It began humming before she turned back to me, leaning against the counter and clearing her throat again with her eyebrows raised.

I didn't get it until I heard the first kernels of corn pop. Wine and popcorn...*ah!* I threw back my head and laughed. "Oh! Yes. Gotcha. Hang on."

I had the show ready by the time Delphine came to the couch with a full bowl of popcorn. I pressed play on *Scandal*, and together we watched Olivia Pope handle shit in the best wardrobe since Audrey in *Breakfast at Tiffany's*. I swooned over her coats, and Delphine swooned over what was under the coats. It felt good to relax, and even better to feel safe.

I yawned deeply by the end of the episode, and despite how I tried to hide it, Delphine noticed. "Go to bed."

Stifling another yawn, I nodded. "Yeah, I think I will. Um, I noticed there is only one bed. Are we sleeping together?" I said with a mock-flirty wink.

She laughed in her pleasant way. "As much as I might enjoy that, ma cheri, I will be on the couch tonight." She produced a nine-millimeter Glock pistol from her bag and laid it next to the popcorn bowl with a solid *thunk*. "No one knows we are here, I hope. But should anyone know and wish us harm, they will soon realize we have teeth and claws." As if concurring, the splash of a large creature in the dark outside roiled the waters.

I loved it when she got all protective.

In my dreams, I fled Randall in a darkened swamp, eventually getting mired in an unseen suck-hole and surrounded by alligators. He easily strode past the alligators to get to me, his hands shaped into reptilian claws that sank into my throat as they smothered me.

I WOKE TO the smell of biscuits and the sound of water lapping the hull. Shaking off the horror of the Randall dreams slowly, I heard Delphine murmuring and realized she was outside. Stumbling the short distance to the kitchen, I poured the requisite coffee and stepped out into an early bayou morning. In the golden light, I could see the boat was situated in a small offshoot of a tributary, almost completely enclosed by land when the level was this low. Cypress and pine woods towered over the camp, closing it in, while at our level, the Cypress knees bent up out of the water. Green vines trailed along the thick ropes holding the boat to the pier. The water level and land elevation resulted in the area where we had parked being roughly even with the roof of the houseboat. Toward the east, the skies were brightening, illuminating pinks and reds overhead as a few clouds floated by.

Delphine was on the phone, and in short order she finished her conversation. Together, we sipped coffee.

"Today, we try the ADA again," Delphine said after the mugs were half empty. "Today we figure out how to fight back."

"Thank you, Del." I had been trying to find a better way to express my gratitude, but it all seemed hollow and insubstantial. "I really don't know what I would do without you."

"You would survive. It's what you do. It's what you have always done. Now go fire up the computer. My friend informs me he has a Tor browser on this system. He says privacy is assured. I have more calls to make."

I knew that Tor was a system for anonymous Internet usage, but beyond that my knowledge was limited. Still, it would be good to check emails and do some online chores. I turned back into the boat.

"No social media," she called out. "And no news articles!"

Reluctantly, I nodded. I really didn't want to know what was being said about me, but I found the idea of checking almost irresistible.

The computer was an old Dell model, probably made around six years ago. Coupled with a satellite connection I knew would be slow. It felt like going back to the days of dial-up modems. To my delight, however, I found the operating system was a bare-bones Linux OS. Delphine's friend knew how to make the most of a little. As the computer booted, I activated my burner phone. I placed a call to ADA Hutto and left a message with my new phone number and a strongly worded request for a callback. Then, I turned my attention to the computer and logged into my new Gmail account.

I had two emails from myself.

The first one had come in at 9:23 p.m. last night and was titled *I'm Sorry*. I opened the mail to find an attachment of the rough draft from my old account requesting reassignment I had all but forgotten about. Oh no.

> *Hey,* the email read. *I came across this draft while working on your laptop. I don't know what to say. I'm sorry I made you feel uncomfortable. I know it is only a job for you, but I really thought we had a connection that was more than patient/provider, especially after everything with Vince.*
>
> *I know having you take care of me made the days easier to get through. I loved laughing with you and watching you do your job. You helped me through Dave's funeral. You really helped me after the funeral.*
>
> *I know you could call it a crush or a rebound since Jenna broke up with me so recently, but I really thought (hoped?) it could be more. I'm so sorry I*

was inappropriate with you. Please don't leave me. I'm starting to get a complex about all the girls I care about leaving. Ha-ha. Joking. But, is there any way we can talk about things? I promise to not be pervy. —J

Fuck. Jason had seen the email I was drafting to request a transfer. I hadn't even thought how he might feel running across the draft, nor considered how he might react. I knew Jason liked me, but other than flirty jokes, he had been entirely appropriate with me.

This was on me. I was the one developing inappropriate, unprofessional feelings. My heart had forced the issue, not his. Guilt pricked at me. I didn't want to hurt him, but I had. I didn't want to be reassigned, but it was the only professional thing to do. This was all my fault, even as he took the blame. Being around Jason made everything else happening around me fade to background noise. *Silly bitch*, I chastised myself. *Don't you know trans girls don't get romances?*

The second email was titled *Can we talk?* It had come in at 11:17 p.m. last night. The body read simply: *Your phone is going straight to VM. Can you call me so we can talk?* More guilt. Now he probably thought I was purposely ignoring him. I glanced at my burner phone and realized I didn't have Jason's number memorized. I dare not risk firing my regular phone up. Delphine would kill me. Maybe I could send myself an email. Jason might be working on the laptop and see it come in.

Jason, I titled it. Have received your emails. Sorry the phone is off. Long story. Please don't think this is your fault. I will be in touch soon as I can. —Z

I pressed send as my phone rang. I didn't recognize the number. Of course, with a new phone and no contacts listed, I didn't recognize any numbers.

"Hello?" Hoping for a stupid telemarketer so I could rage against an anonymous voice.

"Yes, is this Ms. Zoe Calder?"

I didn't recognize the voice, a reedy tone with perfect enunciation, no hint of a Southern drawl of any kind. "It is. Who is this?"

"Ms. Calder, I am Assistant District Attorney Malcolm Hutto. I was given your case and am in charge of the prosecution of Randall Bogen. I received your message."

"Yes. Hello, sir. It's nice to finally make contact with you." I pushed thoughts of Jason to the back of my mind. "I wanted to get an update on how the case was going, and to make sure you knew I didn't send that email the press reported on. It has to be from Randall, doing dirty business with information he got from my phone."

"So you are confirming that you didn't send the email regarding Officer Bogen?"

"No! I mean, yes. I am confirming I did not send the email."

"This is, I must say, highly irregular. I feel compelled to ask you before we go any further, Ms. Calder, would you like to amend your statement in any way regarding what happened? These are serious accusations, and I assure you anything you may be trying to hide—"

Anger rippled like quicksilver down my spine as I interrupted, "Hide? No, I've been yelling the truth at you guys since I woke up in the hospital. Why would I try to hide anything? What use would it be, given the scrutiny I'm about to be under?"

"Ms. Calder, where are you?"

"Where am—? What? I'm in an undisclosed location, hiding from the press after they camped out on my lawn. Why?"

"Again, highly irregular." His heavy breaths were loud, but fuzzy, over the earpiece. "Nothing about this fosters confidence in this case. An explosive email pops up from your own account, with provably false information, and you deny sending it. The press begins to question things, and you disappear. Your phone is off, your vehicle missing, your home abandoned. What am I to make of that? Why are you hiding, Ms. Calder?"

"Why am I hiding? Why am I hiding?!" My voice rose with the frustration swelling in me. "Mr. AD—la de fuckin' A—Hutto, have you seen the articles? Have you seen what the press is insinuating about me, and have you seen the absolutely vile and despicable comments that have been made in those articles?" I took a deep, exasperated breath. "Because I have. And I have heard some hurtful shit in my life, and I thought I had a thick skin. But the shit being spewed about me is something I have never witnessed, and I am simply not able to deal with it right now."

"Ms. Calder, your anger right now doesn't help things. I need you as a witness. But I need you as a believable witness, as a sympathetic witness. I'm sure I don't need to spell out for you how hard these types of cases are to prosecute.

"Now, perhaps you didn't send the email. Perhaps it truly is the work of some depraved lunatic. But I have no way to prove it, and proof—especially in these circumstances—is all that matters."

He paused as if making up his mind. "Ms. Calder, I have decided not to take this case to the grand jury at the moment. For now, we are dropping all charges. We will be investigating further, but at this time, and in the absence of further evidence, I have no confidence I can obtain a conviction against a cop."

"What!" Anger flashed through me like fire and left me shaking. "He's going to get away with it? You have something on him, surely. Something that led the cops to him and led to his arrest. Which I never heard about, by the way. How he came to be arrested. I didn't find him. The cops did. All I did was identify him as the fucker who...who..." Flashbacks exploded in my mind like grenades, making the world tilt and ripple. My heart raced in anger and fear. "Who raped me!" I exploded. "He raped me, strangled and beat me, and the only reason he didn't kill me was because my roommate got home earlier than planned that night. What about the lineup where I picked him out? Or the rape kit? Didn't they do a rape kit in the hospital?"

"Yes, ma'am. Of course. But we still haven't received those results, due to backlog. For the time being, the only evidence we have of any contact with you are log-ins from the dating site. As for the lineup, yes. It seems probable you did meet Officer Bogen at some point; perhaps posing as Arthur Dent online and using a VPN to shield his identifying information, or, and more likely to be argued by the defense, perhaps in the discharge of his duties or in a more *personal* way. You see? It would likely be argued with this email as Exhibit A you wished to punish him or hurt him with a spurious claim. And if that defense is pursued, the fact that an entity claiming the name Arthur Dent used a VPN to interact with your account only muddies the water and adds to reasonable doubt."

"Why the fuck did you arrest him then?" I snarled, fighting to keep him from hearing me sob. I'd be damned if I gave him the satisfaction.

"The fact that he has a Corvette similar to the one you described is what made the investigators push for Officer Bogen's arrest. Again, and I am so sorry to repeat, Ms. Calder, the entire case is circumstantial. Explainable to varying degrees of credulity, and it leaves you quite vulnerable to attacks against your character that I wouldn't wish on anyone.

"What I don't have, pending possible rape kit results, is anything to physically connect Officer Bogen to the location where the attack occurred. Or really, to you in any way."

"Mr. Hutto," I spoke over him. "Please don't let him get away with this. Please. What if he does it again?" I felt as if I was walking a tightrope; pleading for my life, while trying to keep him from witnessing me break down completely. "What if he goes after a 'real' girl next time?"

When I said it, I finally understood what Hutto had been getting at the entire time. "That's what this is all about, isn't it? I'm just some tranny"—I sneered disdain into the word—"and he's a cop, which means he gets out of jail free. Because who is going to believe me against some cop?"

" Ms. Calder"—he was apologetic—"I am limited by what I can prove, and who I have to prove it to. So, yes. Unfortunately, you being transgendered does complicate things. Him being a cop also complicates things. I'm sorry to cut this short, but I am expected in court in a few moments. Goodbye for now." *Click.*

I sank onto the couch, mind blank, eyes unfocused while staring at the silent phone. Numb. My mind kept repeating random bits of the conversation. I sat, beaten and afraid and ashamed and kicking myself for the hope I had let myself feel.

Lost in dissociative thoughts, I glanced at the TV screen, now operating as a monitor. There was a new email from Jason. Shit. I moved over to the keyboard, clicked on the mail as Delphine stepped inside.

> *Re: Jason,*
>
> *Hey! I'm sorry. I don't know what I was thinking, just knew that I liked you a lot. I didn't mean to make you uncomfortable. Can we at least talk about things before you make it official?*
>
> *Full disclosure, I kinda thought you liked me too. But maybe I was reading too much into it. Totally possible. I accept full responsibility for making things uncomfortable for you, and I swear it won't happen anymore. Please know how much I appreciate you, and know I would do anything needed...including not being a moony cow around you.*
>
> *—J*
>
> *PS Vince says hi (he might have a little crush on you as well, lol).*

Suddenly, fiercely, I wanted to see Jason. More to the point, I wanted to lie next to him and stroke his hair softly and watch silly shit on Netflix. God, I wanted to laugh with him, and be safe, and just be a stupid girl hanging out with a guy who stared at me the way he did when he thought I didn't notice.

It was all too much, and I didn't know what to do.

"I heard you yelling on the phone." Delphine broke into my thoughts.

I switched mental gears, preparing myself to break the news to Delphine. "Yeah, that was ADA Hutto. Called me back finally."

"And you yelled at him." She assessed me frankly, without judgment.

"Yep," I said bitterly. "Seems the good ADA doesn't like the situation. He's gonna drop the charges." I shrugged.

The silence from Delphine screamed at high volume. She let it drop without saying a word, and stepped over to stand beside me and rub my shoulders. Her eyes fell on Jason's email as I turned my attention back to it, desperate for a distraction, no matter how painful. She stared down at me, and my puppy dog eyes as I reread the email yet again.

"Oh, cheri. The love you have. It breaks my heart to see you push such a gift away." She sighed and stepped into the galley.

It may have broken Delphine's heart; it shattered mine.

"Any thoughts on the ADA's decision?" I asked while she placed ingredients and spices on the galley counter.

"Non."

"Well that's a first." A weak attempt at a joke.

She looked at me, chef's knife in hand, dark eyes serious. "Until one of us is dead by the other," she repeated her earlier oath. The knife flashed silver as she brought it down to the butcher's block with a loud *thwock*. "Lunch will be ready soon. Perhaps you should respond to the email."

Turning my attention back to the screen, I stared at the blinking cursor. Thoughts and desires about Jason, along with anger and betrayal about the ADA and his handling of the case swirled in my thoughts. I felt paralyzed, as if everything was occurring to me and around me without my input or help. I sat with my fingers poised over the keyboard.

And sat.

After a few minutes of indecisiveness, I got up and went to the small restroom. I rinsed my face with cool water, cupping and filling my hands before bringing my head down to splash the water against my skin. I straightened and caught my reflection in the small mirror. I stared, hating the weakness and fear I saw in the glass. It reminded me of the face that had stared back at me when I had first gotten home from the hospital. Never again would I allow this to happen, I had sworn to myself then. Never again would I be vulnerable.

I stared myself down, repeating the mantra I had chanted that morning. Stared until the fear left my face.

I stared until the anger returned.

Leaving the bathroom, I stalked over to the computer with a purpose. It was time to do something.

Time to fight back.

Chapter Eleven

Jason

HE SAT ON the back porch, savoring the freedom from his bed as he took stock of where he was in the healing process, and how far he had to go. The Monday afternoon sun filtered down through the oak leaves, turning shades of red and yellow as autumn progressed. The latest skin graft, on his right forearm, itched madly. Until he had been burned, he never thought that an innocuous itch could be so distracting and irritating. All in all, he was ahead of schedule in regard to his healing, pleasing the doctors and making his mother beam with pride. His bones were healing well, although he would need further surgery on his right hand to achieve more utility and flexibility, especially before he could get back to the fire department. Still, that was a problem for another day. His shin ached at the site of his tibia/fibula fracture, but the cast had been removed, and he was given a softer walking boot that reached to his knee. The infernal catheter had been removed at his last appointment. Standing on his own for the first time since going to the hospital had been a triumph he had shared with Zoe, even though he felt weak as a newborn and had to use a walker. All that time and effort in the physical therapy room, all those range of motion exercises and manipulations, and all the pain and work were paying off.

Almost every step of the way, she had been there. Cajoling, soothing, encouraging, nagging, stern, and compassionate.

Zoe. God, he missed her already. Learning earlier today she had been removed from his case left him feeling hollow and helpless. His mother had called the agency as she had threatened, probably as soon as she'd left his place. Zoe hadn't gotten the chance to send that email. He hadn't gotten the chance to talk her out of sending it. Between this and Jenna's spiteful confessions surrounding Dave, his feelings toward his mother were volcanic right now. Perhaps presciently, she had been circumspect enough to avoid the house and his repeated calls.

He didn't know when he started to care so much for Zoe. Perhaps it was when she handed him tissues the first day when he'd melted down over the news of Dave's death. Perhaps it was at Dave's funeral when she soothed the young boy whose name she once shared. Or after the funeral, when Vince begged forgiveness, and she reached out for him, and saved them both. Maybe it was when she opened the curtains on her first day back from being attacked, battered but not broken. Even then, he could explain the stirrings away as a crush, a rebound, a harmless infatuation with a woman who cared for him so well.

There were even times, mostly during the ROM exercises that left him screaming from pain and exhaustion, that he still genuinely wanted to hate her. She would not let him quit. But she wouldn't let him go too far either.

Maybe it was his discovery she was assigned male at birth that changed things. His gut-punched reaction when putting the pieces together led to some serious introspection. He watched her with new eyes, watched her grace. Imagined the courage it took for her to claim her identity. Imagined the ambition and sacrifice it took for her to become a nurse. Her androgynous features weren't conventionally pretty, perhaps. But she had poise and confidence, even after the attack, when a new vulnerability set in.

Still, he had been able to keep his thoughts and feelings under control while he was with Jenna. When she broke up with him, it had—after the dust and vitriol settled—left him relieved. He couldn't hate her. They shared a history that spanned a childhood and adolescence, as well as the loss of his sister and Dave. He wished her luck and good fortune. Okay, perhaps with a little comeuppance sprinkled in.

What he felt for Zoe was so much more than he'd ever felt for Jenna. Grander and all-encompassing. It was as if every cell in his body recognized her when she came into the room, surging forward in desire to get close to her. It left him aching and off-kilter.

And it pushed her away.

When he found the draft of her request for reassignment, he'd felt a panic nearly as engulfing as when the floor started to slide under him in the house fire. The thought that he made Zoe uncomfortable left him devastated. She was the best part of this shit show, and he completely fucked it up. When she wouldn't answer her phone he felt betrayed, which he knew was silly even as he raged within himself. He settled for sending her emails to the new account he'd set up for her, hoping maybe she would check it at some point. Her response, short and to the point, had soothed him somewhat, yet left him worried. He knew the firestorm surrounding her was raging right now, knew that he couldn't be her priority.

He scoured the Internet for articles about her, shocked and saddened by the clickbait titles and lurid stories, the before-and-after pics and the copious usage of her previous name along with using words like "his" and "him" in reference to Zoe. He was enraged at the sheer hatred and ignorance in many of the comments left by readers, but it opened his eyes to what she was up against: a world predisposed to hate and despise her, and a canny cop who would use that against her in the most public way.

What pissed him off the most was that it was working. This morning, the DA's office had issued a statement that they would not be pressing charges against Officer Randall Bogen, due to the "current lack of evidence connecting Officer Bogen with the events described by Ms. Calder."

Horseshit. The DA was backing off due to public outcry. No matter the email wasn't from her. Her past was exposed, lies believed, and the majority consensus was that she was doing it for money and made it up to get back at a guy "the dude tried to catfish."

There had to be a way to help. Had to be a way to prove what the corrupt cop had done. He'd spent the weekend buried in the laptop she had left, searching for a thread, something he could pull on that would lead him to Randall's door. After the ADA's announcement this morning, he'd spent hours stalking Randall's online footprint, with an obsession almost bordering on manic.

The need for a mental break was what had driven him outside, finally. Once outside, though, he still found it impossible to shut his brain off. He was counting his breaths in an effort to calm his mind when his phone dinged an email alert. His stomach lurched when he saw it was from Zoe.

Jason.

This is one of the hardest things I have ever had to say, and I am sorry. I have been informed by the agency that my services are no longer required, and my contract has been terminated.

It was never you, never your fault. I know you are wondering why I was planning to request a reassignment. I imagine you feel betrayed, confused. Please don't.

I have to maintain professional and ethical boundaries. And I don't feel I can do that with you any longer. My heart won't let me. You are an incredible person, and it has been an honor and privilege to assist you in your journey back to health. I will never forget you, Jason. Again, my heart won't let me.

I hope you can forget—and forgive—me. It would be best. I'm not sure what happens next, but I don't want it near you. It's ugly out here, but I am finished hiding from it.

You take care of yourself, Merone.
Love, Z

Jason's heart soared, even as his mind screamed at the shitty idea that she would no longer be in his life. She liked him back, and he would never see her again. After some moments, he remembered he still had her laptop, and she or a friend would have to come by to pick it up.

Until then, he planned to scour every goddamned byte on that hard drive for a lead.

He noticed the light through the trees had shifted. It was time to get to work. Back to bed, back to the laptop. He slowly got up, with the new nurse's assistance, and laboriously made his way back to bed with the walker. Finally, all energy drained, he lay back and collected his breath. The nurse—a Nurse Ratchett disciple, he ungraciously concluded—helped him get comfortable. He booted the laptop and delved into the hard drive.

After two hours, he was almost cross-eyed from focusing on the laptop screen. He had installed a utility that went into the hard drive and attempted to recover documents and downloads previously deleted. There were fragments of documents, random bookmarks, and even whole papers she wrote during her nursing classes.

Wait, what was this?

His eyes narrowed as he comprehended what he found. It was a deleted note, fragmented but readable. A warranty confirmation for her phone, and the serial number. Zoe had probably noted the phone's information when she bought it. The warranty had long since expired, and she probably deleted the information after the coverage ended. But there it was, on the screen.

A tiny spark of hope ignited and made him smile. This was a thread. Now, what to do with it?

He booted his own laptop. Within a few minutes of searching, he sank against the pillows, excited and satisfied. *Jackpot!*

The phone had popped up on an inventory list at a pawn shop in Hattiesburg. He double-checked to make sure the serial numbers matched. It was Zoe's phone.

Why would he pawn the phone, instead of simply destroying it? Did he need the money, or was he just arrogant enough to believe it could never be traced to him? Didn't matter. Officer Randall had made a mistake. Jason was determined to make it count.

What should he do with this information? Now that the ADA was backing off the case, he was wary of sending the information to the police. Should he send it to Zoe? It could be problematic if she suddenly popped up with the missing phone. He thought of sending the information to the Hattiesburg Police, but he didn't know anyone there, so he couldn't guarantee they would act on the situation quickly, or at all. The information he uncovered felt as if it had a timer attached, ticking away until it exploded into oblivion, phone disappearing in the hands of a random customer, or too late to help. He turned his attention back to his laptop and started searching. He called up news articles on Zoe, again grimly absorbing the prurient headlines. Filtering the search string down to regional coverage, he skimmed through, hoping for a reporter who handled the story with less sensationalism, more objectivity. After a few minutes, he found a low-key article written by Rachael Callaway, a surprisingly insightful reporter for the *Hattiesburg Clarion Post*. He searched the reporter's back stories, reading older articles with her byline.

She was a good journalist, he realized. Solid writing with heavy emphasis on the facts, and a strong sense of fair play. He dug further into her background, her online details cementing his belief she was Zoe's best hope.

He opened his email and began to compose.

Subject: Urgent info re: Zoe Calder case

Ms. Callaway,

My name is Jason Merone, and I am a firefighter for the City of Biloxi. I was recently involved in a building collapse during a fire and was badly injured. I spent several weeks in the hospital and burn unit, with broken bones and burns over large parts of my body and face. When I arrived home, I needed intensive health care. Zoe Calder was my nurse. I know without doubt that Zoe is not the person who is being portrayed by the press, and I further believe that she did not send the email that outed her as transgender and helped to make this story so salacious.

I would like your help to prove it. I have attached three documents to this email.

One document, a deleted fragment from her laptop hard drive I have recently recovered, contains her Android's serial number and warranty information. This is important because Zoe stated, from the beginning, her phone was stolen in the attack. Finding the phone, even though it has probably been wiped and reset to factory default, may yield important evidence both inside the software and on the phone itself. I do not trust the police to handle this potential evidence properly, as they have shown marked reluctance to even get involved with the case, and the District Attorney seems to be backing away as well.

The second document is a state-required filing from Atwell's Pawn Shop in Hattiesburg, listing the same serial number in document one as being in their possession and still in inventory. If you were to find and purchase this phone, I would defray the expense to your paper and encourage you to find a forensic software technician who may be able to retrieve the information on the phone. I suspect this might help prove that the person accused of stealing the phone was responsible for the email purported to be from Ms. Calder.

The third document is a timeline of events reported to me by Ms. Calder of the night she was attacked. I can personally attest the injuries on her face and throat were evident over a month after she was brutally beaten, raped, and almost murdered.

What I would ask from you is to investigate and report on this with the tenacity and objectivity you have shown in your reporting of other articles I have read in my research of your work.

Thank you for your time.
Jason Merone

Jason added his phone number and attached the documents described in the email but paused before hitting send. What was he doing? *Just send the information to the police. Let them handle it. It's their job. This could be obstruction of justice, evidence tampering. You don't have to interject yourself into this. You don't have to risk this for her. You might not even see her again even if this helps.*

He knew sending the email to a reporter might have consequences. But he had no choice. Zoe was the one at risk here, not him. She had saved his life in more ways than one. This was the least he could do to help.

He sent the email into the void.

THE NEWEST SKIN graft on his arm was close to driving him insane, and he needed to yet again rub the thick bandages over the site, wanting more than anything to scratch down to the skin with his nails, leaving bloody furrows. This didn't feel like healing. This felt like rusty hacksaws gleefully sawing away at his muscles. The pain seemed to be radiating outward from the graft, circling his whole arm, heading toward his elbow. This pain was different, but the new nurse didn't seem worried about it. She checked his arm, applied more ointment and reapplied the bandage, with a promise to call the doctor in the morning if it got worse. He didn't leave his bed, except for bathroom trips, so as to stay close to the laptop. He distracted himself with Netflix, rewatching *Unbreakable Kimmy Schmidt* because it reminded him of the night he and Zoe watched it and laughed.

The anticipation was killing him. Had Rachael Callaway opened the email yet? What would she think of the story? Would she go after the phone? Would she even believe him?

At 7:30, just as this new nurse was going off shift, a ding alerted him to a new email. He opened his account, heart beating faster.

It was from Rachael Callaway.

Subject: Re: Urgent info re: Zoe Calder case

Jason,

Thank you for writing. Have reviewed your documents. Will research further.

R. Callaway

Jason leaned back in relief. Short and to the point. He glanced up as his uncle strode into his room. The night shift was here. They exchanged pleasantries as Jason went to the Netflix queue.

He had grown fond of the evenings that Uncle Billy, Captain William Merone to the world at large, came to babysit. It was only once or twice a week now, but they always had good talks and fun watching mindless TV.

Plus, he always brought beer. Ice-cold IPA's from a microbrewery in New Orleans, lately. Jason wasn't supposed to drink with many of the meds he was taking, but it was nice to break the rules sometimes. They really lowered his tolerance, so he limited the amount he'd have at one time. It had taken Jason a while to acquire a taste for the hoppy, bitter liquid, but now it was his favorite.

Uncle Billy sat on the blue recliner, reached into the cooler he brought with him, and pulled two bottles out of the ice, water dripping off the dark glass as he opened them with a *pisht*. He passed his long arm over to the bed, handing a beer to Jason's waiting hand. They clinked bottles, took long draughts, and sighed in pleasure.

"Alright, kiddo. How's things?" Uncle Billy tended toward the gregarious around him, despite his stern public face, and he was in good form tonight.

"Eh, I've been better. But I've been worse, so all good, I guess."

"Good, good. I just found out about the mess your nurse is in. What's up with that? Kinda feels like a callback to ole Charles. Wonder what he's up to now?"

"Chastity," Jason corrected his uncle automatically. Remembering how they'd treated her felt like failure in the pit of his stomach. "Yeah, kinda similar. Last I heard, she was in Phoenix. But I wasn't ever interested in her like with Zoe. We were just friends. Could be, though, that knowing her helps with this."

"I hear ya. I imagine your mom was beside herself when she found out about it."

Under-fucking-statement of the century. "Yeah." he drew out the word, finishing it with a sigh. "She got Zoe bounced off my case."

"Well, damn. I'm not surprised but—" Billy cut off in midsentence. He gave a low whistle, looking at Jason with one eyebrow raised. "Wait, you like her? As in, like-like?" He must've finally processed what Jason said earlier.

Jason blushed at his direct appraisal. "Yeah. She's...something. But I don't know if I'll ever see her again. Mom and her pocketbook made sure of that."

"Oh, hell. I don't know half the shit you kids get up to, but Jason, let me tell you, son, all I want is for you to be happy. And if this nurse makes you happy—and you think your deep-fried ass has a chance with her—all I have to say is good luck. Go be happy." His eyes crinkled in genuine bonhomie.

Jason paused, getting as close to a smile as his healing face would allow. His uncle's approval meant a lot to him. "Thanks, Uncle Billy. You know what's next, right?"

"Oh, yes. Hit play, por favor."

Jason pressed play, and Uncle Billy's favorite show came on. *Family Guy.*

It was a good night, although the beer seemed to go to Jason's head a little more than usual. Perhaps this batch had a higher alcohol content. He only had a couple but was left flushed and dizzy.

He shook his head to clear the cobwebs. "Whew," he said. "Beer seems strong tonight. Got me buzzing already."

"Lightweight." Billy chuckled. "I should get you something more appropriate for that ridiculous tea set your mother insisted on bringing over here."

Jason laughed, and after a few moments the room stopped spinning so hard, although some dizziness remained. After watching a couple of episodes, Jason was ready for sleep. It was a bit earlier than usual, but was to be expected as he began to be more mobile. He took his Ambien and handed the TV remote to his uncle.

He woke up around midnight, gasping for air and sweating.

"You okay?" Billy asked, flicking on a nearby lamp. "You look like hell, son. Do I need to call someone?"

"Bad dream." He waved off the question. He couldn't seem to get enough air in his lungs. "Thirsty."

Uncle Billy handed him a glass of water from the hospital table. Jason gulped it down. Needing to pee, he looked at the doorway seemingly a mile away. Scooting his legs over the side of the bed, he used their momentum to help him swing his body upright. The room spun wildly as his heart pounded erratically.

"Need to pee," he said.

Billy brought the walker over and helped Jason stand. He got his balance, took a step. The room spun again, forcefully. Nothing made sense. His knees buckled, and he heard crashing sounds seemingly from far away as he collapsed, taking the walker and hospital table with him. He heard Uncle Billy shouting with alarm as he fell. Jason felt the floor on his right cheek as he landed, marveling at how cool it seemed against his fevered skin. His vision tunneled to black.

Chapter Twelve

Zoe

BY MONDAY, I was going stir-crazy, ready to latch onto anything that could possibly save me before I drowned. Hutto's announcement that they were dropping charges left me devastated, even though he assured me the file was still open and would be thoroughly investigated. I knew better.

Sunday, the agency emailed to tell me they were terminating my contract due to "distraction." They didn't feel they could "risk continuing to employ me" due to the "potential issues" surrounding the situation. Unemployed on top of everything else, I was left with an impotent rage that chafed against being cooped up in this small houseboat alone. Delphine had left in the afternoon with a guy who had roared up on a fan boat. She'd kept mum on what she was doing.

"Don't ask, child," she had responded to my question. "Better to not know, in case you get tough questions later." She refused to introduce me to the man on the fan boat, a lean guy in dark sunglasses and camo, with a hard-edged paramilitary look. I got the impression this was his houseboat and not the first time Delphine had been here.

Artists made the most fascinating acquaintances.

She was going after Randall, then. I felt a mixture of grim satisfaction—both a pang I would not be part of it, and disbelief I would condone the extralegal hunting of another, however tacitly. She was clear I was to stay put.

It all felt too passive. Pacing obsessively, I fumed and fretted. I needed to do...something. It was time to fight back!

Hoping a rehashing of the events leading to this situation might suggest a way forward, I opened a Word doc and transcribed the notes I had journaled that sunny day at Java Jane's a lifetime ago. Alternating between paralysis and recklessness, under it all was a growing anger. What should I do? Hide forever? Let Delphine clean up my mess?

Fuck it, let's get reckless. Let's go public. Give interviews to the reporters clamoring for my story. Square my shoulders and meet the spotlight with clenched teeth and demure smile; dare them to do their worst. Tell my truth, however little it might be believed. Was I truly ready for that?

Well, no, not really. But my choices were shit, and the only way out was through.

I began to research reporters who might give me a fair shake.

THE NEXT MORNING, I started packing. I had sent a few inquiring emails to reporters I felt good about. Now, I waited for responses.

Before going public, though, I needed to call Mom. I hadn't told her what had happened to me. It wouldn't change anything, and the call would probably be intercepted by my father. He was the great firewall, separating me from my mom and younger brother. He ruled with absolute sureness that he spoke for God; thus, what he said was ironclad. They dared not disobey.

They didn't want to end up like me. Alone and homeless. Never mind that I was neither anymore. I was the boogey(wo)man in the closet.

Still, I had to try. She deserved a heads-up, and I needed to at least attempt to tell my side of the story before it got splashed everywhere. In case she was worried. Or wondering. Truthfully, I had held off calling her for a few simple reasons: what if she believed I had asked for it? What if she thought I deserved it? Did she even care?

I didn't give a single green shit from a burrito what my high-and-mighty father thought. This would be heralded as confirmation of every thunderous pronouncement of impending doom he had prophesied at me over the years.

Mom was different. Mom always cared, even though she never managed to stand up to the steamroller who was my father. She fretted and reached out at times and sent money when she could sneak any my way. I missed her so damn much it hurt to think about her, even as I hated her for what she had allowed to happen to me.

She didn't have the number to this phone. Which meant my father didn't know it either. So maybe we could talk, even if he went scrolling through her call history later, as he often did.

Nervously, I dialed her number from memory, stomach churning.

"Hello?" At the tentative answer, I had to close my eyes against the onslaught of memories from when she had been my entire world and everything good in it. In that moment, I could see her clearly: long strawberry-tinted hair fading to gray, her face an angular mix of European features and homespun heartiness. She would be in a plain dress, most likely denim. No makeup. No jewelry. Still beautiful.

"Mom. It's me."

"Noa—ah, Zoe? Is that you?"

"Hey, Mom. Are you able to talk? You can just say I have the wrong number if it's not a good time."

The line was silent for moments that stretched to eternity. I heard a sniff on the phone and realized she was crying. Hard. She cleared her throat. "I've been trying to call you," she said, a quaver in her voice. "Oh, my baby, what have you gotten yourself into?"

So she had heard about everything, then. I paused before speaking, my mind racing. "Things have been a little crazy lately."

"Were you raped?"

Hearing it from her shattered me inside all over again. Of all the things I never wanted to be asked by my mother... "Yep."

"Oh god, love. Oh my god. I am so sorry! Oh, baby. Why didn't you tell me?"

I didn't want my asshole father to know and didn't want my mom to think I was *that* kind of girl. "Didn't know how to bring it up. I wasn't sure what your reaction would be."

"I've been trying to call you since I heard. It hurts my heart to think of what happened to you. And it hurts more to think I wasn't there for you when it happened. That we don't have that kind of relationship anymore."

It had been so many years now.

My breathing became shallow; the years of festering hurt and anger pushing to lash out at her; the hope she might still love me urging caution. Taking a deep breath and a ten count, I let her off the hook. This wasn't the time to rehash old family shit. I just wanted her to know I loved her before I stepped back into the real world and whatever waited for me there.

"It's not your fault, Mom. And it's not you. Knowing my father knew and was probably happy about it was something I wasn't prepared to handle. It would've been too much to bear."

"Your father," she said in a tone of such contempt I pulled my phone back from my ear and shook it, wondering if I was hearing her right. "Hmph. I've about had enough of his bullshit."

Wait, what was this? My mother never cursed. To hear her mutter the word bullshit was akin to hearing the pope recite filthy limericks.

"Right there with you," I said flatly.

"Yeah, well, you know how he can be. But lately, he's been...weird. Obsessive and random about things, and a hair-trigger temper. I've never been afraid he would physically hurt me before."

"Gee, I wonder what that's like." Still trying to joke. Joking was always easier.

"Then the press showed up over here on Friday, out of the blue, knocking on the door and ringing the phone off the hook. I was wondering whatever could they want. Then I heard about the cop they arrested, saw what they were writing about you, that you were a whore doing this for money and attention. But you aren't a...prostitute, right?"

"No, Mom, I'm a nurse. A damn good one."

"See, I knew that was wrong. You would never do that, right?" My heart clenched. This was one of the questions I would probably be asked soon, and I dreaded it.

"N-Zoe, are you there?"

"Yes."

"Oh, I thought we got disconnected for a second. But I was saying—"

"Yes. Mom. I meant, yes, I have had sex for goods or services. It wasn't as glamorous as *Pretty Woman* lead me to believe. I never got to drive a Lotus."

The line was so quiet I began to wonder if she had disconnected. Then I heard what sounded like moans coming from a mouth with a hand clamped over it.

She might never talk to me again after this, I thought. Might as well get some stuff off my chest.

"It's called survival sex," I said coldly. If I could keep my cool, I could get the words out. "And when you are a homeless queer teenager with no family, or money, or transportation, or job history, or education, your options get pretty fucking bleak, pretty damn quick." I had to reach down deep to try to tamp down the anger begging for scorched earth before I trusted myself to speak again.

"Yeah, I've given blowjobs because I was desperate for a shower and a fresh razor." *Fuck it. She asked. Blow her up.* "I've been the party girl at sketchy houses with skeevy pervs just so I could have a corner with a dirty blanket and a break from twenty-five-degree rainy nights.

"But you know what? I'm not going to apologize for that. Not anymore. I'm putting it on you. You let my father do this. You stood by." Guess I didn't get that anger under check after all. The spite I threw into my words did nothing to stave off the shame of those desperate times. I should've known I could never fully move past those actions. Once a whore, always a whore, right? No matter that it was for survival. At least I had agreed to those encounters.

Silence on the line and then Mom gave a plaintive sigh. "Yes. God forgive me."

"I'm not a bad person, so you know. I called because wanted to give you and Jacob a heads-up that people might be getting nosy with you guys. And also to tell Jacob he's still my li'l bro and I love him." He didn't deserve this shit either.

"I love you too, Zoe. I pray one day you may be able to forgive me." The words grated at my soul, but I knew she meant them well. It was a bridge I wasn't willing to step on yet, though.

"Maybe we can work on that one later. Take care." Without waiting for a goodbye, I ended the call with a trembling finger. No, I wasn't ready to forgive. Not by a long shot.

AS I CHECKED to make sure I had packed everything I might need, I saw an email waiting in my inbox.

An R. Callaway had sent a message titled *Zoe, I found your phone. Can we talk?* She was one of the reporters I had emailed, but this wasn't a reply to that message.

Here we go. I clicked and read:

> *Ms. Calder,*
>
> *My name is Rachael Callaway, and I am a staff reporter in Hattiesburg for the Hattiesburg Clarion Post. I received an email from a person who stated they had received care from you as a*

nurse, and that they fully believed your allegations against Officer Bogen. They also forwarded information that assisted me in locating your phone. We are having the device examined by a software consultant who specializes in data recovery. We've already found some troubling information.

Would you be willing to talk further about this? My cell number is below.

Rachael

Attached was a photo of the phone, along with the serial number and Rachael's number. The serial number didn't really mean anything to me because who remembers the serial numbers of their gadgets? The phone pictured was definitely mine, though. I recognized the scuff marks at the top left-hand corner of the bezel, and the wear pattern on the home button.

I had to reread the message to fully absorb what was being said. This wasn't a response to the email I had sent. This newspaper had located my phone, and they had found something, thanks to Jason. Maybe something on my laptop had actually helped.

I felt a frisson of excitement, hating the feeling but unable to will it away. What did they find? Would we be able to link it to Randall? Would this nightmare be ending soon? Picking up my cell, I winced at the last number called on the screen and dialed the number Rachael had provided.

"Rachael Callaway," answered a youthful voice in a no-nonsense tone after two rings.

"Ms. Callaway. This is Zoe Calder. I just got your email."

"Ms. Calder, hi!" she said in a much warmer tone. "Yes. Thank you for calling me. Do you have a few moments?"

I couldn't let this anticipation worm its way any deeper. Not yet. I shook my head to clear it before answering. "Yes. I'm wondering how you found my phone. And what you found on it."

"We are working on the story as we speak. The phone is still with an expert, but we've already pulled some interesting information. He's hoping to find more as he digs farther in. Now, Ms. Calder, for the record, are you confirming this is your phone?"

I hesitated. The blunt question brought my guard up. "It seems to be, yes. But it's hard to be sure from just a picture."

"Careful. I like that. Can you confirm, again for the record, that the phone was stolen on the night you allege you were attacked?"

I closed my eyes and spoke through clenched teeth, the memory pinging my anger. "Yes. He threw it in a black garbage bag along with other stuff he had touched in the house. Wine bottles, plates, glasses, and stuff like that."

She didn't respond for a moment, probably taking down notes. When she spoke again, it was in a quieter voice. "Did you know he took pictures with your phone?"

The way she asked let me know she wasn't talking about random landscapes. Pictures? Oh, God. No. Please. No. "I did *not* know that."

"I know you've had it rough lately, and I don't blame you for hiding. But, is there a chance we could meet up? I have so many questions for you, and to be honest, after seeing those pictures, I really want to tell your side of the story. They are...ah...they're pretty horrific."

I could only close my eyes and shake my head at the thought of the types of pictures he must have taken. The memories from that night, never too far away, again began to play an endless loop in my head. The idea that the worst night of my life had been recorded and preserved was a further indignity that left me floundering.

"Ms. Calder?" Rachael's voice brought me back to reality. I didn't know how long I had been silent.

"Zoe. You can call me Zoe."

"Zoe. I'm sorry for what you went through. I would really like to meet with you, if possible."

The panic and indecision was back. Could I just stay on this houseboat forever? "I—I don't know. I'm still trying to process this."

"Do me a favor. Check your email. If you want to help the next girl he comes across, call me back. I'll be working on the story." The line went dead.

I sat, numbed by the information. The message popped up on the monitor, bold black letters reading *Picture (NSFW)*. I stared at the screen as if it were radioactive. If I clicked, I could never unsee it. Fragmented images from that night flashed through my mind. The wine at the deck table outside. The bunched wrinkles of the tarp when he laid it on the floor beside me. The rough texture of the carpet pile on my knees as it bit and burned the skin during my struggles.

I couldn't do it. I couldn't open the image. It might just destroy me.

I had to.

I clicked on open quickly. Rip the Band-Aid off.

The older computer rendered the file slowly, from blocky pixels to a recognizable but corrupted photo. I screamed when I saw the picture, the agony of the image almost unbearable as it echoed through my body.

Randall was mid-penetration, his long arm holding the camera out to the side, while his other hand was bunched in my hair, wrenching my head back awkwardly, displaying one side of my beaten face, noose tight around my throat. He poked his tongue out at the camera, a sadistic, leering grin on his face.

The motherfucker had taken a selfie.

THE ROAD UNSPOOLED in front of the Trailblazer as I drove toward Hattiesburg alone. My thoughts were fueled with murderous fantasies, fed by the music blaring from the stereo at high volume. I found a radio station that played heavier stuff, and it seemed darkly poetic the first song to blast out after the commercial break was Godsmack's "I Stand Alone." The heavy guitar licks and throbbing drumbeat were distorted by the overloaded speakers as I drove recklessly toward Rachael Callaway.

Seeing the picture she sent had fundamentally changed something within me. The agony I felt at seeing the picture had quickly melted from the supernova of fury that consumed me. The legal system hadn't failed me, I reasoned. It had gotten out of my way.

Some things had to be handled personally, and Randall had to die.

I didn't know what Delphine had in mind when she went hunting, but I realized something when I saw that picture: I wanted to watch. I wanted to be the last thing he saw before he left this earth, to watch his eyes fix on mine as the life faded from them and understand his ultimate mistake had been not finishing the job when he set out to kill me.

I had called Rachael back after seeing the picture and set up a time to meet at the paper's office. Delphine didn't answer when I called her, and I left a message. She would be pissed, but I would deal with that later. I forwarded the picture to her and left a post-it in the houseboat.

Grabbing the keys, my purse, and the revolver Delphine had left behind, I got in the truck, leaving my packed bags behind.

The soundtrack on my drive continued with System of a Down, Halestorm, and Rage Against the Machine. I screamed every word to "Bulls on Parade," knifing through curves without missing a beat. It was my armor, and my sword, and I was taking this motherfucker down.

Afternoon was fading into dusk when I arrived at the Clarion Post's office. I tucked the gun back into my purse before exiting the truck.

I was met by a small-framed woman who looked like a college freshman. Her bright-red hair spiraled to her shoulders, but sharp hazel eyes and a calm smile put me at ease as we exchanged pleasantries. Rachael Callaway escorted me past the lobby guard, up to the third floor in an elevator, past a busy open room with desks and computers and people, and into a conference room. The table in the middle dominated the room, tall whiteboards on both long walls. Sconces and recessed lighting replaced the usual utilitarian florescent lights, giving the room a softer feel. Two men sat at one end of the table. They stood at our entrance.

"Zoe, this is Oliver Brooks, our editor-in-chief. And this is Kelly Roberts. He is the consultant who did the forensic examination of your phone," Rachael introduced.

We shook hands and murmured pleasantries.

"Would you like some water? Or coffee?" Rachael asked as she pointed me toward a chair.

"Oh, coffee! Yes, please." Coffee, oh *God,* I needed coffee.

"Back in a sec," she said, turning to exit the room. She glanced back at me from the doorway, measuring me with compassion in her steady gaze. "It's good to meet you, Zoe. Thank you for coming."

After a few minutes during which we made awkward small talk across the table, Rachael returned with Keurig-fresh coffee for us both. I raised an eyebrow at her cup. She laughed at my face. "It's never a bad time for coffee, and newspapers run on it as much as the ink and paper."

Rachael sat across the table and opened her laptop. She glanced over the top of the computer at me, again assessing me. I looked back at her directly, held her gaze. She saw the rage in my eyes and nodded grimly.

Oliver, the editor-in-chief, cleared his throat for attention. "Ms. Calder, thank you for agreeing to tell your story. Rachael will be interviewing you, but we have all contributed questions. After the interview, we will present the information we have gathered so far, both as a courtesy and to hopefully clarify any additional questions that may arise. I am here as a representative of this publication to monitor this meeting and keep things on track. I would request the information you are about to receive be kept confidential until we can fact-check and publish.

"Before we get to the questions, Ms. Calder, could you tell us what happened?"

Still running on adrenaline and high-octane fury, I forgot to be nervous or ashamed. I recounted the events of that evening. Everyone was rapt as I finished, elbows on the table, eyes focused on me.

"Wow," Oliver said into the silence. "Thank you for sharing. Do you need a break before we get into the questions?"

"No." This had already taken so much from me, it wasn't getting a second more.

"Okay. So let's keep it going. Rachael?" He turned the meeting over to her.

She picked up her pen and opened her legal pad to a blank page.

It felt like an attorney's brutal cross-examination. The questions were intrusive and blunt and often circled back to previous queries. I hid nothing.

Rachael flipped the pad closed finally, indicating the interview was over. "Thank you for your candor, Ms. Calder. I can't imagine how difficult this has been." She turned to her laptop, danced her fingers over the keys. With a click, she shared her laptop screen with the overhead projector.

"So yesterday, Monday, I received an email from Jason Merone." The email text filled the screen along the far wall. "As you can see, he was quite certain of your innocence."

I read it with an ache, Jason's email penetrating the cloak of rage I had pulled around myself. Even after hurting him, he still wanted to help me. Once again, I owed him big.

"This is one of the attachments Jason referred to in the body of the email. As you can see, it is a fragmented note containing your phone's serial number," she continued.

The warranty note, I remembered. How long ago had I deleted it? The fact that it was still recoverable on the computer seemed both miraculous and terrible.

"Why did Mr. Merone have your laptop?"

"Because he asked for it." I shrugged. "He mentioned trying to see if there was anything on the drive that might help."

She nodded, opening her pad to make a notation.

"To continue," she said, glancing back to the wall screen. "We verified the phone was listed on inventory at an Atwell's Pawn Shop over on West Pine Street. Got there as he was getting ready to close, but I sweet-talked him into letting me shop for a phone. Told him I had cash.

"Bottom line, that's how we retrieved the phone. I confirmed that it was defaulted to factory settings and wiped, with the SIM card removed. We then reached out to Mr. Roberts, who, thankfully, was available. If he looks tired, it's because he's been working on this phone from around nine last night until about an hour before you got here. He's described the process of what he did, but it went way over my head. The upshot is, we recovered pictures. You've seen one; there are a few more." *Click, click.*

Even through my rage, the pictures that flooded the room still shocked me. I sat and stared at them, a half-dozen pictures of Randall brutalizing me. I stared and committed them to memory. Each and every one would be answered for. I swore it.

This time it was Kelly, the phone tech, who cleared his throat. "To add to the growing pile of evidence, I can verify this phone was powered on and geo-located on the night of your attack. The signal bounced off the nearest cell tower in Dantzler, Mississippi. It's dark after that."

Dantzler. Where Randall lived.

"It's also become evident that there is more than meets the eye with Officer Bogen." Rachael took up the narrative again. "The hourly rate for the attorney he retained along with the cash for the bond he posted doesn't add up. Now, he does own a thirty-acre farm-ranch near Dantzler that he inherited from his parents after their death, but putting it as collateral wouldn't yield enough to make the bond. Not with cash. And there are no records of any sort of lien being placed against it. So we've been digging further into his background." She nodded over to Kelly.

"He lives pretty close to the bone," Kelly said. "No big expenses. No listed property other than the farm, truck, and the Corvette that led the detectives to him. Searching for him online reveals nothing, really. We're pretty sure he uses a VPN when online, which is pretty smart. Keeps him anonymous and his traffic private. It means there is no way to prove the person you interacted with was actually Mr. Bogen. But then he made a mistake and pawned your phone, thinking the data wipe made everything go away. Smart move, dumb move."

I swallowed around the lump in my throat. They really were digging; they believed me.

Rachael jumped back in. "It's like he is being told what to do in some cases, and winging it in others. Nothing concrete we can point to, but it's beginning to smell an awful lot like there may be an organization behind him. And I'm not talking about his brothers in blue."

"So, not just a corrupt cop, but like, super-duper bad guy then?" I responded.

"Yeah, something like that. It's going to take a while to unravel everything, I think." Rachael ended the presentation, clicked off the overhead projector. At her response, I sensed the mood of the room change. What was I missing?

The editor at the table spoke up after clearing his throat. "Ms. Calder, again, I wish to stress this was a courtesy to you. The evidence is overwhelming as to what occurred the night you were attacked, and I can only imagine what you must have gone through since." He paused, took a sip of water.

I watched the buildup with fascination and growing dread.

"But in light of the potential of additional malfeasance on the part of Officer Bogen, and in light of the ethical concerns that publicizing this information may have an effect on his rights to a fair trial, I have made the decision to hold off on publishing this story until we can investigate Officer Bogen's extracurricular activities further. If we can link him to a criminal syndicate, and prove it, it may help to expose and prosecute additional people involved. I don't want to expose him as just a rapist if we can also expose him for criminal acts under color of law.

"We will, of course, be forwarding this information to the District Attorney's office. And we will hold their feet to the fire and insist on justice for you. But at this time, we will not be going public with this."

Just a rapist? Fuck you, Mr. Brooks. The blood in me ran ice-cold after his ponderous statement. After a moment of thought, I realized I didn't care. It didn't change my plans.

Mr. Just A Rapist had a debt to settle, and I intended to receive full payment with interest.

I left the room without another word. Rachael followed me out.

"I'm sorry," she said when we were alone in the elevator. "I was outvoted. I have the article written. I was ready to publish. I pushed to publish, even with the strong indication that he is connected. But Oliver has Pulitzers in his eyes. We've heard whispers and rumors about a drug network, but nothing we could pin down. This might be the wedge we need to blow it up, make a big stink. Get awards, put the newspaper on the map."

"I understand. Why go after 'just a rapist' when he could be so much more?" I said with heavy sarcasm, even though the numbness had started to form back in my stomach again.

To her credit, Rachael winced. "He— I'm sorry, yeah. He can be tone-deaf sometimes. He's a good editor. I disagree with his decision, but I see his point. And it's his call."

The elevator dinged, and the doors opened to the lobby. Rachael lay her hand on my shoulder. "Zoe, you have the worst poker face. I could practically read your thoughts. Be careful, whatever you have in mind, okay? Just...be careful."

She disappeared behind the closing elevator doors, and I was alone again.

I made my way back to the truck, locking in the silence, when I closed the door and sat brooding. Everything had changed, yet nothing had changed at all. The knowledge that he was possibly connected meant I needed to be more careful, but I was still going after him. The tantalizing promise that a newspaper knew the truth of my story meant nothing if they didn't publish the article. I would still be the *catfish tranny whore*, as the Internet collective in their wisdom had decided to call me, until the truth came out.

I checked my phone. Fifteen missed calls from Delphine and another twenty texts. She'd made it back to the boat, then. She was worried about me, but she was also pissed.

I called her phone, but it went straight to voicemail so I left an update.

The fury of the day ebbed away as I sat in the silence of the half-empty parking lot. Anger takes a lot of energy to maintain, and I could feel exhaustion creeping in around the edges.

I needed more coffee.

As I started the truck, the phone beeped a low battery warning. My charger was packed with the rest of my stuff. Still in the houseboat. Fucking brilliant, as always. I needed to keep enough juice to make or receive phone calls, in case Delphine called me back.

Wait. I had a spare. Thinking back to the night Delphine had brought us to this truck, I glanced down at the center console. Opening it, I found my real phone and battery. I wasn't hiding anymore, might as well have my usual phone up and running. I snapped the battery into the Samsung and turned it on. As the phone booted, I drove into the Hattiesburg night, looking for coffee and Wi-Fi.

I STOPPED AT a Starbucks on Hardy Street right before closing. I ordered a plain coffee and loaded it with sugar. Pulling out the phone, I noted the massive number of missed calls and checked the voicemail. It was full. I checked text messages, deleting the ones from unknown senders without reading.

There was a text from Jason last night.

I went still, noting the pull from my heart and the thrill I got from seeing his name on my screen. I opened the text.

Ms. Calder. This is William Merone, Jason's uncle. I tried to call you but the phone went straight to VM, which was full. Wanted to inform you that Jason is in ICU with MRSA. Not expected to last the night. Thought you might want to know.

The world faded away until there was only the bright screen of the phone, the words in black on the white background, unchanging even as I wished them away. No. Fuck no. Not Jason. My heart couldn't take another blow.

I sat, paralyzed and uncomprehending, until a barista, still pimpled from a difficult adolescence, touched my shoulder. "Miss? I'm sorry. We're closing now."

Foggy, I looked up. Focused on him with glassy eyes, I finally nodded my understanding.

Walking back to the truck, I read the text again. And again.

I needed to see him if possible, to say goodbye. Mr. Just A Rapist could wait.

Pointing the truck toward I-59, I drove south in silence. Toward Jason. Toward home.

He was probably dead now. And bitterly, now that it was all too late, I faced the bald truth.

I was in love with Jason Merone.

Chapter Thirteen

Jason

DRONING HUMS AND mechanical beeping ushered his way back to consciousness. It felt like deja vu. Hadn't he done this already?

He thrashed against the tethers stuck in and on him, trying to grab the invader in his throat that pushed air into his lungs in a maddening metronome. His hands were restrained, his struggles ineffective. His mind blossomed into panic, heart rate spiking, causing the beeps to increase tempo.

There was a flurry of activity. Masked faces floated in and out of sight, concern and compassion in their voices as they assessed this new development.

"Jason," an authoritative voice called out. "Hey, hold on, now. Calm down. You're in the ICU, and everyone is here to help you. But I need you to relax. Just relax, buddy."

Uncle Billy. He recognized the voice. So he was in the ICU. Again. Fuck.

He opened his eyes, the light hurting even though it was dim in the room. He located Uncle Billy, shot a question with his eyes.

Relief colored Billy's voice as Jason calmed. "Welcome back, kiddo. You scared us pretty good," he said. "Your mom's on her way. Why don't we let the doctors and nurses do their thing, and then I'll tell you what happened, okay?"

Jason gave a slight nod, his mind still swimming, thoughts still jumbled. The activity continued, nurses and doctors talking above him. Finally, a doctor spoke to him.

"Jason, I'm Doctor Eubanks. You seem to be feeling better. You were really fighting the ventilator pretty good just now. Do you feel up to getting that tube out of your throat?" His no-nonsense manner helped calm Jason a bit.

Again, Jason nodded as best he could.

"Okay. Give us a few minutes. Try not to fight it if possible. We'll have it out in a jiffy."

A jiffy turned out to be at least twenty minutes later. Finally, the tube came out, leaving him breathing on his own. He took a deep breath, exhaled. And again. He couldn't describe how good it felt to breathe by himself.

With the tube removed, there was no need to restrain his hands, so they were freed as well. His hand, he realized. They only freed his left hand.

He glanced at his right arm. The gauze was wrapped tightly around his elbow, and past the elbow...there was nothing. The rest of his arm had been removed. New panic bloomed, his eyes wildly searching for Uncle Billy as he reached across his body to touch the nub where hand and forearm had once been.

"Shhh. Hey, calm down, buddy. I know that's an ugly surprise. But you contracted a raging case of MRSA, and this was the only way to save your life. The main infection was hunkered down in the skin graft you had on your right arm, and there were cysts and pockets of infection that were spreading through the rest of you. Some of it traveled through your bloodstream to your heart and tried to shut it down. We damn near lost you. Had to do CPR on you all the way from your bedroom floor to the ER, where the doctors brought you back with some fancy gadgets and lots of drugs. You've been fighting the infection and in and out of consciousness for about three days now."

Jason went still, absorbing the information. "MRSA," his uncle had said. *Shit.* A Methicillin-resistant staph infection. He looked at the bags on the IV pole, two smaller bags clustered around a large bag of saline. Broad-spectrum antibiotics, he figured.

He knew MRSA was deadly, and he was at high risk. It was one of the things Zoe had been vigilant about, always cleaning and wiping and spraying. His replacement nurse, well, she had a bit more relaxed approach to things.

And in less than seventy-two hours after Zoe's departure—at his mother's insistence—most of him had wound up here.

The pain he'd gotten used to over the weeks and months flared up again. It was the pain from his now missing right forearm that pissed him off the most. He knew about phantom limb syndrome, but it didn't seem fair that he still had to deal with pain from an extremity he was no longer attached to. Worse, the damn catheter was back in. He sighed and took in his surroundings, squashing the trepidation trying to take seed in his gut. Feeling sorry for himself wasn't going to help anything.

It was a small hospital cubicle, dominated by the bed he was in. Lots of blocky medical equipment and monitors set up for his life support arranged around the head end of the bed on both sides. His uncle was there in full gown and facemask, as if prepared for surgery. Everyone else around him was fully gowned as well. He noted a glass wall beyond the curtains. He was in quarantine.

Uncle Billy had stepped to the end of the bed and was absently patting his feet in an awkward attempt to comfort Jason as he tried to piece together the night he had collapsed. He could feel the bruise on his cheekbone from the meeting of face and floor.

He would never be a firefighter again. Not down an arm.

The dawning horror hit him like a wrecking ball; a swooping inevitable arc crashing into him, leaving plans and dreams and hopes in rubble. He'd known getting back on the line was a long shot and used the improbability of it to fuel his PT and ROM sessions. Had taken the times where the pain felt like clawing, fire-spewing banshees screeching for release as a badge of honor. A measure of the fight it would take to reach his goal.

At least this way he wouldn't ever kill anyone on the scene again. There's a fucking bright side to everything, right? Fucking fuck.

Uncle Billy continued to pat his feet until he moved, curling into himself like a salted slug. Right now, he hated Captain William Merone. Right now he was the fire department, the ideal he could never achieve. He closed his eyes and shut the world out.

The crack of helmets and pads slamming together in his mind nearly drowned out the monitor beeps in his mind. *The gap opens in front of him, and he rushes to fill it. The running back hits like a freight train, impact leaving him on his ass and unable to properly breathe. "That's what I'm talking about!" the coach is yelling, but for some reason he looks like Uncle Billy and has a fire department badge clipped to the waist of his sweatpants. "Jason, take a break. You can watch from the bleachers."*

Permanently.

Damn.

He was gonna need to call Vince soon, wasn't he?

"OH, MY POOR baby. I thought we had lost you. And your arm! I tried to ask for more time to see if the medicines would work and keep us from having to amputate, but they were pretty clear that was what was causing you to be so sick. I'm so sorry, honey."

His mother had arrived, bringing his phone. It had been cleaned and bagged and allowed in after strict protocols rendered it safe. He clutched it like a lifeline, as she fussed about the room, fluffing his pillows and interrogating any hospital staff as they entered. She was a whirl of worry, distracting him. He grew irritated at her presence, like she was the itch that caused all this. He still hadn't forgiven her for when Dave died, much less getting Zoe fired. Which, let's face it, was probably why he was in this bed with fewer parts than he was used to.

He ignored her frittering as much as he could. The phone came online, and he saw the missed texts and calls. So many from friends, especially Vince. Several from Rachael Callaway. And two from Zoe.

He checked the texts from Zoe first. *Thank you for letting me know, Captain Merone. I will be there ASAP.* The message was in response to the text Uncle Billy had sent the night he fell ill. She had sent it on Tuesday night, late. He opened the next one. *Jason, I hope you get this someday. Because that will mean you didn't die. I wasn't allowed to visit. Please don't die. Live the best life you can. And know that I care so very much for you.*

What happened? Why the fuck hadn't she been able to come and see him?

He checked the texts from Rachael. She reached out for further comments and clarifications. She had more questions, and it was clear she was onto something big. Maybe Zoe would get justice soon. He'd call them back when he was alone.

For now, his mother fussed and fluttered around the room. Her hair was frizzy and strands were sticking out from her head.

"Mom, I know you're tired. I'm still here, I'm in good hands. You should get some rest."

She stopped and simply stared Jason. Her shoulders slumped and she took a shaky breath. "I thought we were out of the woods, until Billy called me in the middle of the night. It scared me so much. I don't think I can physically live through losing another child."

She stepped to Jason's bedside, putting her arm on his right shoulder. Her eyes met his, and the steel normally in her gaze melted to a vulnerability he didn't know what to do with. "You are not allowed to die before me. Do you understand? I couldn't handle surviving your sister and you. It's too much to ask of anyone."

It wasn't often she showed this side of herself. After his father went to jail, she worked with single-minded obsession to provide a good life for him and Christi. His sister's death had nearly broken his mother. It was sobering how many times she came so close to being completely alone. How stressful had this been for her?

Maybe she made some mistakes, but so had he. Didn't everyone? Despite everything, she was his mom, and she cared so much in her own little ways.

He held his hand out for hers, pulling her in for a hug, pain be damned. He couldn't remember the last time they had hugged.

"Okay, I promise not to die first. Hell, I'm starting to feel indestructible. Immortal, even," he said in mock bravado, needing to lighten things somewhat.

"Hmph. Well, you better be. As long as I'm around." Her voice caught a bit, but she played along.

Reluctantly, Jason ended the hug. The stress and fear from this latest scare left its mark on her, the fatigue and worry draining away her usual vitality. "Mom, you look like you need to sleep for a month. Go home. I'll be okay now. Promise. Indestructible, remember?"

She promised to go home and rest, but it took another twenty minutes and three more hugs before she actually left.

When he was alone, Jason tried to get busy on the cell phone, but soon realized his room was a dead zone. It must be close to the X-ray and nuclear medicine area. Everything on the phone was from before it was allowed in with him. It was merely a paperweight without access to calls, text, or Wi-Fi.

Early the next morning, it was clear to the medical staff that Jason was responding to the antibiotic supercocktail, and the MRSA was being eradicated from his system. They decided it was safe to move him to his own room.

He arrived in the private room just after noon. Sunlight flooded in from the south-facing windows, causing the soothing blue and green walls to glow with welcome. It had that antiseptic hospital smell, of course, but was larger than the cramped cubicle he had been in, with fewer machines measuring every little function of his body. This room was progress; it meant he wasn't dying anymore.

There were still strict protocols for visitors to adhere to in defense of his compromised immunity, but at least there were fewer restrictions on his visitors and the time they were allowed to be around.

The first person through the door was Vince. "Holy shit, you're still alive. Damn good to see you." His smile was genuine. He pumped Jason's left hand awkwardly, then gave him a playful punch in the shoulder. "They limited your visitors while you were in ICU, so I let your momma and Captain Merone and the other guys from station seven take the slots. I got the impression you weren't doing much talking anyway." His words tumbled out doubly quick, his relief palpable at seeing Jason back in the world. He turned to grab the visitor's seat, sliding it across the floor closer to the bed with an obnoxious screech.

I wasn't allowed to visit, Zoe's text echoed in his mind. "Zoe? Did you see her? Was she here?" Christ, any mention of her short-circuited his brain.

Vince's grin faltered. "Oh, yeah. She was sitting with Captain Merone when I got there. They were talking MRSA, how it spreads, how fast. Talking about your chances of pulling through. I was upset when I got there, but hearing that conversation and seeing Captain Merone with funeral home brochures totally fucked me up. I'm sorry I didn't visit, but I reckoned if this was it, there were people ahead of me who deserved to say personal goodbyes."

"Dude, we've been through enough fuckery you ought to know that's bullshit," Jason chastised his friend with a joke. Then he turned his attention to the thought forefront in his mind. "Zoe said she wasn't allowed to visit."

Vince nodded sadly. "Well, shit, yeah, that's true. By the time your momma got here, the waiting area was full of firefighters, and Zoe was down the hall by herself. Everybody knew who she was, if you catch my drift. Not just the nurse thing, but the news stuff. So there were already a lot of mean looks.

"Your momma got here, and the first person she saw was Zoe. Holy shit, I've never seen anybody hit pissed that supersonic quick. She didn't even break stride. Just walked up to Zoe and slapped her across the face with a smack we all heard. 'Catfish tranny whore,' she said. 'How dare you show up here?'"

"Everybody spilled out into the hall, and your momma stood up straight and noticed. She pointed her chin at Zoe and told us, 'She is NOT allowed to see or visit my son. Can someone get security to escort her out?' Then she turned and took a seat in the waiting area."

"Zoe, bless her, took her hand off her face, covering where she got slapped, and waved the guys off. 'No need. I'll leave. Sorry to intrude,' she said and walked off with her shoulders slumped. I'm too polite to say what got said about her after she left." He nodded solemnly at Jason's stare, shrugging sadly.

Jason'd promised to forgive his mom, but this news made it hard. The fact she breezed through the door right then didn't help. He kept his temper, barely, the sheet-white guilty look Vince blanched helping turn the heat to humor.

RACHAEL CALLAWAY ARRIVED a little before one, after an advance call. He insisted on privacy, and his mom followed behind Vince to the cafeteria. Rachael's curly red hair and freckled pale skin attested to her Irish heritage, and she moved with energy and purpose.

"Jason? Hi, I'm Rachael," she introduced herself. She took in his appearance, winced with sympathy. "Jesus. Glad you're still with us."

"Me too," he said. "How did things go? Did you find the cell phone?"

"Did we ever. Holy shit! Do you have any idea what kind of can of worms you opened?" She bounced on her feet, then sat and produced a small notebook from her messenger bag.

"Did it help? Are they going to nail the bastard?" The eagerness was trying to rip itself from his already sore throat. Zoe was going to be okay!

She looked up from the notebook, "About that... I mentioned a can of worms? We started doing some digging into the background of Officer Bogen, and things just aren't adding up. We forwarded the evidence we found to the DA, but we are currently holding off on publishing the article until we can find out more about him."

"What? What's happening?"

Rachael told Jason about finding the phone, the pictures they found on it, then meeting with Zoe, and the editorial decision to pursue the story further before publishing. Jason listened with growing incredulity.

"So, you're saying it's highly probable this psycho douchebag is, like, a mafia-connected kind of guy? And you have proof that this guy raped Zoe, but you aren't going to publish because there might be more?" His voice rose in anger and frustration. "Her life is fucked right now, and you could at least help repair some of the damage to her reputation. She's lost her job over this, for Christ's sake."

Rachael raised her hands in a placating, defensive manner. "Jason, I'll be honest. It sucks, and I wanted to publish, but I was shot down. I disagreed then. I disagree now. I can't control what the DA does with the evidence we sent, and I can't control what the editor chooses to publish or when. At this point, all I can do is find what I can, as quickly as I can. Can you help me? If so, I have some questions."

Jason stared unblinking at Rachael. She met his gaze fully, waited for his decision. Finally, he nodded curtly. Placing the pen on her notebook, she began asking questions.

Chapter Fourteen

Zoe

DANTZLER, MISSISSIPPI WAS a small, sleepy area located about thirty-five miles north of Biloxi and just south of Hattiesburg. I was still in the Trailblazer, traveling through the rural farmlands of my rapist's hometown. The afternoon was still early, and the humidity was seasonably low. I had driven past his residence a couple of times, eyeing his house and the property. It was an old farmstead in need of major repairs, with a tin-roofed barn off to the side and large open fields still bearing scars from the crops of seasons long past. With no vehicles in sight, all was quiet on the property.

The phone rang from the console at my elbow. I glanced at the caller ID. Hutto. What the hell? How did he know to call this number? "Hello?" I answered.

"Ms. Calder, this is ADA Hutto. May I ask your whereabouts?" Punctilious as ever, I wanted to punch him square in the face.

"Why? What do you care?"

"Ms. Calder, I have been informed that you are in a place you have no logical reason to be in. Are you not currently in Dantzler, remarkably close to Officer Bogen's residence?"

How does he know? A chill skittered up my spine, along with the feeling of being watched. I stayed silent on the line, an involuntary admission of guilt.

"Ms. Calder, I don't know what you have in mind," he said after I refused to answer, "but you don't need to be where you are. Please leave Dantzler, and please forget whatever plans you had in mind for Officer Bogen. There have been some developments. Can you give us the time we need to dot our i's and cross our t's?"

He was confirming having received the information from the newspaper, then. "And when those i's are dotted, are you going to do a damn thing?"

"Ms. Calder, the information I have received is quite compelling. So much so, that I can surmise why you are there in Dantzler, and though I strenuously object, I can understand what must be driving you right now."

"So now you believe me?"

"Ms. Calder, I have always believed you. I apologize if it may have seemed otherwise. Now, I have asked the gentlemen behind you to escort you out of Dantzler. They are taking time away from observing Bogen's home to do so. Please drive safely, but expediently, so they can get back to their duties."

I'd guessed the observers were why he knew I was there. The big news here was, finally, someone believed me. Listening to Hutto on the phone, I felt the killing rage bank down to a simmer. Delphine and I promised to give the justice system a chance first. If it fell through again, we could always go find our own justice.

The black Equinox in my rearview mirror shadowed my progress out of Dantzler. I reached the end of the road and turned right on Highway 59 to go south, toward Biloxi. The truck reached the road about thirty seconds later, turning right, as well. After a few moments, the truck sped off past me and turned left at a turnaround in the road between the lanes. I continued south.

I called Delphine and brought her up to speed. She was still pissed that I'd left the camp without a check-in plan but was somewhat mollified when I told her about what Rachael Callaway had uncovered, and about the recent conversation with Hutto.

"Well, perhaps finally we have some good news. If there are cops watching the farm, I can assure you it's a recent development," she said. "What are your plans?"

"You know me. I'm winging it right now."

"Mm-hmm. Not your best trait, I have to say. Keep your head down, and stay out of trouble."

"What are you doing? Are you back at the camp?"

"Non." She didn't elaborate. "Why don't you call that reporter? See if she has anything new."

Nice change of subject there. I knew there was something she wasn't telling me. My stomach flipped with uneasiness. "Okay. Hey, no felonies right now, mmkay?"

"I have no idea what you mean, cher."

"I'm saying be careful, Del." If she got herself killed, I'd bring her back and kill her myself.

"And you, cheri." I hated the sympathy in her voice, as if she was worried. The phone went silent, and I tossed it into the cupholder with a jangle of loose change.

I went through the Whataburger drive-thru, when I got into Biloxi, having a mighty need for greasy meat patties and salty potato sticks. I parked while munching my fries and called Rachael.

"Zoe, hi," she answered.

"Hey Rachael. I was calling to check in, see if you were able to find anything new or exciting for the article not being published." I tried and failed to keep the frustration out of my voice.

"Well, nothing provable to this point. A lot of speculation and innuendo, mostly. I was finally able to interview Jason Merone though. That may be helpful at some point."

My heart stuttered. "Wait! You talked to Jason? Like, he is alive and talking and *alive*?" I sputtered, sure she must be talking about another person as the information sparked through me.

"Yes. It seems likely he is going to pull through. They took him out of ICU and put him in a private room. And may I say, that boy is sure hung up on you. You must be an outstanding nurse."

Oh my God. Jason was not only alive, he was out of ICU! I talked some more with Rachael, filled her in on what had happened with the phone call from Hutto, but my mind was flustered. She sensed the disconnect, I'm sure, but asked several questions. Finally, she ended the call with assurances she was working hard on the article.

Jason had pulled through. The news left me stunned.

I needed to see him. His mother had stopped me from visiting when he was unconscious, her anger at the situation finding a scapegoat in me. She'd been vicious, calling for security and demanding I leave. I didn't argue. I'd simply left, texting Jason from the parking garage before I headed into the coming dawn back to Hattiesburg.

It struck me again, as poignant as the first time, that I was in love with Jason Merone. And I wasn't his nurse anymore, so the ethical issues no longer applied.

I pulled out of the parking lot with a squeal of tires. I had a boy to see.

"COME IN," SAID the voice, at my knock on the door. Jason's voice. My face flushed as I prepared to enter the room and see him, unsure what would I say if he had visitors.

I swung the door open and walked in. The masked superhero was alone, TV blaring some sitcom.

When he saw me, his face lit up with pleasure as tears glinted in his eyes. His left hand came up in a wave and he beckoned me over. I walked to his bedside, letting him drag me into a full embrace.

I gasped when I saw his right forearm was gone. "Oh my god, Jason!" Now I had tears. It wasn't fair. He had been through so much, and now, to have to go through this? Seeing the stump where his hand and forearm had been, seeing the bandages, made me feel guilty. As if I were personally responsible.

"What, that old thing?" he said with a cavalier smile. "It was time to get rid of it anyway. Damn thing was trying to kill me."

"Jesus, Jason. I'm glad you're not dead." I could feel a goofy grin on my face.

I let him hug me again. It was a strong hug. A hug that pulled me close to him so he could whisper in my ear, "I'm kind of in love with you."

I carefully slid my arms around his neck, leaning into the hug. I whispered back, "I'm kind of in love with you, too, Mr. Merone."

I wanted to kiss him—to hell with the consequences— to lose myself in this moment with this man. To have him kiss me back harder, to let the thrill of it thrum through me until the world faded away and left only us, only this moment. But we couldn't. Not yet. With his infection still ongoing, along with his compromised immunity, it might be fatal. I closed my eyes and bit my lips against the frustration. To be this close to him and still not able to truly touch him was an agony I hadn't prepared for. I looked into his beautiful eyes and saw the resignation in them as he groaned in frustration. *He'd wanted to kiss me too! God, this* really *wasn't fair.*

I settled for stroking the tufts of hair that poked out of the top of his mask, melting inside when he rested his head on my shoulder and sighed in pleasure.

A knock at the door and the entrance of a nurse interrupted us. She checked vitals and gave Jason more medicines in his IV bags. As she was preparing to leave, Jason's mother walked into the room.

She was obviously thrown by my appearance and our closeness. "Jason, hello," she said, without acknowledging me.

"Mom, hi," Jason said tightly. "It's nice to see you, and I love you, but Vince told me what happened in the ICU waiting area, and I think you owe Zoe an apology for what happened."

Damn, he got down to business in a hurry. I hadn't had a clue that was coming.

"I will not," her voice rose an octave. "My god, Jason. Think about what you're doing. You're a hero, for goodness sake. You are a Merone!" she said with exasperation in her voice. "You don't have to affiliate yourself with this—this—"

"Lady, Mom? Is that the word you're choking on?" He was inexorable, and his defense made my heart flutter.

"Yes, well, I suppose we have different ideas as to who can call themselves a lady. But no, the words I was choking on were catfish tranny whore. You know that's what everyone calls her now?"

"Be careful, Mother. I know about the nickname. It's stupid and juvenile, and neither part applies," Jason warned softly. "We went through this with Chastity, remember?"

"As if I would forget that. Charles seemed a decent enough person—"

"Chastity, Mom."

"Fine. Chastity seemed like a good person but had to have some screws loose in his head to go be a firefighter and then decide to say, 'Oh, hey, I'm actually a girl.' Uh-uh. Doesn't work like that, and we both know it." Her face twisted as if she'd bitten into something sour.

"How many times have we had this discussion? Just because you don't understand it doesn't mean she was crazy, or wrong. Chastity was a friend, and a good firefighter, and a good person. I miss her. This thing with Zoe is different. I love her. Am in love with her."

"You...what?!" Mrs. Merone sputtered, all decorum lost as she turned beet red. "You love this...this...person?" The stricken look on her face would have been comical in any other setting.

"No, Mom," he said in a weary tone. "No. I love this girl. This. Girl." He raised my hand still clutched in his to underscore his point. "She makes me happy and helped me heal and made me laugh, even when I felt like I was still on fire. She went through hell, with me, and in her own life, and she still did her job. She's tough, but in a good way. In a way that makes the world better. Even when people do shitty things to her, she still does good things, and my life is a hundred times better when she is in it. She's the one who made me want to fight to stay alive. Hell, even Vince is halfway in love with her, and not just because she saved his life too. She is the one who let us know that things can be—will be—better. Just by being herself."

I hadn't known Jason could be so eloquent. Neither had Mrs. Merone, judging by her thunderstruck face.

Jason added into the silence, "Mom, I love you. But right now, I'm waiting for an apology for what happened in ICU."

Her eyes met mine, and I could see emotions warring in them. I struggled with my own, as well. She had gotten me fired, openly mocked me and other women like me, and had publicly slapped me. I wasn't in a forgiving mood. Did I really want to try things with this guy, while dealing with his mother the whole time? Fair question, and one I needed to really consider.

Jason stared at Martha until finally she pursed her lips. "I'm sorry." She didn't look at me when she said it.

Nope. Not near enough.

"Well that apology meant fuck all," I said. Martha's gasp at my language gave me a thrill of satisfaction. "What exactly are you apologizing for? For slapping me? Or for getting me fired? How about when you called me catfish tranny whore in front of everyone in the waiting room? Why don't you spell it out, Mrs. Merone? Which parts are you apologizing for?"

I took a breath, wondering if I had just demolished everything I was starting to build with Jason. I glanced over, surprised to see the gleam of pride in his eyes.

The silence carried as she considered me, measured me. After a huff, she squared her shoulders and faced me dead-on. "Zoe, I am truly sorry. For all of the above and more. It's possible my words were more hurtful than I intended." She turned to her son. "Jason, I only want you to be happy, and if...if Zoe is what you want, then..." she trailed off, waving her arms in surrender. She looked back at me and added, "Don't you dare hurt my boy."

Jason squeezed my hand at her tentative overtures. I squeezed back, lost in completely new waters I had no map for navigating. Jason broke into a big grin he pointed at both of us.

"I love you guys!" he proclaimed to the room at large.

Guess the pain meds the nurse had topped him off with were kicking in. I smiled and shook my head. I loved that wonderful, magnificent bastard too.

Mrs. Merone quietly took a seat, pointing her attention to *The Big Bang Theory* on TV. With an icy detente achieved, we watched TV until Jason's loud snores filled the room.

"Zoe? Can we talk outside?" Mrs. Merone asked after Jason's snores were well-established.

Now what? "Sure."

We stepped into the hall. I wasn't sure what to expect, but my guard was up. The last thing I expected was the gentle shoulder squeeze she gave me.

"That outburst back there finally cleared up something that has been bugging me since you started working with Jason."

"Ah, okay. What?"

"Who you've reminded me of. I couldn't put my finger on it till tonight. Now, I can't believe I didn't see it immediately. My daughter, Christi. I think there's a part of me that's known all along. Maybe it's why I wanted to hate you, even before everything happened with...you know, the attack. And after, with the news."

Well, that was unexpected. "Um...I...ah...don't quite know what to say. Does Jason? I mean, is that why he—?"

"Is that why he likes you? I don't think so, dear. I can't speak for him, of course."

"I saw her picture. She was beautiful. I don't think we look anything alike."

"No, no, it's not a physical resemblance. It's how you interact with the world. Mostly sweet and a little naïve, until a line gets crossed. And then a take-no-prisoners attitude ready to burn everything down. That outburst earlier... I could've sworn I'd had that very conversation with Christi." Her shoulders softened, and a hint of tears shimmered in the corner of her eyes.

"I would've had to apologize to her after, as well. There's no excuse for how I acted. I'm sorry for being cruel to you, especially when you came when he was in the ICU." She looked at me directly, her face open and begging for forgiveness.

Dammit. I still didn't want to like this woman, but I felt the ice thin a little.

Before I could reply, my phone started buzzing in my pocket. Saved by the bell, I thought as I checked the caller ID. Delphine. "Sorry, I need to take this." I turned away and answered. "Hello?"

"He is here, mon amie. The little shit stain. He has come home to his farm, in Dantzler. You have a decision to make. Quickly, child."

I knew immediately what she was offering. Kill Randall and never have to worry about him again, or roll the dice with the DA? I walked a few steps from Mrs. Merone for privacy.

Everything in me screamed for murder. To tell Delphine and her mysterious friend to do their worst. Fuck him up, let the crows have his meat and his blood feed the weeds.

But I couldn't. I couldn't ask the friend who had saved my life to kill for me.

Sweet and a little naïve. Shit.

"Del, I love you, and I want to say do it more than you will ever know. But, no, I can't ask you to do that."

"Say no more, child. We shall stay here through the night. If you change your mind..."

"Ah! Don't tempt me. Let's give Hutto a chance."

Delphine was silent a beat. "As you wish, mon amie. Where are you?"

"I'm at the hospital."

"Of course. And how is Jason?"

"He's good. He's gonna pull through. Oh, and...ah... he loves me."

I could almost hear her smile over the phone. "Mon amie! This makes my heart happy. Such beautiful news. Rest well."

Stay with Jason, it was. "Be careful!"

"Always."

I put the phone away, walked back to Jason's mom, and gave her a light hug as my answer. We walked back into his room and settled in to watch TV while he snored loud enough to wake the dead.

IT WAS NEARING ten in the evening, and I was preparing to leave Jason when my phone buzzed a text alert. It was Del. *Call me when you can. Urgent.*

Jason was asleep, so I scribbled him a cutesy note for when he woke up. Then I waved goodbye to Martha. She waved back with a wan smile. The truce still held, tenuous as it was.

I waited until I was back in my truck in the parking garage before I called Delphine. When she answered, noise poured out of the phone. Sirens and yells competed with a crackling roar that could only come from a very large fire. I heard a car door shut, and the noise dampened a bit.

"Del?" I shouted for the third time.

"An unexpected development, cher," she answered. "It seems we weren't the only ones eager to meet with Bogen."

"What the hell is going on up there? It sounds like a war zone."

"The good officer's house is currently going up in very large flames, fed in no small part by the propane tank in the backyard." She spoke tersely. "We've been up on a slight ridge observing. We were going to wait for the middle of the night to move in to see what we might find in his car and home. But about an hour ago, the sheriff's office arrived with several men geared for combat. They surrounded the house, knocked on the door to serve a warrant, and suddenly there were shots fired, smoke from the house, and then a large explosion from the propane tank."

"What?! They had a shoot-out?" I could hear the incredulity in my own voice. What the actual fuck was happening in my life?

"Indeed. The house was fully covered within a couple of minutes. The SWAT team had to fall back. The fire was just too big, too fast. No sign of Randall. A few minutes later, firefighters and more police showed up. I count three different volunteer fire departments out here, along with Dantzler PD, and ATF. Exciting times, yeah?

"At this point the house is pretty much done, and I think the firefighters out here are treating this as a training exercise and excuse to pump water. No one came out of that house, cheri."

I sat and absorbed the news Delphine had given me. No way he could survive the fire she described. Of course, I wouldn't be satisfied until his body was identified. "Del, are you sure you saw him go in the house? And he couldn't leave without you seeing it? Are you sure he's dead?"

She answered in her blunt way, "No, child. I am not sure he's dead, because I have not seen his body. But I am sure I saw him go in, and I am reasonably sure he did not leave. I will stand watch here and see if they find his body. The flames are dying down, and the cleanup should commence soon enough."

"Okay, thanks for the hopeful news. Can you keep me posted?"

"Of course."

I sat in the truck, eyes blurred and unfocused, lost in thought. Randall was possibly dead. Randall, dead! A part of me felt as if I should be ashamed of the triumph raging through me. But the primitive part of me howled in glee. I pumped my fist. Then reminded myself that nothing was confirmed yet. Everything seemed so surreal, it was like a movie script of my life. Torn between relief, joy, and a touch of guilt, I started the truck. No more hiding, time to go home.

The press was gone when I arrived. Thank God.

THE NEWS THE next morning confirmed what Delphine had reported. Officer Randall Bogen was killed when his house caught fire during an attempted arrest by the Dantzler Sheriff's Office.

On the same day, the Hattiesburg Clarion ran a damning article outlining the case against Bogen regarding my rape. The selfies Randall had taken, edited for publication but still shocking, exploded across the wires like a bombshell.

I was vindicated. ADA Hutto had pursued a warrant based on the information the paper passed along to his office. He was the one who insisted on a SWAT operation to serve the warrant, and that decision probably saved lives. Bogen was not going to go without a fight and had rigged the house for a suicidal last stand. Had they merely sent a couple of cops for a courteous arrest, it would have been deadly for them.

From pariah to hero overnight. It felt slightly better to be a hero, but the anxiety was almost the same as when the world had been out for my blood. My reputation, destroyed overnight, might take years to rebuild. And I was still unemployed.

Amid requests for comments from media, I fielded calls from my mom—asking if I'd seen the news—and Delphine, checking in on her way to the houseboat to get the items we had packed. Then, a call from Rachael.

"Hey, girl! Did you hear the news?" The excitement in her voice was evident.

"Yes. And I read your article as well. Thank you. For working on it, and for being fair. And also for censoring me out of those nasty pictures. I hope you get lots of awards for it."

"Well, thanks. Yeah I hope so too. I had to write like a banshee to get the article in before deadline. Everything popped out there in Dantzler, and suddenly the editor wanted to publish to get the scoop. So we put the corruption stuff to the side for now. We're still working on that angle though."

"I can't really blame the editor, although I still want to. It really looks like you put the Clarion on the map. I'm seeing your article everywhere." There was a strange disconnect for me. Between the me I was then, and the me I was now.

She sounded so thrilled. "It's pretty exciting, I'll admit. I wanted to make sure you were doing okay."

"Thanks for checking. It's a bit disorienting. I'm just glad it's finally over."

Rachael went serious. "Honestly, Zoe, I wonder if it is. Over I mean. Maybe for you, hopefully for you. But there's still some seriously nasty stuff behind this guy. Keep being careful, okay?"

A red flag waved itself in front of my face at her words. "Jesus, Rachael. What do I need to worry about now?"

"No, no. Sorry about the pessimism. I swear I'm not trying to rain on your parade. I'm just in a mood today. How's Jason?"

"He's recovering, getting better. I'm about to swing by and check on him." I still wanted to know what the fuck she meant, but my words weren't really working.

"Well, we wish him a speedy recovery. We owe him big. Also, I would absolutely love to do a feature on him. He's quite a guy."

"I'll let him know," I replied, goofy grin plastering to my face as I thought of seeing him.

We ended the call.

It wasn't over yet.

Rachael had claimed to be in a mood, but the premonition sent a chill through my body. I shook my head to clear the thoughts. Time to do something I knew would cheer me up.

Time to go see Jason.

Chapter Fifteen

Jason

EVERYONE WAS TALKING about his girlfriend when he woke up. This time, though, it was in a good way. Or, at least, a better way. The comments sections online still had all the various phobias he had come to expect of the good trolls of Internetville. But now, he could find glimmers of respect for the lady he loved; an acknowledgment of the difficult time she went through and the truth of what had occurred.

He was oddly proud of her. Proud she had kept her wits about her through everything and hadn't broken or lost her sense of self. She was strong, but still so sweet. Also yes, really fun to look at.

He woke that morning with less pain than he expected. His eyes found the note from Zoe, and he reached for it with his right hand out of habit. The distress when he remembered the hand was gone was sharp and savage. He retrieved the note with his left hand, flipped the folded page open with a thumb and wrist flick.

Jason,

This is so much more than I ever imagined. I will see you as soon as I can tomorrow. Rest well, keep healing. I Love You, Z

He reread the note, then turned on the TV to catch up on news and wait for Zoe's arrival. He was glued to the reports for over an hour as he gleaned information about what had happened to Officer Bogen. He read the article from Rachael Callaway.

He had helped, he realized. He might no longer be the heroic firefighter running headlong into blazing infernos, but he could still find a way to help those he loved.

For the first time since the fire, he was starting to feel he could be okay. That he could not only live, but thrive, be successful, and be loved.

She walked in around midmorning wearing the blue scrubs with pink piping she'd been wearing the first day they'd met and carrying a box of Shipley donuts. The smell hit him as she set the box down and opened it. Suddenly, he was voraciously hungry, lunging for the box and, in the process, almost spilling the coffee she brought.

"Hey!" She laughed. "Easy. Don't spill the coffee. Or I'll make you clean it up yourself." Her teasing words and dancing eyes breathed a giddiness into him.

He grinned a mischievous smile, cocked an eyebrow, and waited impatiently to be served.

Together, they ate donuts, and drank coffee, and watched the news. Conversations sparked by random commercials or interesting news items quickly devolved into bantering sessions full of double entendres.

He drank her in. She caught him staring and gave him her best sultry-vamp look before laughing it off, setting his heart racing. She shifted her body toward him, and her face grew serious. "So, obviously you know about my, ah, less than common configuration, shall we say? And unless I'm wildly misreading the signals here, it seems you would agreeable if there were some...physicality involved soon."

"You do circle a subject when you're uncomfortable, don't you?" Jason teased. "Ask your question, babe."

She hesitated, but only for a moment. "Have you thought about being with me? Realistically, thought about being with me? I mean, sometime in the future when the doctor clears you for...ah...fun stuff?"

More often than would be considered healthy. "I've thought long and hard about it," he answered innocently, staring at her until she caught the joke. "The answer is yes. I have thought about being with you physically."

"Ugh. And you seemed so normal." Her wink gave away the joke.

"Babe, I wasn't normal before the fire. After...hell, what do you think a guy stuck in bed for so long is going to get up to in his head? Especially given what I had to look at every day." His face was blooming red; he knew it. Her delighted laughter didn't help matters either.

AS THE DAY progressed, they fielded visitors who came to check on Jason and wish him well. The responses from Jason's friends and work buddies to Zoe's presence ranged from acceptance to badly disguised discomfort. Martha seemed at least resigned to her presence there, and Delphine beamed like a lighthouse when she dropped in.

When Dr. Eubanks came by to examine Jason, he pronounced that, given the current rate of improvement, Jason should be cleared to go home in a couple of days.

It was a day for good news all around.

As the sun set outside, and dusk settled in, Jason took a moment to reflect on his situation. He ached with the realization he would never fight fire again and ached at the loss of his arm.

But he was still alive. The surprise was that he was grateful to be alive in spite of the pain and the lost dream. He was in love. He was healing. And for the first time since the fire, he could accept his life. He wanted it to continue, no matter how much it hurt to be in his body. For the first time, he was curious to see what was next.

He noticed Zoe yawn for the third time in half an hour. The happiness on her face didn't hide the bags under her eyes. "Go home, love," he told her. "Get some rest. You've earned it."

She looked at him with a tenderness that made him giddy. "But I like being here. It's my favorite place in the world right now."

"What? Have you lost your mind?" he said with disbelief. "It's a hospital. It sucks here."

"But you're here. My favorite place is where you are."

My God, I love this corny woman, he thought, even as he hooted in derision at the schmaltzy statement. "Go home, love," he repeated. "I'll still be here tomorrow."

Reluctantly, Zoe left.

As always, he appreciated the view as she left the room.

When the door closed behind her, Jason was alone. He shut off the TV, the phone, and all the lights he could reach. Alone in the dim quiet, Jason began to make plans for a life he hadn't expected to want so fiercely.

Two days later, Jason went home.

IT TOOK A full month before the doctor pronounced Jason 'virtually' free of MRSA. A month where Zoe held boundaries firm. No kissing. Not much touching. Lots of handwashing and disinfectant spraying. The house was kept spotless, and had been deep cleaned by professionals before he got back from the hospital to eradicate any chance of the MRSA still being a threat to him here. It had worked, finally. The decolonizing treatments, the antibiotics, the precautions and semi-quarantine he'd suffered through had paid off.

He couldn't even play it cool when he'd called Zoe to tell her the news. "Guess who got cleared for takeoff?" he said as soon as she'd answered. "Come kiss me!"

Now he waited for her, recalling her excitement at his pronouncement, and how much his heart had lurched at the realization she was as giddy as himself at the idea of finally being together.

Zoe arrived when the nurse's shift was ending. She glided in, wearing a maxi skirt, which almost brushed the floor, and an embroidered peasant blouse, her skin glowing and still smelling of the chlorhexidine she'd showered in. She caught him looking at her and gave a curtsy. "Do you like?"

"Every inch," he sighed with pleasure.

"Mmmm," she purred seductively. "That's my line." She laughed at his shocked expression.

"Lord, girl," he choked out at the blatant come-on. "I don't know if I can keep up."

"Oh, I'll make sure of it." Honey dripped from her words, melting away rational thought.

He turned serious, meeting her eyes. "I don't want to do anything that makes you uncomfortable, or reminds you of—you know—him. It."

"I know, Jason. It's one reason why I feel so comfortable around you." Just like that, the sex kitten was gone. She ran a hand through her still slightly damp hair, the darkened strands mixing with the lighter bits of her dried hair. "I was kidding with the whole seductive thing. Kind of. I want that with you, but honestly, I'll have to take it slow. I really don't want to go too fast, and I'm not sure what my reaction will be when I'm with you the first time. But I want to be with you. I want that very much."

"Okay. So we take it slow, then. Netflix?" Anything, just to be with her.

"And chill," she purred in seductive parody again.

Laughing, Jason logged into Netflix while Zoe excused herself to the bathroom.

She came back in a burgundy-colored chemise that set his heart racing, then slid under the crisp cotton sheets of his bed. They cuddled while watching *Notting Hill*. He always felt somewhat guilty about loving this movie so much, but discovering it was one of her passionate favorites, as well, changed his mind.

It was a perfect choice, at least until the end, when Julia Roberts was lying with Hugh Grant on the park bench, pregnant and serene. As the credits rolled, he felt her shaking, heard her sniffling. He reached over and grabbed a tissue from the box strategically placed nearby before the movie. Gently, he corralled the tears that spilled.

"Sorry," she said as he dabbed at her face. "I always forget about that part, and it kills me every time."

"Aw, babe, I'm sorry. It got me choked up, too, the first time I saw it."

To his dismay, he heard her cry harder, felt her pulling away, shoulders curling forward. "Babe? Are you okay?" he asked, concerned.

"I will be," she answered as she blew through another tissue. "I love this movie so much, but I swear I always block the ending from my mind."

He didn't quite understand. It was sweet and heartwarming, but why block it out? "The ending? You mean, the two of them on the park bench?"

"Yeah, actually, the three of them."

And it dawned on him. "Oh, you mean because she's pregnant. Why is that so sad?"

"Because it will never be me," she sobbed, turning to bury her face in his chest and curl up against him. "I don't get to be a mom like that. I won't ever know what that feels like."

Jason didn't speak, because there was nothing he could think of to make her feel better. He simply wrapped his arm around her as best he could, even as the wounds and burns protested, and held her as she wept.

After a couple of minutes, she raised her head to Jason. The vulnerability on her face made him ache. "Jesus, I'm sorry. I'm not sure where that came from. That ending always hits me in the gut, but I never boo-hooed over it so hard before."

"It's okay," he reassured her. "I can only imagine what that must feel like." He watched her face open to a thought.

"Oh," she said quietly. "Oh. Hell."

"Tell me," he said. He stroked her hair with his hand and caressed her cheek.

"It was always hypothetical before, a problem for another time. I never met anyone who made me think of family and babies. Never had anyone who made me want that so hard. Until now. Until you." She looked up at him with such love in her puffy eyes, he wanted to cry.

At a loss for words, he softly kissed the tears on her cheek. A thrill ran through him as she sought his lips with her own, sorrow suddenly flaming into desire as he accepted her, all of her, in this moment.

The everything of her left him lightheaded, wanting—needing—more. Running his finger under the spaghetti strap that looped her shoulder, he pulled upward with a meaningful tug. She blushed for a moment, pausing before pulling the chemise over her head with a swish and letting it drop to the floor in a silken puddle. Her look as she presented her nakedness was a challenge, the slight tremor in her hands as she expertly helped him remove his clothes the only clue to her nervousness.

She shouldn't have worried. She was flawless. He was the one worried, as his own anxiety at being disrobed left his whole body trembling.

"What?" he said at her silence.

"I want to see you. All of you. May I?" Her fingers caressed the bottom edge of his compression mask, leaving no doubt what she was asking of him.

Panic. Did she really know what she was asking? The hour or so every day he was able to remove his mask was his favorite, the only time he fully felt the air on his face. This was different. Taking it off in these intimate moments with her would leave him completely naked, vulnerable in a way he had never been before. Deciding to trust her, he squeezed his eyes shut before slowly nodding his consent. He kept them shut as she, like so many times before, gently gathered the edges and began to peel upward. Finally, the mask fell away, but still he kept his eyes shut as she hovered over him. Finally, he screwed up the courage to open his eyes to her.

The lust in her eyes was something he was completely unprepared for: a pure, raw wanting he had never expected to see directed at him again. He felt himself fully rising to ready as she carefully traced his lips with a finger, whispering fiercely, "Baby. My beautiful baby."

She leaned down to meet his lips with hers, her kiss deeper, sweeter, more urgent than he'd ever known before. He matched her passion with his own, the usual awkward fumbles of new partners amplified by his recent limitations. Patient and responsive, she let him lead the way as he explored his ability to both feel and give pleasure. Slowly, inexorably, they moved together, ever closer. His burns screamed and recently broken bones protested the exercise, but he would not stop. He felt her yield to him, then felt her stiffen against him when her thoughts went dark.

Feeling her panic, he stopped. He couldn't bear to cause her pain in any way.

She read his thoughts. "How did I get so lucky?" she murmured.

"You obviously have very low standards." His cavalier response brought a smile.

"Well, so do you." Her smile belied the sharp retort.

"No, dahling," he said in a faux-haughty tone. "I expect only the most premium of things in my life. Bentleys and Cristal, G5s and Dalmore scotch. Even my Band-Aids are gold leaf."

"Ah, yes, well, perhaps I should see myself out, then."

"No need. I'll just have the butler escort you. Oh, Jeeves! Jeeves, my good man! Please escort this obvious peasant from my sight."

Her laughter was musical. "You always make me laugh."

"And you always make me happy." *I'm the lucky one,* Jason thought, dimming the lights in the room. *What did I do to deserve you?*

Together, in the dark, they caressed. Slowly at first and then with increasing need. They took from each other and gave themselves, blurring the lines of where one stopped and the other began. He gasped when she took his member in her hand, rigid with need and desire, sighed when her mouth enveloped him with wetness and suction. She brought him close several times, backing off before he went over the cliff. Then she had a condom and lube in her hand, holding them up to him in unspoken question.

His moan answered her question better than his enthusiastic nodding. Careful to avoid the burns on his lower right leg, she climbed on top when he was ready. Then, positioning herself above his hips, she opened to him, teasing him with a sultry gaze as she slowly took all of him, pausing when he was fully inside. After a few moments of stillness, she looked down at him with a cocked eyebrow and unconcealed hunger. She twitched her hips, wringing a gasp from him.

Licking her lips, she ran her hands down her body and then up his, pinching his nipples along the way. She bit her lips and began to grind a secret rhythm until, faster than he thought possible, she took him over the edge. She writhed against him with screams of pleasure, matching his orgasm with one of her own, as he came with a thunderous intensity that left him weak and gasping for air.

WITH A TWITCH and a gasp, Jason woke. His eyes fuzzy, he looked around before focusing on her. She had changed back into her regular clothes, probably not wanting to be almost naked in front of the nurse when she arrived for the morning shift. The air on his face reminded him they had fallen asleep together before replacing his mask. Whoops.

"Good morning, beautiful," she sing-songed, smiling at him.

"Hmph! Lies. All lies." As she helped him back into clothes and placed the mask back over his face, he sniffed the air. "I smell coffee."

"It should be about ready."

She came back with coffee, and Jason groaned with pleasure. "I love you."

"I love you too."

"I was talking to the coffee."

"You ass!" She laughed, punching at his shoulder playfully.

They drank coffee and greeted the morning with kisses and cream-cheese bagels. The day nurse arrived, and Zoe gathered her things. She furrowed her brow when she picked up her phone.

"Everything okay?" he asked at her look.

"I'm not sure. I have a missed call and a couple of texts from Mom. I'll call her when I get home." She walked over to him, kissed him in a way that made him want an encore of last night right now, new nurse be damned. She smiled at his eagerness. "Down, boy. I'll see you tonight, okay?"

Fuck yeah.

Chapter Sixteen

Zoe

ONE YEAR LATER:
Nashville, Tennessee

The antiseptic smell of a hospital filled my nose, and my vision was hazy as consciousness returned. Trying to lift my head, I jerked with reflexive panic as the room spun. A calming hand fell on my shoulder, helping to anchor me to reality.

"Welcome back, love. It's okay. You're out of surgery now." I recognized that voice.

"Mom?"

"Yes. I'm right here with you. We're in the recovery room, and they'll get you to a private room in just a bit."

Surgery? Oh! Memories stitched themselves back into place. Surgery. I had gotten gender confirmation surgery. The ugly, dangly parts of me were gone. The relief was indescribable, but everything was still suffused with a dream-like quality that left me afraid I would wake to discover it was a cruel trick. After making sure I was truly in reality, I laid my head on the pillow and cried. Mom handed me a tissue as the joy and happiness streamed down my face.

Within an hour, I was transported to my room. After the orderlies left, Mom set about fluffing pillows and adjusting sheets, helping me get comfortable in bed.

The knock at the door was followed by the entrance of a stunning bouquet of pristine white roses. I smiled at the *Congratulations* sash draped across the gorgeous flowers. The bouquet was set on the window sill, and Mom grabbed the card.

"'Thinking of you,'" she read. "Hmm, not signed. But goodness, isn't this lovely?"

They were. "Probably from Jason. He was really bummed I wouldn't let him come."

It had been the worst luck, timing-wise. The widely renowned facial plastic surgeon in New Orleans Jason had waited so long to see had finally been able to schedule him. The day after my surgery. His waiting list was almost as long as the list for my own surgeon, and I had forbidden him to reschedule. It meant too much to him, a sentiment I shared in regard to my own surgery. My call to let him know I was awake went to voicemail.

"How's your pain?" Mom asked as I set the phone down.

"So far, so good. I really expected worse."

"That's good to hear. Zoe?"

"Yeah?"

"Thank you for letting me be here. I love you."

"I love you, too, Mom." The meds were making me sleepy, and I slurred the words as I started to drift off.

Before I could fall asleep, though, I needed my plushy. I groaned, gesturing at my duffel. Mom reached into my bag and handed it to me. I cuddled it to my chest, smelling the cologne Jason had spritzed on it before giving it to me, laughing at Mom's confusion as she regarded the doll.

"Jason gave this to me to be here for him at the surgery." I held it up so she could see it better. "It's supposed to remind me of him."

"A hockey player?"

"Ha! No. It's Jason. Jason Voorhees. From the *Friday the 13th* movies? It's exactly his kind of humor. And I love it, because it makes me laugh and smells like him."

"Oh! I get it now. He's a keeper, isn't he?" The gentle smile she gave me made me giggle. Keeper, goalie, keeper as in keeping him, definitely.

"I think so," I could no longer hold my eyes open. "That boy in Biloxi is probably a keeper too." I couldn't resist joking, although I wasn't sure if I said it out loud before sleep swept me away.

I woke alone, with a note from Mom saying she had stepped out to get some food. My cell phone was nearby, so I called Jason. No answer again, so I called and updated Delphine, preening at the pride in her voice. Then, alone in my room, I thought back over the events of the past year.

I HAD GOTTEN up early and started the coffeemaker, that morning after our first night together. Came back into his room and watched him sleep.

He wasn't a pretty sight, by any means. The scars on his face and neck were lumpy and red, calling attention to his missing ear and erratic hairline. His missing forearm still broke my heart. His bandages were soaked through, and his muscles were tensed against the ever-present pain, even in his sleep.

But he had become the most precious thing in the world to me. Beyond the fact this man had offered his life to the protection of his community, and that he had helped me find my stolen phone and nail a bad guy to the wall—a bad guy now in the cemetery, where he'd never hurt anyone again—he also made me laugh. Even when I tortured him to help him heal, he made me laugh. Our personalities meshed and complemented each other's, and I never tired of being around him.

Perhaps I could've found someone prettier. I would never find someone better.

The morning after our first tryst together, I had called Mom. Her missed calls and texts felt urgent.

She answered on the second ring. "Zoe, hi." Her voice was shaky but determined.

"Hey, Mom. What's up?"

"I'm...not very proud of myself right now."

I stayed quiet. Where was this going? I walked over to the couch with my coffee and took a seat.

She waited a moment before speaking again. "The last time we spoke, when you told me about some of the things you had to do just to survive, I was disgusted. I hate to admit that, but I was. And then when you put the blame on me, I was shocked and angry. My first thought was 'How dare you?' But then, it got me thinking, real honestly and deeply. If it had been me in that situation, if I had a mom who did and allowed the stuff I allowed to happen to you, I'd blame her too. And rightfully so."

"Kind of late to the party," I said, harsher than intended. The postcoital glow I had brought from Jason's was rapidly fading from this call and making me grouchy.

"When I stopped being angry," she forged on, ignoring my prickliness, "I got so unbearably sad for you. For all you've had to go through, and my part in it. I let your father throw you away like—like some kind of defective merchandise. I professed to love my children unconditionally, but really there were so many stupid strings attached. Because of me, your life was so much harder than it should have been. All I can say, Zoe, is I am so sorry."

"Sorry?" The word set my teeth on edge. "What do you want from me, Mother? Just wave my hand and provide absolution for all the shit I went through so *you* can feel better?"

"I thought I was doing the right thing, not that it's an excuse." Shame threaded her voice, but she seemed resolved to face hard truths without getting defensive. "Your father and the church convinced me that we were doing this in the spirit of love. Tough love, yes, but love. 'Love the sinner, hate the sin,' they would always say. So I went along, even when it tore my heart apart. *I went along*, and I will carry that regret to my grave."

Apologies, first from Mrs. Merone and now Mom, left me off-balance. I was used to spite and passive aggressiveness from disapproving people; I knew how to handle that after lots of practice. Accepting a mea culpa was something I wasn't quite as well-versed at.

Mom took a deep breath in the silence, then plunged ahead. "God doesn't make mistakes. And he made you exactly the way you are. We were just too close-minded and scared to see it. What we did was out of hate and spite and fear, and I see that now. I hope one day you can forgive me, but I would understand if you don't. All I can say is this: I swear to you, in front of God Almighty, I will never again hurt you for who you are. Going forward, I will love you the way I should have all along, and I will never again be ashamed of you.

"You will always have a place in my heart and in my family. And if anyone else has a problem with it, they can just piddle off. I swear it, Zoe. I love you."

I didn't know how to respond. Choking on the lump in my throat, I sank onto the couch, curling my knees to my chest as if to protect my heart.

"I love you, Mom," I blearily confessed. "I've missed you. So much."

"I missed you too."

There was one major doubt niggling in my mind. "What about the asshole?"

"Your father? Well, he can get in line, or give up half his stuff when I leave."

I'd almost choked on my laughter.

We talked for over an hour more; there were still so many things that needed to be said. Still, by the time the call ended, I felt like I had a mom again.

The search for work didn't take long. After getting me fired from the nursing agency, Mrs. Merone helped me get hired at the burn center in Gulfport, using her influence to push for a quick hire.

That meant I didn't need to dip into savings, and I finally accumulated the money needed for surgery. Due to the relative scarcity of doctors specializing in this type of surgery, the next available date was the following summer. The wait was excruciating.

After neglecting her for months after the rape, I reacquainted myself with my bike. It took a few sessions with Dr. Jones, my therapist, to finally stop associating my bike with the assault. The buzz-by when Randall sent me into the grass was every bit a part of events, and it had taken a long time to feel brave enough to ride again. With profuse apologies to Eowyn for my neglect, she treated me to such a lovely expedition on that first ride back I knew I was forgiven. Physically, I was in the best shape of my life, in preparation for the surgery. Mentally, I was also healing, but more slowly.

Jason was a big part of the process. His healing progressed, as well, to the point he no longer needed a private nurse. He also started going to a therapist to grapple with the mental health issues that arose as a result of his injuries, his guilt over the death of David and the child they'd found, and the loss of his dream to get back to firefighting. In its place, he had thrown himself fully into learning to code and develop software. Then, finding a gifted mentor in Kelly Roberts, the software forensics expert who retrieved the data from my phone, he began to focus more on penetration testing. Kelly introduced him to the darknet, and the myriad programs designed to breach security, crack encryption, and grab sensitive information. He also taught Jason the legalities, ethics, and code of conduct expected for those who wielded that power for good.

He even proposed once, on the celebratory evening he was cleared to stop wearing the compression mask on his face, near Christmas. Panicked and sure we would break up in the aftermath, I'd turned him down. I wasn't sure why, then or now. Even when I brought it up with Dr. Jones, I couldn't figure out any answers. Thankfully, he handled the rejection with grace, and our relationship continued.

Reconciliation took a while, and the process was contentious, but Mom stayed true to her word. She became my fiercest supporter among the family and had initiated divorce proceedings against my father after he went into a thunderous rage at her change of heart. It must have been a shock to him to discover what he thought was a dormouse had turned into a lion in front of his eyes. She forced him out of the house and took half of the marital assets in the process, as promised. I was the only one who truly knew her secret inner terror, her trembling fear as she faced his wrath. I knew how much courage it took for her to claim her life and family for her own, free from his abuse.

My father blamed everything on me, of course. At times, I would hear apocryphal stories, furtively delivered by a couple of sympathetic friends left behind and still attending church there, of sermons delivered from the pulpit lashing out against "sexual deviants and perverts" and those who supported such people. I was mocked and ridiculed, held up as an example of what Satan would do to those who turned away from "the true path." At first, I'd been distressed to hear about the energetic bigotry from my father, then had come to laugh at the ignorance, and finally, left feeling sad for the hatred that separated us. He was an asshole, but he was still my father, half of the reason for my existence. In some ways, I missed him. Well, mostly I missed the misty image I had of him from early childhood, when I thought my daddy hung the moon.

But now, I had my mom. She was a newer, better version of herself, and happy to have a daughter. Jacob, now twenty-two, and close to his degree in accounting, was still unsure and tentative around me, but that seemed to slowly get better with time. This year had found me surrounded by love, protected from hate, and, simply, happy.

It was a good year.

SURGERY WAS THE cherry on top of the happy sundae. Of course, with the pain flaring up as the meds wore off, it didn't feel like a cherry. It felt sharp-edged and fragile, with pain in new intensity in new places. But still, I could smile because I finally, truly, felt as if I belonged in this body.

A quick knock, and Mom swept in with bags from a local greasy spoon. She walked in, leaving the door open as she set the food on the hospital tray. I wasn't really hungry, until the smell hit me. Then I was ravenous, impatiently waiting as Mom set iced tea in front of me and dug through the wrappers.

"Well, someone looks hungry," said a voice at the open doorway. The speaker leaned nonchalantly against the doorframe, with a bemused face.

Jason. *Jason was here!*

I didn't—couldn't—say anything. I simply raised my arms to him, a goofy grin on my face. He limped across the floor to me—no walker or wheelchair for this guy anymore—and carefully wrapped me in a hug. "Jason! Oh my god, I can't believe you're here. Why are you here? What about the surgery?"

"It can wait. I made the doctor reschedule, because no way was I going to miss being here. He juggled some things, and now I'm scheduled for day after tomorrow. Sorry I couldn't get here earlier. The flight schedules out of New Orleans were atrocious. How are you feeling?"

"Better, now that I know why you weren't answering your phone." He leaned over me, and I kissed him hard enough to make Mom uncomfortable. She politely cleared her throat, although it took a couple of times for us to catch on. We grinned sheepishly as Jason stood back up. Noticing me eyeing the food on my tray, Jason opened the container and let me eat.

"Thank you for the flowers," I said through a mouthful of burger, motioning my head toward the roses on the windowsill.

"Ah, those are pretty. But not from me. I came straight over from the airport, so I didn't get you anything yet. The card didn't say who it was from?"

"It only said 'thinking of you,' and it wasn't signed. Thought maybe you had called them in and decided not to sign. Could they be from your mom?"

"Maybe. Doesn't feel like it though. She's pretty strict about the etiquette and meaning of things. I don't think she would have gotten you white roses. Not really appropriate for this situation."

"You'll have to fill me in on this etiquette stuff one day," I said, then turned back to Mom. "Do you think it could it have been Asshole...er...my father?"

Mom shook her head. "That's not something he would do, dear."

"Well, what the hell? Do I have a secret admirer? Delphine swore they weren't from her." I was puzzled, though not enough to devote much more worry to it.

Together, we watched TV as I began to heal. The pain meds gave me the giggles and gave everything a bright, happy sheen as the man I loved spent time getting to know my mom.

The next morning, Jason flew back for his own rescheduled surgery.

TWO WEEKS AND one rather uncomfortable plane ride later, I was back at home. Mom helped me settle into bed, under the watchful gaze of the guardian angel Delphine had painted for me. It was Mom's first time seeing the painting, and she was struck as speechless as I had been when I had first seen it.

Word got out that I was home, and the friends I had reconnected with after the attack came by to say hi and congratulations. They were met by Delphine, who plied them with her delicious food and various liquors, and everyone stayed until it was a full-on party. I was brought into the living room and placed on the couch. I sensed a feeling of expectation in the air, though I didn't know why. When Jason showed up, the festivities seemed to kick up a notch. The crowd parted for Jason, still sporting bandages on his face from his surgery, as he came to the couch. "Welcome home, love," he said in my ear as he hugged me. Then he stepped back and sank to one knee.

The crowd went completely silent. My mind went completely blank.

"Zoe," he began, "when I met you, I really wanted to hate you and didn't make a secret of it. But it was like my soul recognized you. Like my heart took one look at you and said, 'oh, there you are.' It just took time for the rest of me to accept it and come around. I didn't believe in soulmates, and I still struggle with the concept, to be honest. But seeing you that first time, and getting to know you as you helped me heal, tells me there might be such a thing as fate. Because I knew you as soon as I saw you."

I sat in frozen silence, my thoughts in a frenzy.

"When I'm with you, you are all I think about. When I am away from you, the clock in my head ticks off the minutes until I can be with you again.

"Zoe, I want to spend the rest of my life with you, however long or short it may be. I want to make a family with you, no matter what it looks like. You make me happy, and you save me over and over from the dark parts of myself. From those parts that want to give up when I go to dark places, or when I feel like an absolute gargoyle. You remind me I am loved, and at least one person in this world finds me beautiful." As he spoke, he pulled a royal-blue, velvet-covered ring box out of his pocket, nerves causing him to bobble it slightly as he opened it with his hand. It trembled, along with his voice, as he pushed the open case toward me. "Zoe Calder, will you marry me?"

The silence was only broken by a gasp from Delphine at the sight of the gorgeous ring nestled in the Tiffany's box.

I had turned this man down already and still wasn't sure why. Everything within me pushed for yes, but I couldn't say yes if I didn't know why I once said no. Then, suddenly, I understood. I was afraid. For me, marriage equaled family, and family equaled hurt and rejection. It wasn't that I didn't trust him, but past experiences left me determined to never let anyone have the power to hurt me like that again. What had changed was that Jason had simply kept loving me. After I had rejected him, he still let me know in a thousand large and small ways he loved me. I didn't have to be afraid of him, I knew bone-deep. This man would never hurt me. Now, as the silence stretched into discomfort for everyone, I knew I was ready for a lifetime with Jason Merone.

He waited, face slowly blanching at the idea he may have made a mistake. "Yes," I said, only for Jason, and he deflated as he released the breath he was holding. Then, "Yes!" again for everyone else. The crowd erupted into cheers, and Delphine popped the cork on a bottle of champagne, the first bottle of many that flowed throughout the rest of the evening. Jason slid the understated, yet decadently expensive ring on my finger, then sat next to me on the couch as the engagement party cranked back up. All too soon, yet not soon enough for the sore places on my weary body, the party died down. Jason helped me to the bedroom, but I waved off his attempts to stay. There were procedures I had to do for postsurgical care, and I was uncomfortable with him being there for them, at least for now.

After everyone had gone home, including Mom and Jason, I sank into the blissful quiet of my room. My heart was full of love, but my body was a dead battery, all energy spent. Still, I had dilating to do. Unpacking the set of surgical dilators, heavy acrylic cylinders with a rounded top in three graduated sizes, I selected my current size and prepped for the session. Dilating was necessary to maintain and improve the depth of my new vagina as it healed. While not painful, it wasn't especially fun, and I was required to do this three times a day for about fifteen minutes each time for the next few weeks.

Before I could insert the green dilator, the phone rang on my nightstand. Not wanting to be interrupted, I reached over and pressed the side button to mute the ring. When the phone rang again, I checked the ID, which read Unknown, so I sent it to voicemail. The phone immediately rang again. Groaning in irritation, I answered. "Hello?"

I heard breathing on the line. *Pervert.* I pulled the phone away from my ear to jab End Call.

"Zoe." The voice stopped me. Ice ran down my spine. "Congratulations on your new pussy. Did you get my flowers?" The caller was sinister, menacing, and adrenaline flooded through me.

"Who is this?" I demanded, hoping I was wrong. But I knew that voice.

"Oh, you know me. And I know you, if you catch my drift." The chuckle was ugly, the meaning clear. "Not sure when, my dearest darling, but I'll be taking that new equipment for a test drive before I finish what I started. Congratulations on your engagement, by the way. See you soon." The phone went quiet and the call ended. My heart thudded, and I couldn't catch my breath, terror blooming into a full panic attack as I screamed loud enough to bring Delphine into my room at a dead run.

Randall.

He wasn't dead.

And he was coming for me again.

NO ONE KNEW anything. The police had come out at our call, but a search of the premises turned up nothing in the way of clues. They were polite, but my insistence that a dead man called me didn't create the alarm in them that it had in Delphine. They were more inclined to believe it was a troll from Internetland looking for laughs.

Jason came back immediately, a solid, calming presence, and refused to leave me. After the police left, Delphine brought out her guns, handing one each to me and Jason and putting the other two on the kitchen bar.

I chuckled with gallows humor at the guns. "Not sure these will work on a ghost," I said.

"I want to know what happened," Delphine seethed. "I know they brought a body out of the house. But whose body? What the fuck is going on here?"

Jason stayed quiet as Delphine and I paced. He sat pensively, staring into space. Finally, he spoke. "Please don't get mad about this question, but are you sure it was Randall? How did you know?"

Off guard, I tried to understand why he was asking. "Because he called me. I know his voice, way better than I want to. It haunts my dreams."

"Okay," he said. "I wasn't trying to make you feel bad, or call you a liar. If the voice had been synthesized or disguised, then it may have been a troll fishing for a response. But this is different. If he's still alive..." he trailed off, face grim.

"If he's still alive...what?" prompted Delphine.

"If he's still alive, then he had to have help. Most likely from a governmental authority of some sort. DEA or FBI or some other alphabet soup department. No way anyone local could pull off that level of deception."

"Help. Help, what do you mean, help?" I asked sharply.

He sighed and ran his hand through his hair. "Well, I would bet the crime organization Bogen worked for has seen a sharp increase in arrests and business disruption, using information only he could provide. What if they put him in witness protection in exchange for his information? What if the events at his home were just for show? For any other cops who might have been involved, or higher-ups in the network?"

Blood running cold, I contemplated the speculation. Could they have possibly sprung this motherfucker loose simply because of the information he could give? It didn't seem likely, but I couldn't think of another scenario that squared what had happened at Randall's farm and what I had just heard on my phone.

Delphine weighed in. "It seems a likely thing, cher, what he says. And if it's true, we have other problems."

"Oh, wonderful. This sounds promising."

"Cher, if he went into witness protection, he is someone completely new. Remember, Randall Bogen is dead, buried, with a death certificate. Witness protection would give him a new identity, and it would be a closely kept secret. So, we have no idea what his name is now, where he is, or how to begin to try to find him. He is, as you said, a ghost. How do you catch a ghost?"

Jesus. Terror threatened to overwhelm me again. *How do you catch a ghost? Where do you start?* "So, what? I have to wait for him to decide when and where he wants to kill me, then hope I get lucky? I was lucky once. Not sure I get to walk away from him a second time." I was shaken to the core, images from that night flashing behind my eyes.

Jason stood and walked over to me. "You're shivering," he said. "Come here." He held me as I buried my face in his chest and willed the fear-trembles to stop.

Over at the bar, there was a *snick, chink* from the Glock Delphine held as she removed and replaced the full magazine; then again as she checked the other one. I felt no safer with the guns in the house, but it was at least some small measure of protection. After a couple of minutes of leaning into Jason's chest as I wrestled with the images Randall had left me, I raised my head.

"So what do we do?" I asked.

"We find him, cher, ghost or non. And then we finish the job," Delphine answered.

"And for now," Jason said, "you are never to be alone. Ever. Until he goes away permanently."

I nodded my agreement, exhausted, but now too terrified to sleep. "Shower. Hot. Long. I feel cold and dirty."

"I'll wait for you in the bedroom," Jason said.

When I got into the bathroom, I left the lights off and showered in the dark. It was a soothing practice I had discovered back in childhood on the nights when my anxiety and depression were at their worst. Making the shower as hot as I could handle, I stood under the water, letting it run from the top of my head down my body. The foreign feel of the engagement ring on my finger was a reminder that Jason proposed—and I accepted. The emotional whiplash of this evening was too much. The water washed over me, and all I could do was breathe and pray for numbness.

Too soon, the hot water was gone. Still in the dark, I put my furry robe on and made my way back to the bedroom. Jason was waiting. The thought brought a small ray of happiness to my dark place.

Right up until I walked into the bedroom to see him cozied up on the bed next to the surgical dilators I had forgotten all about after the phone call. This mortification made the night complete.

Red-faced, I made my way to the bed to grab the hunks of plastic and put them away.

"What are those?" Jason asked in wide-eyed innocence, and I couldn't tell if he was joking or not.

I blushed deeper. "It's, you know, for my surgery. Er, for my new, you know...my hoo-ha." How did I go from fearing for my life, to being so embarrassed I wanted to die? And why was I suddenly blushing and stumbling around words like a twelve-year-old?

"Your hoo-ha?" Jason laughed delightedly.

"You know what I mean."

Jason gave one more chuckle before dropping the innocent eyes and turning serious. "How are things down there? Does it hurt a lot? Are you okay with, you know, the results? How do you feel?" He pulled me into a spooning cuddle on the bed, his arm wrapped around my waist. He wanted to hear my thoughts; wanted to be there for me.

Wanted to be my husband.

That he wanted to spend the rest of his life with me still flummoxed me. I melted against his body heat, feeling protected. Feeling loved. Even after a year of this relationship, I still marveled at his ability to soothe me, to make me feel cherished and loved and hella sexy.

Of course, there was no way to feel sexy when my new private parts were on fire, and I was exhausted and scared to death.

"So, were you finished with these?" Jason asked, indicating the dilators.

"Well, no. Cuntwaffle called before I could do my session."

"Cuntwaffle?" he asked.

"Delphine's nickname for him," I explained with a shrug.

"Ah, I see." Jason held up the green dilator. "Want me to help you finish? I mean, I know we can't really have, ah, relations for another few weeks, but maybe we could make some of these sessions more fun than clinical, yes?"

"Damn, don't remind me about the weeks we have to wait. Okay, I'm not saying your offer isn't tempting, because when you say it like that, I get quivery. But to be blunt, it looks like raw beef down there right now, and I'd be even more embarrassed than I have been already."

Jason kissed my ear and then the nape of my neck just below it. Softly, oh so tenderly. "But I like hamburger," he whispered seductively.

"But not raw! It's more like steak tartare right now," I shot back.

"Mmm..." he rumbled in his chest, the vibrations sending tingles throughout my entire body. "Steak," he finished in a Homer Simpson impression.

Trying to stifle the laughter bubbling up was no use. I laughed out loud with my whole body, oddly delighted to be with him in this moment.

Lying back, I let him help me finish the dilating session. He made it seductive and tender, his kisses bringing tingles to the new parts of me, and by the time it was finished, I had somehow relegated Cuntwaffle to the back of my mind.

THE NEXT DAY began a quest for answers. I called the District Attorney's office and left a message for ADA Hutto. Delphine called her mysterious friend from the fan boat and left to meet him. Jason reached out to Rachael.

Rachael was at the house within two hours, which meant she must have left almost as soon as Jason called. She arrived just after ten in the morning.

"Congratulations on your surgery," she said, striding into the kitchen where I was trying to make decent toast. She noticed the ring on my finger and gave me a thumbs-up. Then, it was down to business. "Now, what the hell happened last night?"

She listened intently as I told her about the phone call, taking notes on her ever-present notepad. Her face twisted into a frown. "Holy shit," she muttered, mostly to herself. "You're sure it was him?"

"Positive. His voice is seared into my brain. 'This doesn't end well for you' he said when he finished raping me. Can't exactly forget what that sounds like. It was him."

"Fuck," she said. "Holy fuck. This is crazy. If he's not dead, who did they pull out of that house? How did they make it look like it was Randall? What the absolute fuck is going on?"

I kinda liked the foul-mouthed side of her.

"You said he sent you flowers?" she asked. "When was that?"

"Right after my surgery. When I got to my room out of recovery, an orderly came in with this big bouquet of white roses. The card said 'thinking of you' but wasn't signed."

"White roses, huh? That utter twat. Shit. Bet he laughed a lot at that joke."

"I'm sure he did. But why white roses? That's what I don't get. Were they on sale? Or was it the bouquet that caught his eye?"

Jason leaned on the kitchen counter, pouring coffee into one of our blue mugs. "I can tell you why, but you won't like it."

"Oh, God, what? Tell me."

"I told you my mom is into the etiquette of things and is always proper, right? She used to go on about what each flower symbolized. White roses have several meanings, such as purity and innocence, but the meaning to apply here is they also symbolize the worship of someone in death. An undying love that endures, even beyond the grave."

A shiver wrenched through my body, the audacity adding to my panic. "Fucking asshole! I'll bet he did get a big laugh out of that." The fear gripping me last night was back, and then some.

Rachael eyed the coffee pot. I walked over and shakily poured her a cup.

She accepted the mug from me and took a sip. "So, it seems we have a stalker who is supposed to be dead, but isn't. And this person has threatened to kill you. You know, the first time I met you, I could tell you intended to go after him and rid the world of a scumbag. I didn't completely approve, but I understood the sentiment. But now—and if you repeat this I will swear you are lying—but now, I understand. If it were me in your position, I would do the same damn thing. Shit, he's like the Terminator."

"And now he's a ghost," I said. "New name, new ID, new location. How do we find him? Can you help?"

"I can try. But honestly, I don't know." She was blunt. "If he is in witness protection like you're thinking, it would be rather difficult to suss out his new name and location. They keep that shit on lockdown. And..."

I was really starting to dread these trailing sentences. "And?" I prompted.

"Look, I don't know an awful lot about witness protection, so take this with a grain of salt, okay? But, if he is in witness protection, if he had all this information and helped take down some shadowy syndicate, I would think he has immunity from prosecution. Probably, and especially, including your rape.

"And honestly, he might not have even committed any new crime yet. I mean, he's probably skirted the line contacting you like this, for sure. But I doubt it's anything that would stick, even if you found him and had a friendly prosecutor ready to go to the mat for you." She shook her head, sending red curls bouncing.

"Oh, this gets better and better," I sighed, putting my head on top of my arms on the table. "So he can terrorize me and stalk me, but there isn't anything anyone could do until he kills me." The coffee sat sour in my belly.

"I hate to break bad news to you, but if this guess is right, then that's probably the way of it."

I noticed Jason had set up his laptop on the dining room table, coffee nearby, and it was clear he was getting settled in for a long session. He looked up at my questioning glance.

"The flowers. Maybe we can find out who called in the order, or at least what card was used," he said. "Hopefully, we can find a rabbit hole that leads somewhere."

Rachael nodded approvingly. "Meanwhile," she said, "I'll put in as many Freedom of Information Act requests as I can think of regarding this whole debacle. Maybe we can uncover something that way."

"Is there anything I can do to help?" Still weak from surgery, I was starting to ache badly and wanted nothing more than to sink into bed and sleep the exhaustion and fear away.

Racheal spoke to Jason instead of answering again. "Hey, would you be willing to go through these files we've put together on the crime network we suspect he's involved with? Some of it's from old-fashioned journalism and some of it's from Kelly, our forensics guy who isn't available to us right now. There's something there, I'm sure of it. Maybe you can work some kind of magic. See something we've missed."

"Hell, yes. There's room for another laptop at the table," Jason said, then focused on me. His gaze softened. "Go to bed, love. I don't know how long this will take, and you look like death right now, no offense. I got your back."

"Fuck that," I said, determined not to be dismissed. "Rachael, do you mind showing me those files while Jason works his voodoo?"

Chapter Seventeen

Jason

THE FLAMING MONSTER in his nightmare had Randall's face last night.

Now, as Rachael and Zoe set up their laptops at the table beside him, Jason tried to forget the terrifying images and focus on the laptop in hopes of finding something that might help end this nightmare. All those hours studying while he healed, all those hours spent navigating the darker side of the net with Kelly needed to pay off. Zoe was in mortal danger, and the thought of losing her was completely unraveling him. He tried to hide his fear around her, not wanting to add to her anxiety, but wasn't sure how successful he was.

In the year since their relationship kicked off, he had fallen ever more in love with Zoe. She slowly allowed herself to be more open and vulnerable to him. She was like a precious jewel, each facet of her personality taking its turn in the light and adding depth and clarity to the overall sparkle. To think some psychopath seemed dead set on taking her left him with a sense of dread and fear.

It also pissed him right off.

He would not allow anyone to hurt her, not without a fight. Not without using every bit of treasure and talent at his disposal. Kelly may have been a forensic software expert, but he also knew some deep and dark shit. Shit he'd taught to Jason. He clicked across the keys furiously, searching. Testing.

The flowers Zoe received had been left in Nashville, but she kept the card. The card had a gold-embossed imprint of the local florist that filled the order, Hearts In Bloom, and there was a phone number. There was an old adage the fire department used when entering a building: "Try before you pry." Often, firefighters wasted time and caused unnecessary damage to a property by using an ax or pry tool to open a door that was unlocked and easily opened. Bearing that in mind, he first called the company, politely asking for the identity of the person who requested the order. The order was called in anonymously. A card had been used, but the mature-sounding woman who spoke with him politely suggested a warrant would be the best way to obtain the requested information.

So now we pry, he thought as he approached the florist's database. Patience was necessary, as the programs took time. He would set a program to run, take a sip of too-often cold coffee, and then review files with Zoe and Rachael.

It took three hours to find a way into the florist's system. An hour later, he was able to access the invoices. The purchase had been made with an anonymous prepaid Visa gift card.

Dead end.

Jason leaned back, frustrated. There had to be a way to find something. Just a small thread he could find and pull on.

A blue plate with a ham sandwich landed on the table beside him, with a *thunk,* as a gentle hand caressed his shoulder. He glanced up at Zoe, smiling.

"Here. I'll bet you haven't eaten all day," she said, ruffling his hair, sending good shivers down his spine.

No, he hadn't eaten today, had he? He took a break to eat the sandwich, needing to clear his head, get some distance from the puzzle. Think of something clever. "Any response from Hutto?" Jason asked, his mouth half full of sandwich

"No. He's in court all day, according to the office. I'll try him again later this evening." She passed her hand through her hair distractedly.

He pulled her close, his arm wrapping around her waist. "Feeling okay? Physically, I mean."

"Ha. Everything is sore and tender, and I get exhausted with a walk to the mailbox, but I'll be okay. Any progress on the flowers?"

"Dead end for now." His tone was more curt than he wanted it to be. "I'm not giving up," he added quickly. "There has to be something."

"Thank you for doing this." She hugged her elbows with a distant stare, fear blanking her face into lost resignation.

He couldn't take that trapped animal look on her face. Fuck this. Break time was over.

Shoving the half-eaten sandwich away, he shifted back to the computer. A thought sparking his fingers clattering across the keyboard. "Maybe I can trace where the damn thing..." he muttered as he sank back into the zone.

DUSK WAS SETTLING in before Jason closed the laptop. It had been a long day, and the pain kept at bay by his concentration swept back in with ferocious intensity. He got lucky again.

But he dreaded the conversation he was about to have with Zoe.

Delphine returned at some point while he worked, but he wasn't sure when. He only realized when he heard her conversing with Zoe and Rachael in the living room.

Jason slowly got up, stretched his back, made his way into the living room, and groaned as he sank down on the couch.

"Oh my god, love. You must be in all kinds of pain." Zoe fretted as she noted his tentative movements. "Can I get you something? A drink or a Percocet?"

He waved her off. "No. I'll be okay. Just forgot to move around like I should. I'll be fine soon."

"Okay. You have any luck?"

"Yes," he said carefully. "Well, some. I know who bought the card that was used for the purchase."

"Who was it?"

"How did you do that?"

Zoe and Delphine asked simultaneously.

Rachael whipped out her notepad.

He decided to answer Delphine first, since it would lead to Zoe's query. "Okay, so I decided to go back to find the information the florist stored on the credit card. Might as well try to see where that information led, right? Now, I'm not brave or stupid enough to try my hand at penetrating the Visa firewall, especially since there would probably be a dead end there even if I took the risk. If whoever bought the gift card used cash and fraudulent data to activate it, there wouldn't be any information to find. Still, I wanted to see if there was anything I could use. Took a bit, but I finally caught a little break. The older system the florist uses asks for the billing zip code and stores the info. That would have to be the zip code used when the card was activated. The zip used was 39475. Mississippi, obviously. Purvis, Mississippi, specifically."

"You mean Randall bought the gift card about eighty miles from here?" Zoe said.

"No," Jason said, still not answering outright, as he weighed the information. "I don't think Randall bought the card. He may have used it, but he didn't buy it. Once I had a zip code, I started doing some thinking and poking around a little bit. Purvis, as you know, is a tiny little town. A grocery store, a couple of dollar stores, some fast-food chains. A couple of red lights.

"Here's the thing, and here's where we got lucky: there is only one place in Purvis selling that particular Visa gift card: Tatum's Grocery Store. It's directly across the street from the bank. That got me thinking: what if someone was buying these cards for Randall, activating them, and then sending them on? The post office is right behind the grocery store a street over. What if they had a PO box there, so they just used the zip code out of habit? Or maybe Randall told them to. If he is receiving and using multiple cards like this, it might make sense to specify the address used for the dummy account opened when the card was activated."

"Money laundering. That's what you're describing." Rachael glanced up from her notepad.

"Right," Jason agreed, delaying the inevitable as long as possible. "Cash only gets you so far these days. A dead guy would need a way to still be able make purchases. A gift card could be a way to do that.

"Anyway, I wormed into Tatum's system. It's fairly sophisticated for being a small town. Everything is digital and stored on a server with off-site backup and redundancy. It took me a bit, but I got into the backup. I found pretty quickly I could search purchases by item and get a shot of the receipt. So I started searching for purchases of gift cards starting with your surgery date and working backward." His audience was rapt, letting him tell the story as his dread built at the coming revelation.

"It was a Hail Mary pass, I freely admit. Then something caught my attention from about a week before your surgery. A purchase of five one-hundred-dollar cards. And that was it. No other purchases on the receipt. It was paid with a debit card, not cash. So it was easy to get the name on the card."

"Who was it?" Zoe asked again, breathlessly leaning forward in anticipation.

"It was a charitable organization, a 501(c)3 called Hands Helping the Hopeless." He watched Zoe, wanting to know if the name meant anything to her, but her face revealed nothing except excitement at the news.

"Oh, shit." Rachael said. "So it *is* money laundering. We knew that had to be happening, but couldn't really narrow down how." She noticed Zoe's inquisitive look. "Probably worked like this: bad guys give ill-gotten gains to an altruistic person, the nonprofit operator, who deposits it as a donation. Then when Mr. or Ms. Change-the-World makes a withdrawal, that money is tax-free and available to forward the mission of the charity, all nice and neato. So if said Hopeless Hands purchases gift cards, they can just say 'Hey, we distribute gift cards to down-and-outs needing money for shelter and food.' Then they give the cards to the bad guys, and they have their money cleaned and available to forward their own altruistic agendas."

"Thank you, Ms. Wikipedia," Zoe said dryly. It was clear the drawn-out story was making her impatient.

It was killing Jason, too, as he stalled to delay the inevitable. "Right, so, the obvious thing was to see who was listed in the IRS filings. I imagine there are several types of these charities floating around because there are forms that have to be filled out. The lower the contributions or income any one charity has to report, the less scrutiny the treasury is liable to bring to bear."

"Yep," Rachael said with cynicism beyond her years. "Any wonder now why Mississippi leads the nation in drug use *and* per capita charitable giving?"

Well, she was definitely the right journalistic choice. "So this particular charity was listed as a religious organization..." Jason paused for a moment, saw Delphine's dark look flash understanding.

He had known Delphine was starting to puzzle over the way he was telling the story. Could tell the sensitive artist had picked up on his discomfort. Somehow, following his story and how he told it, she knew. He confirmed it to her with a sad purse of his lips and slight head nod.

"What?" Zoe asked, in puzzlement at the brief exchange. "Who? Who was it?"

He stared at Delphine, pleading with his eyes. *You tell her.*

Delphine simply looked back at Jason. "Non, mon ami. Is your story. Finish it."

Fuck. There was no easy way out of this. Jason gathered his courage. Took a sip of water. "Okay, well. Shit. The charity is listed as an outreach of a church, which listed the pastor as the head of the board. The other names on the board were fictitious, or at least I couldn't find anything on them online. But the chairman's name..." Jason blew out a sigh. "Fuck. It was Jonathan Calder. It was your father."

Jason watched the emotions play across her face. Puzzlement at first, then confusion, leading to a head-shaking denial. He watched the comprehension that her father was laundering money for the monster who wanted to kill her started to sink in.

"Oh. Shit," she said weakly, and he knew if she were standing, her knees would have buckled.

"The hell? Why would he do that?" Zoe shot panicked glances between the three of them.

Delphine went the direct route. "You should ask him, cher."

Jason nodded. "Yeah, I think so too. What the hell is he doing?"

She sighed, seeming to curl up into herself. She looked like such a lost little girl that he wanted to take back the entire story. Wanted to whisk her away to a safe place where nothing, no one, could ever hurt her again.

She caught him staring, but misinterpreted his look as pity. Anger flushed her cheeks. "What? You don't think I can handle this? You think I'm just some poor thing who can't deal with a father who hates me?" Her brown hair swished around her as she pushed it back out of her face, leveling her glare entirely on Jason. He met it with a slight smile, relieved at her fire. "Shit. I got over him a long time ago. You tend to not give a fuck about someone when they toss you out of the house at sixteen because you're too faggoty for them. So yeah. Let me pay this asshole a visit. Just be sure you have bail money for afterward. What's the fucking address?"

"I will go with you, cher," Delphine said into the silence after her outburst. "For your safety. And his."

"I'm going to start digging into this and a whole bunch of other 501(c)3's back at the office, starting now,"

Rachael said, and her eyes sparkled with glee. "This is huge, and this is going to be a lot of work."

"I'm coming too," Jason said quietly. No one argued when they saw his face.

He had hated hurting her like this, but it was good to see her response. To see her move beyond the fear.

It was good to see the fighter in her roar back to life.

Chapter Eighteen

Zoe

JASON HAD LEARNED the house my father was renting since Mom had kicked him out was about a mile off the main road in Magee. It was a town slightly larger than Purvis, about twenty minutes to the southeast. Gravel crunched under tires as I turned down the long driveway to a small, trim rental house, a few miles outside the city limits. It had taken just over an hour—and half a lifetime—to get here.

Delphine and Jason remained quiet during the trip, which I greatly appreciated. Memories of a childhood endured, rather than enjoyed, galloped through my head. Memories of never being enough, of being told—in ways large and small, physical and emotional—I was less, always less.

Now, I was back to face my father.

This time I wasn't a child.

Now, there was hell to pay.

The ranch-style house nestled at the end of a circular drive about a quarter mile off the road, pine trees densely looming around the property in a teardrop shape. Jason stood close to me as I banged on the dark-oak door, while Delphine hung back near the car. She'd brought her gun and held it close in her purse. It was Friday afternoon, his usual study time for Sunday's sermons, so I guessed he would be home. The door opened, and Jonathan Calder stood framed in the doorway.

He had his plastic-grinned welcome face on as he opened the door, every inch the ebullient pastor. As he realized who I was, his expression went wild, before settling on haughty.

"Noah. What can I do for you?"

This was the man who terrified me growing up? Though I hadn't seen him since the day he threw my toothbrush at me in silence while I hurriedly packed my suitcase for my one-way trip out of his life, I still had that imprint of him in my mind as a powerful person who bent the world around him to his will and could not be defied. But I had made my way through the world since then and dealt with things far worse than him. I had no fear of him now. Only pity for the petty tyrant standing in the doorway.

"We need to talk," I said bluntly. He had aged, badly, since I last saw him. I remembered him as tall, intimidating, with a rigid bearing and straight dark-brown hair shellacked into place by loads of hairspray; remembered him as powerful and self-assured. Now he seemed frail, brittle. His hair was almost completely gray, and his eyes were watery and held hints of madness. "Why are you buying Visa money cards, and who are you sending them to?"

Emotions flickered across his face: fear, puzzlement, anger, and unexpectedly, guilt. He raised himself to full height and tried for bluster. "Why would you care? Why are you here? Hiding behind a black woman and a one-armed man, no less. Am I really that scary?"

Taking a step closer to him, I made him shrink back, instinctively. It irked him that I noticed it. I could see it in his eyes. I stood on the porch silently, demanding an answer.

He blew a put-upon huff. "The church has a charity. We buy gift cards to help support people down on their luck. You came here to talk about the charity?" His face turned sly. "Why? Do you need money? Down on your luck, huh? I warned you so many time—"

But I wasn't a scared teenager anymore, and I couldn't care less about his attempts to deflect. "How you know Randall Bogen?" I interrupted.

His face blanched. I had struck a nerve. "He's dead, isn't he? That was the guy who was killed at his house about a year ago, right? The cop." He spoke faster, refusing to meet my eyes.

"Yeah. That's the one. Do you know him? Personally?"

"Nope," he said quickly. "Don't know him. Now you and your friends can git. And don't come back unless it's to repent your sinful ways. Not that the God I serve would forgive you." He sneered, stepping back to shut the door.

I placed my foot on the threshold, and Jason leaned on the door to prevent it from closing. "Uh-uh. You don't get to just dismiss me. Not today. I was happy to leave you alone, but that wasn't enough for you, was it? No, you had to go and start sending money to the guy who tried to kill me, and I need answers. Delphine!"

She strode into the house behind us, a tawny cat prowling silently. The condition of the room and the kitchen beyond as I pointed him to the couch was jarringly disordered; the complete opposite of the bucolic image presented outside. Dirty clothes covered the kitchen table, and plates and pots choked the sink, still encrusted with remnants of ancient meals. Garbage spilled from the overflowing trashcan, with fruit flies flitting around it. In the living room, magazines and paper scraps lay everywhere, among the flotsam of half-assembled appliances. Mud-crusted shoes were in the middle of the floor, each mate separated and lying somewhere else. It smelled horrible, the stench a miasma of rotted food and unbearable body odor mixed with a sharp ammonia scent that assaulted the nose, like cat piss, but worse.

"What...the utter...fuck?" I said, waving my arms to indicate the house. He had taken a seat on the couch—on the edge because of all the junk parked there. Delphine and I remained standing. No way was I trusting any of this near my surgical site. He shrugged, all bluster gone, as if sitting had caused him to keep falling inward, a slow-motion implosion. Still unwilling to look up at me, he started gathering papers and magazines from the couch, as if to tidy up a bit.

His movements were jumpy, and he scratched at himself in various places as he pushed at junk piles around him. I shot a look at Delphine, *What the hell?*

Meth, she mouthed silently back. Jason had already caught on, nodding at Del's lip movements.

Suddenly, it all made sense. The mess, the lack of hygiene, the jittery movements. It was as if barging into his lair had pulled back the curtains on his public persona, revealing a pitiful addict.

The silence spun out as he shuffled and scratched. Finally he stopped, glancing at Jason from the corner of his eye. The pity that played over his face after looking at Jason left me seething.

The muddy shoe I kicked to get his attention skittered across a glossy fashion magazine before coming to rest against half of a George Foreman grill. "Do you need help?" I asked coldly.

"No, I'm fine," he mumbled. "It's just a little messy in here. I was going to clean it up tomorrow. Why don't you say whatever you came here to say and then leave me be?"

I hesitated, the rage and questions needing to be asked temporarily forgotten at the sight of what my father had become.

"Jonathan, how long have you been using?" Jason asked gently.

He sniffed a short inhale, started biting at the red, angry cuticles on his thumbs. He seemed to be having an inner dialogue, and after a moment he jumped from the couch. Delphine put her hand in her purse, shifting slightly into a more balanced stance. She didn't draw the gun, but she was ready. He noted her movement, registered the hand in the purse, and his eyes narrowed as he realized what it meant. She motioned her other hand downward at him to sit. He sat and slumped, first from his shoulders but continuing down until his head rested between his knees. Soon, I could hear strangled sobs coming from him.

"Oh, God, God, merciful God," he said piteously, raising his head a little but refusing to look at anyone. "I messed up. I'm sorry. Everybody is going to hate me. What will the congregation say?"

"How long?" Jason asked again. The sharper tone told me I wasn't the only one warring with anger and empathy.

"About two years, I guess. Probably more."

"Meth?"

"Among other stuff. But mostly, yeah."

"Why?" I was utterly perplexed by the person sitting on the couch. Strangely, I felt no triumph or elation at what he was now. Only pity.

He took a moment to answer. "I had to have neck surgery for a pinched nerve about four years ago. It worked, at first, but after a while the pain came back, and I needed pills again. But the doctors decided I was drug-seeking and started weaning me off. It was unbearable pain, and I had to get some help somewhere. So I asked around and got a hookup. At first, it was just a little weed, and that seemed to take the edge off, but then I couldn't get any more pills from the doctor, and every other doctor I went to brushed me off. I was stuck with the street stuff. I tried heroin, but it made me nauseous, and coming down was brutal, and I started thinking maybe I was getting addicted. I talked to my cousin about it one day, looking for help. He had been injured on a construction site a while back, had major back pain and other issues. I thought maybe he had some pills or something. But he told me, no, what I needed was ice. Took a second to realize he wasn't talking about cold water, but really pure meth. He said the pain was mostly in my head, and the ice would help with that. It was the only stuff that worked."

"Surely someone noticed?" I couldn't believe what I was hearing.

"I was able to keep it under wraps; even your mother didn't know about it." As he spoke, a strange grin ghosted across his face, as if he was proud of that accomplishment.

"Right. Good job on that." My sarcasm wiped the grin off his face. "Get to the part of the story where you're giving Randall money."

His eyes flitted up and over each of us before looking down at the floor again. He shrugged and continued, "I had to get more and more to keep the edge off. Plus, I never really got off the smack, which was the whole reason I started on the...other. I started putting some 'on the books,' you know, get some now and pay later. The bill started getting heavy, and people got nervous. One day, this cop pulled up at the house, in uniform and everything, and started leaning heavy on me. Said I had two days to settle things. I had to do some fancy stuff with the church books to cover it. Two days later, he came by and took my money."

"Randall." My voice sounded empty even to my ears.

"Yeah. Him."

"Is that when you set up the charity-laundering thing?"

He nodded slowly. "When I paid the past due, yeah. We went to a house; he wasn't in uniform this time; he got me high for the first time in days. He was just drinking beer, sneering that he never touched the stuff I was doing. But still, we started talking as he got tight. I told him how much paying all that money at one time hurt. He laughed. Like he got off on my misery. Gave me instructions on how to set up the charity, how the laundering thing would work. It wasn't like I could say no."

Jason had a dangerous look. "Jonathan, so far this has all been about you. What I want to know is how Zoe got dragged into your mess."

"He got to talking about my family one day. Ruth's favorite grocery, Jacob's baseball practice times, that kind of stuff. It was bald threat. He promised if I tried to go to the police, if I tried to shut down the charity or blow the whistle, hell, if I tried to go to rehab, he would 'take care of' my family." Clamping his mouth shut as if he had already said too much, he glanced around at the mess of his house and sighed as if seeing it for the first time. Then he hung his head again and began to unburden himself once more. "But he only knew about Ruth and Jacob. I never told him I had another son."

My stomach clenched, the exclusion even now a sharp hurt.

"There was a time a while back that things got a little rough. He went at a junkie who owed money, pretty hard; was looking at a police brutality complaint, maybe charges. So things were looking dicey for him, and he was trying to game out escape options. Said what he needed was a new ID."

Jason figured it out before I did. Rushing forward, his hand was a blur as he punched my father. "You fucking piece of shit." He punctuated each word he spoke with cracking hits that made the man's head bounce. "She's your *daughter*."

I went to stop Jason before I felt a touch on my shoulder. Delphine shook a silent no at me.

Jason stepped back, breathing hard. Jonathan lay back against the couch, blood gushing from a broken nose and busted lips. "Go on," Jason said, his voice low and deadly calm. "Finish this fucking story."

My father didn't fight back; only tried to cover his head as Jason had swung at him. He slid bonelessly off the couch to the floor. Swiping at his nose, using his forearm, he fixed his gaze on Jason's shoes, then started mumbling through his puffy and broken lips. "When he said he needed an ID, I told him maybe I could help. I said I had a son who wasn't using his anymore. Told him I had the birth certificate and social security card. But there was a catch."

Now I understood. And the world darkened to a scarlet rage.

"I was still alive. That was the catch, wasn't it?" I spoke fury into each syllable. "I had a different name but was still using the social security number. The only way to be sure nothing bit him in the ass later was if I was dead." I hadn't been a random hookup for Randall. He'd targeted me after a conversation with my father. He'd planned to kill me all along.

My sperm donor nodded, still staring at Jason's shoes.

"So what happened next?" I said.

"He called the next day and said his boss gave the green light to set up a contract for five thousand dollars. As if he were doing me a favor. Said to make sure I took the birth certificate and social security card and leave it in a drawer in the desk in my church office. He said he'd get it when it was convenient for him."

My father paid to have me assaulted and killed. The horror of the revelation was a bright starburst blotting out rational thought. I turned to Delphine. She was a coiled spring on a hair trigger, gun out and focused on my father.

Jason spoke in the tense silence. "When did Randall get back in touch with you?"

"After everything happened and everyone thought Randall was dead, I started to breathe a little easier. But then, about three months later, I got a phone call. Randall. Couldn't believe it. He said he was spilling everything to the cops and bragged about being untouchable. Said he was taking people down unless they paid him enough to keep quiet, on top of the money being funneled through the charity. I knew it was true too. There were lots of arrests. Everyone was on eggshells, and it was impossible to get any product. I got so desperate, I tried cooking some of my own stuff.

"So now the church is dead broke, and they'll know it soon. It's all falling down around my ears and won't a damn one of those guys get a speck of dirt on them from it," he said in a bitter, aggrieved tone.

"You danced to the tune." It was a savage thrill to throw the adage he had so often used on me back in his face. "Now you pay the piper."

I looked at my friends. They stayed quiet, letting me gather my thoughts. "Okay, here's what happens next. We are going to go talk to Mr. Hutto at the District Attorney's office, and you are going to tell him what you told me. And you are going to help us find this man. And when we do, you testify. Or take your chances with this drug cartel. What do you think they'll do after we go to the DA?"

He looked up at me, fear and resignation on his face. Finally, he seemed to arrive at a decision and made an affirmative nod. "I'll go to jail, won't I?"

"Yeah, probably. Embezzlement, money laundering, murder for hire," I ticked off the possible charges on my fingers. "There's a lot to answer for. But maybe you can get a deal if your information helps find and stop this guy. Hopefully, we can get you into rehab. Do you want to get help?" As angry as I was, if I could help him get clean, I felt obligated. He was still my father, as much as I loathed him.

"Yes. God knows, yes. But he said he's got immunity or something."

"Not from shit he's doing now. Immunity from past crimes maybe, not from crimes committed after going into witness protection, if that's what happened." I was starting to doubt Randall was still in witness protection, if indeed he had ever been. All the more reason to get my father protected.

After a tense moment of silence, I made a decision. "I'm going to call Hutto," I said to Delphine. Then to my father, I said, "You get a shower and clean up. We'll take you with us, but not smelling like that. Do you have any clean clothes?"

He nodded and headed toward the bathroom down the hall as I called the ADA. After three tries, Hutto finally answered. I sketched out what had happened and filled in the information my father had given us.

"Is he willing to testify?" he asked, clearly shocked at the fact Randall was still alive. He hadn't returned my calls earlier.

"Yes, and I'm bringing him in from Magee right now to surrender. Should be back in Biloxi in about an hour and a half. Can we meet you somewhere?"

"Okay. Okay. Why don't you take him to—"

A gun blast shook the house, and I dropped the phone as I was knocked to the floor, Jason lunging to cover my body with his. Delphine whirled, gun pointed as she advanced down the hall. It came from the bedroom. I knew with gut-cold certainty what it meant, even as my brain sputtered and reality tilted.

I grabbed the phone as Delphine got to the door. Jason slowly stood and helped me to my feet. On the line, Hutto was repeating some unheard question. Delphine kicked the door open, crouching in a shooter's stance as she crossed into the bedroom. She backed out slowly, motioned me to stop as I started to head down the hall. "Non, cher. You don't want to see. Trust me."

"Could you send police and EMS?" I interrupted Hutto on the phone.

His usual unflappability was long gone. "Ah...yes...ah. What? What's happened?"

"Pretty sure my father just committed suicide."

"Oh...ah...yes...um...where are you? I'll ring them immediately."

"Seventeen Spencer Abney Lane, in Magee."

"Yes. Very good. Okay." The line went dead.

In the aftermath, I grappled with the shock of the events. Decided I needed to see him. He was my father, after all. A detestable human who had nevertheless been painted into a corner by events that snowballed out of his control. It seemed important to bear witness to the end of his life. Over his protests, I broke free of Jason and walked down the hall.

"Cher," Delphine warned. I ignored her too.

I stood in the doorway, absorbed the grisly scene, and the too-still body. After a moment that would forever be seared into my soul, I turned around and walked outside. Plopped down on a porch step. Waited for the circus to arrive.

Chapter Nineteen

Jason

AFTER THEY WERE released from the scene, Delphine drove home. Zoe sat in the back with Jason. She said nothing, staring into the distance as she leaned against him.

In the year they'd dated, he'd heard stories of the man who had tried to break her. Horrific stories, told humorously or ironically. He had no love for the man and would waste no tears on him. Hell, his knuckles still throbbed from the punches he bounced off the guy's skull. The foremost worry in his mind was how this would affect Zoe. Would she feel guilty, feel she had driven him to it? What went through her mind when she saw her father in that final scene? Would she change? How?

The worst of the situation was they were no closer to finding Randall. How many potential clues and information had died with that single shot?

They got home just before midnight. She walked gingerly, exhausted, obviously sore, and needing help inside. She had overdone it so soon after surgery. He helped her into the house, shoulder under her arm, straight to the bedroom.

"Need a shower," she muttered. "Stink." She barely opened her eyes. He wasn't sure how much of this disconnect was from the physical pain and fatigue and how much was due to the events of the day.

It was true. An unpleasant odor clung to them from the house. He undressed her on the bed, surprised at his efficiency with one hand and an elbow. He helped her into the shower, running the water until it grew warm. He turned to leave, to let her have some space.

"Please don't go," she said quietly from behind the shower curtain. "I don't want to be alone." The gentleness of her voice damn near broke his heart.

"Okay." Jason sat on the commode to wait for her. He heard sniffling before a quiet sob lanced his heart. Without thinking, he stepped into the shower with her, still clothed. She turned to him, wrapping her arms around his chest and holding on tightly.

"I shouldn't have gone in," she said as the water cascaded down her back. "But I thought I needed to. Needed to see him, see how it ended. God, that was a mistake." She shuddered.

He shushed her gently, soaping her down. She responded with sighs and soft moans, her trust in him and vulnerability a gift as precious as any he had ever received.

After the shower, he tucked her into bed and stripped off his sodden clothes to lie next to her. As she dilated, she touched him often, as if to reassure herself that he was real.

"He was never going to love me." She sighed, almost to herself. "He was my daddy, and he threw me away. But I always hoped things could change. Maybe that's why he called me that last time, I thought. To warn me about Randall. Maybe he wanted...I don't know. He's really dead, isn't he? And he never even called me Zoe."

Jason snuggled against her, sharing her pain as best he could. He shed no tears for the dead man, but there were plenty for the girl who had lost her father long before today.

THE SLATE-GRAY sky spit drizzle as Jason and Zoe, along with Delphine, entered the church. It was her first time back since she had been thrown out of the family and shunned ten years ago.

Zoe had been a bundle of nerves that morning. Changed her outfit three times, her movements choppy and clumsy. She was going home, and she was preparing to be hurt yet again by those who subscribed to the fire-and-brimstone version of Christianity she'd grown up with.

"You don't have to do this, love," Jason said after her second outfit swap. He was edgy and irritated, but trying not to show her. He would have been much happier to skip the funeral, much happier knowing Zoe was sheltered from the straight-backed judgments of those in the cultish hive, along with the threat of Randall looming over everything.

"I do," she answered. "I have to be there for Mom and Jacob. You're the one who doesn't have to go."

That was false. If she was going, he was. No way was he letting her be alone right now. He kept a respectful distance, as she prepared for the day, but hovered close by for support.

They drove to Foxtrot, Mississippi, a heavily wooded, sparsely populated town barely large enough to be incorporated. It was a two-hour journey north through back roads and farmlands, past small clearings with asphalt and washed-out diners next to laundromats and gas stations with analog dials on the ancient pumps. It reeked of poverty and pride.

They arrived at the church about twenty minutes before the scheduled start of the service. The church, with a stereotypical steeple built almost forty years ago, looked tired and dismal, the whitewashed clapboard dingy and peeling. The gravel parking lot was less crowded than Zoe expected, given the sudden death of its minister. Small knots of people milled around outside, and Jason felt an anxiety that surely matched hers.

He was still trying to get used to being looked at in public, being seen and judged on an appearance that was different from most. He'd needed to learn how to let ugly comments and stupid jokes slide, and how to deflect ignorant questions and answer innocent ones. Zoe helped him with it because she had been there. It got much better for her, as her transition progressed and hormones and time worked their magic. He, on the other hand, was not aesthetically pleasing. His scars still stood out in sharp relief, discolored skin crinkled in strange ways, missing ear, missing hand. His image was startling, and he understood that. Still, every double-take, every sharp breath that occurred as he passed felt like a branding iron to his heart, hurting him and marking him as different. At times, he longed to be the person he was before the fire, beautiful and whole. Here at the church, though, Zoe's appearance would likely be more distracting and comment-worthy than his.

Zoe parked as far away from the building as the parking lot would allow, and they walked to the church three abreast. It reminded Jason of something out of *Reservoir Dogs*, the gang walking as if they owned the world. Jason and Zoe held hands as they entered, and Delphine led the way. The crowd parted for them, unsure at first of who they were or why they were here. Already, they could hear the whispers and mutters as they progressed toward Zoe's mom and brother.

Decades of bad carpet and aging pews had its own smell, Jason decided. A blind person could wake up in an empty church and know exactly where they were, based only on the smell.

Even for a funeral, the vibe of the gathering was off. The circumstances of Pastor Jonathan Calder's passing must have shocked the church-goers, and they didn't know how to react. They responded to the presence of the three friends exactly as Jason had feared: double-takes, gawking, and judgmental stares.

A hush fell at the entrance of a new mourner. ADA Hutto walked in alone, his suit a tastefully tailored navy-blue three-piece with black pocket square and gray textured tie. He strode to the pew where the family in mourning sat.

"Mrs. Calder," he said with gravitas to Zoe's mom when he reached her. He laid a comforting arm on her shoulder as she made to stand up. "No, no. No need to get up. I just wanted to extend my personal condolences. I was on the phone with Zoe when...well, when everything happened."

"Ruth." My mom spoke for the first time. "You can call me Ruth. We were in the process of getting divorced, so I'm not really comfortable with the Mrs. or the Calder."

"Of course," he said warmly. "Ruth. I'm so sorry about what happened."

"Thank you. Would you like to sit with us?"

He nodded his assent and made his way to sit beside Jason and Zoe.

Together in the long pews, the friends and family of Ruth Calder sat in silence as the funeral began.

THE HEAVY MOOD lifted somewhat on the drive home. Darkness had fallen several hours ago, and the twisting country roads were inky black. Jonathan Calder was buried, followed by a reception at Zoe's childhood home. It was an awkward and unpleasant time for everyone. Zoe was alternately ignored, misgendered, and judged. She simply rolled with it, while Jason devoted considerable energy to simply keeping his peace.

A thin, beak-nosed man had tottered over to them at the reception and launched into a diatribe in baleful tones. "You are an abomination, and a disappointment to your father," he'd intoned.

A gaggle of mourners stopped picking at the bland casserole to watch the show, making Jason's fist tighten. "You are going to bust hell wide open, and I pray it happens soon." His words were pompous. He was a deacon there at the church, would probably be the next preacher, Zoe told Jason later. This was his idea of an audition.

Zoe had simply turned on him with her highest megawatt smile and sweetly replied, "Oh, thank you, darling!" Drawing the darling out an extra couple of syllables, she added, "So nice to know I'll be among friends. I do hope they seat us away from your table there."

The deacon's startled face was priceless. Delphine's throaty laugh in response to the deacon's shock only added to the humor, leaving his face bright red as he stuttered for a response.

"Stand down, little man," Delphine had purred to the Ichabod Crane look-alike, her voice dripping honey and arsenic. "And back the fuck up."

He harrumphed but skittered away toward Ruth, his Adam's apple bobbing furiously. She simply pointed him to the front door of her home with a calm glare. He left in disbelief, but he hadn't said another word.

The laughter in the car, talking about it as they drove home, was cathartic. Zoe relaxed, and Jason could almost see the weight of years lifting off her shoulders. Her father could never torment her again. Could never torment her brother or mother again.

Zoe's phone trilled in the center console. She pressed the button on the steering wheel to answer. "Hello?"

"You had a lovely home." A man's voice boomed out over the speakers. "Hope you had fun with your dead daddy. I left you a present in the glove box." The call ended with a beep

Zoe gasped and jerked, sending the car rumbling onto the gravel median before she regained control and rolled to a stop.

Delphine, in the passenger seat, opened the glove box.

The 'gift' was a white rose, a red Bic lighter secured to the stem with twine. A note attached near the top of the stem read 'thinking of you,' with a smiley face.

"My house," Delphine said sadly as she twirled the rose. "He said we had a beautiful home. Had."

"Oh god," Zoe said and floored the gas pedal. The Sentra responded with increasing speed, hurtling through the darkness as Zoe drove through the twists and curves at the sharp edge of the car's limits.

Delphine called the police. "Hello? Can you send someone to my house to make sure it is okay? Someone has just made a threat on it, and I very much believe them."

"Okay, ma'am. What is the address?"

She gave the operator the address, face turning worried at the silence.

"Ma'am, can you give me your name and confirm that address again?"

Delphine did so and waited. Something was definitely wrong.

"Ah, Ms. Roulet, I am sorry to inform you, but that address is the location of a fully involved structure fire. We have multiple engine companies on the scene, and they are doing all they can, but it was going pretty good when they got to it. Are you nearby? Do you know if anyone may have been in there?"

"No. The house should be empty. I'm about—" She looked to Zoe for an estimate. "—thirty-five minutes away."

"Okay. I'll let the police know you are on your way. I'm sorry to give you this news, ma'am."

"Fuck!" she swore as she ended the call. "Fuck, fuck, fuck."

Jason hung on tightly in the back seat as tires squealed through another curve. Meanwhile, Delphine looked over at Zoe as she set up the next curve. "Our home is on fire, cher. Step on it."

Somehow, Zoe coaxed the car to go even faster.

ONCE THE CURVES evened out a bit, and Jason could catch a breath, he called around to some buddies on the

Biloxi FD. It took four tries before he found someone to answer.

"Stanley, hey. It's Jason, Jason Calder. Hey, what can you tell me about the structure fire at sixty-seven Azalea Lane?"

As he listened, Delphine watched him. He tried to keep his face neutral, but given the news, it was almost impossible.

"Thanks, man," he finally grunted. "Yeah, come by anytime. We'll have a beer." He ended the call and informed Delphine and Zoe grimly, "It's not good. It went up fast; nothing they could do. It's gone."

"Fuck." She looked down at the white rose still in her hand. "It's a terror campaign. He wants you beaten and terrified before the coup de grace."

Zoe said nothing, gave no indication she heard, even as she absorbed the thought that the painting over her bed was no more. It was the knife left twisting in her belly; Del's efforts and expertise and art had simply been kindling for the fire that claimed almost everything they owned.

The car chased its headlights as they made their way home.

Chapter Twenty

Zoe

THE HOUSE WAS smoldering when we got there, rubble with a few skeletal beams left stubbornly standing. Ash hung in the air, the smell a mix of charred wood and soggy trash fire. Only a few firefighters from two engine companies remained on the scene, and they turned their efforts to churning through the debris to make sure every ember was extinguished. Klieg lights illuminated the work area, throwing shadows and flattening the scene into two dimensions of hyperbright and pitch-dark.

I was homeless. Again. The feeling was a mix of resignation and nostalgic familiarity. Everything was gone. Even Jason's truck and Delphine's car were burned out husks. I thought again of the beautiful painting Del had given me, now so much ash. My heart ached.

The fireground was Jason's beat. I watched him stride into the working area, walk up to the battalion chief at one of the engines. Soon the firefighters were crowding around him, cycling through to give fist bumps and bro hugs before going back to the dwindling work. It was a tiny glimpse of the Jason he was before the fire savaged his body. His movements were languid, and his stature had a bearing of ease and confidence.

In those moments, it was clear Jason was born to be a firefighter. He would have been a captain. Chief. He would have led more men into infernos, and they would have followed him through hell. Seeing him there in his element, the pride of what he was and the grief at what he had lost eclipsed my own concerns.

Delphine and I sat on the hood of my car, watching the firefighters and waiting. I ached, the site of my recent surgery screaming bloody murder and reminding me that my dilators had also been in the house. After about ten minutes, Jason turned and came back to us.

"It's pretty much what would be expected for a fire like this," he said. "Lots of flammable liquids all over and then poof. Hot fire everywhere all at once. Even if we had engines in the yard before the match was tossed, I doubt we could have saved it." He gave a quizzical look at my expression. "What?"

"You said 'we.' As if you were still a firefighter. No, wait, that came out wrong." I said quickly when I saw the hurt on his face. I took his hand, brought him close. "I'm just realizing that you are still a firefighter at heart. Watching you with the guys, and how you moved out there, it's not hard to see what sort of firefighter you were."

"Uh, thanks?" He still wasn't getting it.

"What she's saying, cher—" Delphine interjected. "—rather inelegantly, I might add, is that she now has an inkling of who you were before she met you. And in that knowing, she is profoundly moved by your sacrifice."

"Oh, er—"

"I only meant—"

Jason and I said at the same time.

"Shush, children," Delphine interrupted. "In times such as these, lips have better uses than speaking."

She was right. There in the dark, away from the klieg lights and the activity they shined on, Jason drew close to me, and I told him of my pride, of my love for him, my hurts and hopes. His eloquent replies took my breath away, and we told each other much more.

All without saying a word.

THE SUNRISE WAS a mockingly beautiful counterpoint to the ugliness in front of us. First a dark-reddish tinge spread across the sky and then lighter reds and pinks that reflected off the gulf clouds as the light strengthened. I felt the woods around me wake up, and the new day was off to the races.

The first order of business was to find a place to stay. We went to Jason's to have coffee and figure out how to start the process of recovering from the fire.

Over coffee, in the subdued quiet of the aftermath of a stressful night, I brooded. So many people had been hurt and changed because of me: Del was homeless, because I got horny; Mom and my brother were dealing with the loss of a husband and father, because I was who I was and couldn't *deal* with not being comfortable with myself anymore. And Jason. Jesus, Jason lost an arm because I wasn't there to take care of him like I had promised to do. Everyone around me was hurting and lost because I kept fucking up.

The only way to fix it was to go and be by myself. Maybe Randall would find me, maybe not. But if I were by myself, at least no one else would be hurt or killed.

Jason cleared his throat in the silence as he set his coffee down on the table and reached out to me, trapping the engagement ring on my finger and twirling it around. "Stay with me. You and Delphine. My place is yours."

I'd known the offer coming. It was a reasonable response. We were engaged, and I was homeless. It was logical, simple. I just hoped I could do this without hurting his heart too much. "Jason, I...I don't know. Maybe I should go hide somewhere by myself."

"No. You can't be alone. Are you forgetting the guy who wants to kill you so he can set up shop somewhere with your identity?"

Of course not. It was the biggest reason I wanted to get away from everyone. "No. But, Jason, I can't. I won't."

He frowned, furrowing lines between his eyebrows. "What? Why? We, um, we are engaged, aren't we? Like, spend the rest of our lives together, grow old and sit in rocking chairs on the porch, engaged?" The hurt on his face ripped me apart, but a Jason alive and angry was worth so much more than a dead fiancé.

I closed my eyes against the horrors of my imagination—my father's savaged head after the fatal gunshot, with Jason's face superimposed on it, a gleeful Randall standing over him. No. I couldn't bear anything happening to him because of me. Getting him away from me was the best way I could love him. My heart thrummed as adrenaline raced through me, and my breath grew shallow.

"I can't explain it. I really can't. I love you, but I thought we would have more time before we moved in together. I don't think I'm ready for this yet. This...living at your place. What if...what if we learn we can't stand each other? What if we just can't live together? What if this relationship ends because...because you leave toothpaste in the sink and leave the cap off the tube?" Telling him the real reason would only piss him off, and that was a fight I couldn't deal with in this state.

"I'll try to be more considerate with my hygiene," Jason responded drily, a glimmer of anger underpinning his confusion.

"You know what I mean. What if there's a deal breaker that we didn't know would be one until after it's too late?" My breathing was ragged, full on fight-or-flight mode engaged.

I could see Jason struggling to keep the anger from showing on his face while he talked to me. "Zoe, I love you. I promise that won't change if you move in with me."

"What if..." I started, and trailed off.

"What if?" Jason asked and waited for an answer.

"What if...what if you decide..." Fuck. I wanted to do this without hurting him, but he wasn't going to give any other way. Fear urged me on, burning inside me until I felt like I was going to end up as wrecked as my house. I could handle anything if I knew Jason was okay. "What if I'm not, you know, woman enough for you? Jason, I know you're different. You've proven it. But, what if? If you change your mind, decide to kick me out, I'm back in a place I swore I would never be again."

Mission accomplished. Jason had never been truly angry at me before, but there was no doubt he was pissed. His face was flushed, setting the pale scars into sharp relief. "Damn it, Zoe. I asked you to marry me in front of your friends. I have never, ever been ashamed of you. I never thought I *could* be ashamed of you." He shook his head.

I swallowed hard. His hand raised as if he was going to touch my shoulder, but he clenched his fist by his side instead.

"That you think I could ever be so callous and ugly as to just change my mind and dump you out on your ass...

Fuck, Zoe. That's not me. That has never been me." He wiped at his face, and when he looked up at me again, there was no doubt he was crying.

His voice broke. "I love you, but damn. How could you think that? Why would you think that?"

Anything I could say in response was swallowed by the shame I felt seeing his hurt. My eyes blistered with tears. Of course, Jason wasn't like any other guy I had ever met. That's why I didn't deserve him. And why I couldn't get him killed.

His anger deepened at my silence. "Fine. Have it your way. Go find a hole to hide in. I don't care." He stalked off to his bedroom, the door slamming shut, taking all the air in the room with him.

I moved toward the bedroom, but Delphine stopped me. "Cher," she said in a disappointed tone, "I'm not sure why you needed to hurt him, but you've done a good job."

"Me? Why? Because I couldn't bear to see him hurt or killed?" His anger was starting to rub off on me, and I spoke harshly.

"Just so, mon amie. What was offered to you was more than a place to stay. He offered everything he has to make sure you are provided and cared for, with full knowledge of the risks. He offered it to his fiancée, who only a few days ago accepted his proposal of marriage. So, yes, he is angry, and I don't blame him.

Jason is a good man, one of the best I've met. He loves you and offered you his world. I can see what you are doing, and I can imagine why. But to him, it probably feels like you shit all over everything for no good reason. Is that fair to him?"

Del saw right through me, I realized, letting the tension fall from my shoulders. Maybe it wasn't fair to him, but neither was him dying to try to protect me. Crap. I blew out a long sigh. "Fuck, Delphine, I'm more terrified of Randall hurting Jason than getting to me again."

Delphine gave me a wan smile. "He loves you. He knows the danger, and you love him. So now you can either get over yourself and take a chance with the beautiful boy in that room, or let fear kill the best thing to ever come into your life."

I looked over at his bedroom door, shut to keep me out. She was right. But the fear of losing him broke me in places I had long thought banished to the dark.

"Okay," I grudgingly nodded. "Damn it, you're always right. But I'm terrified."

"Because you've had to learn not to be vulnerable. Letting him assume this risk with you is, in essence, trusting him with your life." She took my hands in hers, and I met her dark-brown eyes. I expected judgment, or pity, but found only love.

"What you've done, transitioning, is such a raw and scary thing. And to be rejected by so many for it? That leaves scars, cher. You've had to plate those scars with armor just to survive, and you've done well. I have always been proud of the person you are, but the scars...? They don't heal until you take the armor off."

I hated crying, hated being the girl who was so emotional all the time, but Delphine's words had me leaking and sniffling. "God, Del, what if he doesn't like me anymore? What if he's changed his mind?"

"He hasn't." She reached out and tucked a lock of my hair behind my ear, her hand trailing down my shoulder.

"How can you possibly know that?" I tilted my head toward the comfort of her touch, raising my shoulders.

"He didn't ask for the ring back. I think he's in for the long haul, cheri. Are you?"

The question cut straight to the heart of my problem. I wanted someone to see all my flaws and love me anyway, but when I actually found that person, I wanted an excuse to push them away. My life was colored by the fact that those who were closest to me were the ones whose rejections hurt the most. The ones who promised unconditional love put the highest terms on the price tag. So I simply learned to be alone, to never let anyone close, because I didn't know if I could get through that again. This situation might be the opposite side of that coin, but it was still the same coin.

Twisting the engagement ring on my finger, I thought about the question Delphine had asked. *Are you in for the long haul?*

I realized I was.

For Jason, I would risk everything. Including letting him risk his life if that's what it took.

The phone rang, crashing me back to reality. ADA Hutto's number showed on the caller ID, which for once, I thought to check. "Hello, this is Zoe."

"Ms. Calder," Hutto said, "I understand there was some excitement after the funeral."

"Yeah, you could say that."

"This has turned into some nasty business. I'm so sorry for what you are going through. I'm calling to inform you I have been working closely with the investigation of your father's death, since it seems he was in some way involved with Randall Bogen, even after the officer was supposedly dead and buried. It's set me off-kilter, I can tell you that. I've had the authorities there going through the house searching for anything that might help shed light on where this man might be. I have received some interesting information, Ms. Calder, but I'm not completely sure how to decipher it. Would it be possible for you to come by the office and take a look?"

"What is it? What did you find?" I couldn't let myself believe that this really might be a break. Could it really be true we were close to catching the bastard?

"It seems to be coded in some way, and I'm sure we could get it sorted and figured out. But I don't know how long it will take. It may be that you know what this means. Or perhaps at least help get us going in the right direction. You don't have to, of course, as my next step would be to ask Mrs. Cald— Ruth."

I didn't want Mom involved in any of this. "When would you like to meet?"

"I have time right now, if you are available."

"I'm on my way. Give me half an hour?" Nothing would stop me from getting there if it meant I could help put an end to this nightmare.

"Very good, ma'am. I'll let Stacey in reception know to expect you."

I hung up and looked at Delphine with a gleam in my eyes. "Hutto's got something promising out of my father's house. Thinks I might be able to help figure it out."

"Ah, very good news. I wish I could come with you, but Stephanie will be here soon to take me to meet the insurance adjuster at my place. I would love to see what secrets have been unearthed."

"I'll let you know as soon as I know what it is." I promised.

I walked to Jason's door. Knocked. "Jason?"

"On the phone," he said. After a moment, the door opened. He had the phone cupped to his left shoulder. "What?" Yep, he was still pissed.

"Hutto at the DA's office has some sort of evidence he wants me to take a look at. I'm about to go over."

"Okay, well, can it wait? Rachael is on the phone, going over the files they've managed to obtain. She says there isn't much there; we were going to go over them together."

"Well, I told him I would be there in about half an hour. Sorry, I didn't realize you were on the phone working on my stuff." His assumption that I'd wait when this was so important grated at me.

"It's fine. Is Delphine going with you? I don't want you by yourself."

"No, she's about to be picked up to go deal with the house."

"I'll go with you then. Hey, Rachael—" he said into the phone.

"No! Jason, I'll be okay. With the DA on this, I don't think Randall can afford to mess with me right now. He wants me terrified, right? Scared and looking over my shoulder? I don't think he's going to try anything so soon after burning the house down."

"Zoe," he said in exasperation. Then he had a thought. "Oh! Maybe Vince can drop you off. That way you can leave the car here, and when you're finished I'll come get you. Remember, never be alone."

That was sensible, and my irritation melted away. Vince was happy to pick me up, even offering to wait with me. I waved him off with assurances Jason would be picking me up.

The office of Assistant District Attorney Malcolm Hutto was more luxurious than I anticipated. Oriental rugs protected a nice gray carpet and anchored the dark cherry furniture. The office was as prim and proper as its current resident.

The receptionist, Stacey, had escorted me right back to the office when I arrived, and Hutto greeted me within five minutes, striding into the office while removing his suit coat.

"Ms. Calder," he said as he hung the coat on a stand in the corner. "Thanks for coming over. I know things are rather tumultuous for you right now."

"Of course, anything I can do to help. What did you find?"

"It's quite interesting and feels important, but I can't quite figure it out. Oh, where are my manners? Would you like something to drink? Water? Coffee?"

"Oh, coffee would be nice, thank you." I wondered where he had this strange thing hidden.

"No problem, Ms. Calder. I could use some as well. Please give me a moment. I'll get it myself. Stacey is about to go to lunch."

With his permission, I used his en suite restroom while he went for coffee. He came back soon carrying two steaming mugs on a silver tray. He handed one to me, pointed to the table in the corner that had sugar and powdered creamer among the cut crystal decanters of expensive-looking booze. I sugared the coffee and returned to my seat.

Hutto was placing manila files full of paper on the desk when I turned my attention back to him. "So, I admit I didn't want to believe you at first—that Randall Bogen wasn't dead. It's, well, it's rather unbelievable. His body was pulled from his house, identified by a medical examiner and federal authorities. They don't make these kinds of mistakes."

I sipped coffee, watching him begin to sort the files as he laid out the case. This was probably what he was like in court, laying out the foundations before getting to the juicy stuff.

"So it made me wonder," he continued. "What if it wasn't a mistake? What if they—*knew*—Bogen was alive? What if they made it happen? What if it was a way to get him into witness protection without anyone local being the wiser? And what if Bogen decided to squeeze some of his previous associates and let them know they were going down if they didn't play ball with him? That, I strongly believe, is where your father came in." His voice took on a droning quality, and I found it hard to concentrate as he talked. I was tired, deep-down-to-the-bone tired and having trouble keeping up with the conversation.

"We knew thish ow aredy," I said, horrified at the slur in my words. Man, I must be more tired than I'd thought. I clumsily reached for the coffee and knocked it onto the rug. "Oh! Shorry. M' bad," I apologized to Hutto, mortified at the accident.

He looked back at me, only this time it was as if he had taken off a mask I didn't know he was wearing. The gun he placed on the desk yawned with a languid threat. He smirked at me. "It's quite alright. We'll get you cleaned up."

I tried to run, but my body wouldn't do what I wanted. I tensed in the chair and then slumped back down as the room spun. What the hell? What was happening?

Hutto walked over to me, slapping me hard across the face. My head bobbed and lolled on my shoulder, and I discovered I could no longer move on my own. "Did you like my coffee? I put a little something in it for you."

The world was going dark around the edges, and I was no longer in control of my body. He grabbed me by the throat and pushed. I found myself on the floor, no memory of falling, the patterns on the rug under my cheek dancing and whirling as if alive. Moments after hearing Hutto speaking over the phone in garbled tones, I heard the office door open. The visitor walked into my line of sight wearing paint-splattered coveralls and those Doc Martens.

Randall.

Fucking Randall. My vision began to tunnel to black. Randall wins. People like him always did.

Chapter Twenty-One

Jason

HE LISTENED ON his cell as Rachael went over all the information her expedited FOIA requests had achieved. There were files on the investigation into Zoe's rape, police and fire department reports on what happened out at the farmhouse in Dantzler, as well as Bogen's personnel file. The files were heavily redacted, and there was nothing new to be gleaned.

Finally, they had to accept the fact: they wouldn't find Randall in here. They couldn't even confirm that Randall was in witness protection. Jason was dead on his feet after the eventful night before and couldn't imagine how Zoe was still coherent.

"So it seems likely he was placed in WITSEC, but there won't be any confirmation," Rachael continued. "I don't know where to go next. Simply put, I don't know how to find this guy. How's Zoe?"

She was probably going to be the death of him. "She's holding up, but it's getting harder for her." Not that it was easy for Jason either.

Rachael made sympathetic noises. "Yeah, this has to be really tough for her. God, could you imagine being in the middle of this shit?"

It was a rhetorical question Jason didn't feel compelled to answer. Instead, he turned his attention back to the laptop, and the files. "Fuck, let's go over everything again. From the top, when I found where the stolen phone was."

They went back to the beginning.

AFTER ANOTHER HOUR of rehashing the information they'd compiled, Jason was getting frustrated. There was simply nothing there that could be used to find Randall. He needed a break.

"Hey, Rachael, I'm gonna take a break, check in on Zoe."

"Sure, I'll bang away at this a little more. I'll call you if I find anything."

He got up slowly and carefully stretched, trying to get some of the stiffness out of his joints. He refilled his sweet tea and called Zoe.

No answer. Hutto better have something good for them. Jason was still aggravated with Zoe, but that was secondary to finding the guy trying to kill her. They couldn't fight if she were dead.

The possibility left him cold and shaken. He tried her phone again. Voicemail.

Back to work. He opened a file from Rachael they had picked over and pecked at, but hadn't exhaustively searched. It was two gigs worth of data marked *forensic results, Z. Calder phone.*

The file was the data that had been recovered from the phone after its factory reset. This was the file containing the pictures that turned his stomach and made him angry enough to commit murder. He didn't want to look but forced himself to go through them again, searching for something, anything. He scrolled through, zooming and enhancing.

He learned nothing new, but now he felt slimy and dirty. He opened another document in the file, full of text messages. Here was a private glimpse into the world of Zoe, as she communicated and reached out to friends and took care of her business. Most of the threads were corrupted, so he was unable to follow all the conversations. But this peek into her world washed the slime away, even as he harbored some guilt for pilfering through her past. This was undiluted Zoe, professional at times, upbeat and happy, innocent and even a tad naïve. If ever he forgot why he loved her, he promised himself he would just think back to these texts.

He went through them and smiled, opened the next one, laughed. Opened the next one, and felt the world drop away.

Daddy, why would you do this to me? Lmao! It's done, but interrupted before disposal. Send the cash to MH for the job. Or don't. I'm sure you know what happens if you don't. Hey, justice is blind! Hahaha.

Jason rubbed his face, blinked and reread the text. This had to be from Randall, sending a message to Zoe's father, seemingly believing she was dead. Demanding payment. Jesus.

He called Zoe again. It went to voicemail immediately. A ball of worry started to bloom in his stomach.

He called Rachael, told her about the text.

"Holy fuck," she said after she found the text on her end. "Her father paid for his daughter to be killed? Jesus. Who does that?"

"I don't know. I'm kinda glad he's dead though. Sick bastard." His stomach gnawed at him.

"Wonder who this MH is? He seems to be the boss, or at least the money man. And Jonathan obviously knew who MH was. Mentioning it like that was a bald threat, and an order. Send the cash, or else. Jonathan had to know who MH was for that to be effective."

"*Justice is blind.* What was that about?" Jason wondered aloud.

"Seems odd, given the context, but you know, the guy is a cop. Reckon how many times he said that on the job and laughed to himself?"

"*LMAO*, he said. Laughing my ass off," Jason said, fresh rage rising in his voice. "God, I want to find this asshole so bad. How did this guy keep his job for so long? Surely there was suspicion about him. I mean, this guy is muscle for a network operating the drug trade around here. Wouldn't there be some alarms at some point?"

But there was. Zoe's father had spelled it out, hadn't he? "Oh shit! Rachael, check Bogen's personnel file. Specifically, the time right before Zoe was attacked."

"Hmm, let's see..." she muttered. The clattering of keys came over the phone's speaker. "Ah, here we go. A complaint about two months before the attack. Leroy Brecken. Scumbag arrested for distributing meth near a school zone. Claimed he surrendered, was cuffed, and then peppered and punched and kicked repeatedly before being placed in the car and taken in. Whew, mugshot looks like a methed-out scarecrow went through a cheese grater. There's some prime road rash on his face. Had to go to the hospital later that night, internal bleeding from a broken rib."

"That has to be the one. Let me guess, he recanted?"

"He did. Stated he had taken some LSD that day, was combative, and didn't want to be arrested. Arrest report reads along those lines."

"Hmmm. Any other black marks in the file?"

"Actually, yeah. Another excessive force complaint."

"What was that guy's story?"

"Girl, actually. Terri Brownloe. Arrest warrant served after traffic stop. 2011. Two shots to upper torso after gun was pulled, according to records. She claimed she didn't have a gun, at first; said it was planted. Later stated she had a gun but wasn't intending to use it. Mug shot...oh, hello. Damn, she could be the poster child for one of those faces-of-meth PSA's you see sometimes."

"So, both are obvious junkies, not too much of a leap to assume they had dealings with the network."

"Not much of a leap at all."

Ideas sprouted in his mind, and he clung to their threads of hope. "Wonder what happened to them?"

"Let's check...whoa, okay, Leroy pleaded guilty to a reduced charge of possession, sentenced to jail for three to seven; never made it out. Found in the shower with extra holes and not enough blood. Case is still open. Killer wasn't found, at least not officially."

"Convenient. What about the girl, Terri?"

"Pled to felon in possession of a firearm, served three years before parole. Whereabouts unknown. Currently wanted for violation of her parole. How much you want to bet she's crossed the River Styx?"

Jason listened to Rachael as the ball of worry grew. Why hadn't Zoe finished her meeting yet? What was going on there? This didn't feel right.

"Jason, are you still there?" Rachael asked.

"Yeah, oh, sorry. I'm waiting for Zoe to tell me she is finished with her meeting with ADA Hutto. It's going on two hours. Would've thought she'd be done by now."

"Yeah, no kidding. Isn't this the same guy who stonewalled her initially after she was attacked? Seems a strange turnaround..." she trailed off with an odd note in her voice. "Wait a minute. Hold on. Hutto? That's who she went to see?"

A shiver went down Jason's back as he connected the dots with her. "Yeah...him. Hutto. Malcom. Oh no, god no. Fuck!"

"MH. Malcolm Hutto. Shit! 'Justice is blind.' Son of a bitch!"

"I've got to go get her. Now." Jason jumped up, grabbed the keys for the car, his mind whirring in disbelief.

"Okay, okay. Let's keep our thinking caps on while you drive."

"Yeah, okay. Let me call you back."

Jason ran to Zoe's car, heart racing. He adjusted the seats and mirrors, fumbled with the Bluetooth pairing, finally getting it.

"Okay," he said to Rachael as he sped out of the driveway. "What do I do when I get there? What's my next move?"

"Good question. Finger's crossed she's still in the meeting. Fingers crossed that we're going off half-assed, and MH is someone else. But, Jason, I gotta tell you: Hutto was the prosecutor for both of those cases that involved complaints against Randall. He was the one who made those plea deals. Cock your head a little, squint your eyes, it looks like he could be protecting a dirty cop. Now why would he do that?"

"Because the cop is his muscle. Shit, Rachael, I let her walk straight into the lion's den." His mind repeated a string of fucks—over and over again.

"Beat yourself up later. Let's get to Zoe first." Rachael's tone was calmer but did nothing to ease his panic.

"Okay. Hell, I gotta call Delphine. She needs to know about this."

"Yeah. Do that. But keep in touch. I'll be nosing around some more, see what we can find on Hutto."

Jason ended the call and reached out to Delphine. He relayed the new information as he wove through the traffic that grew more dense as he got closer to the downtown area.

She cursed fluently in Creole as he told her what he and Rachael had discovered. Then she grew quiet. "I should have known this. I should have seen it. How close are you?"

"About ten minutes at this rate. Any advice on what I should do?"

"Play it straight for now, I think. Keep these cards close to the vest. You're just picking her up. Be careful though. I don't think he will mess with you, as it would raise a proper stink. But if he feels threatened, thinks you know things, no telling what happens."

"Right. Jesus, I hope she's not dead." *Don't be dead*, he pleaded with Zoe in his mind. He needed to make up with her.

"Nor I, cher. Best not think such things right now. I'm going to go for now. I have people to call, favors to ask."

She hung up, and Jason drove toward the DA's office.

The building was a large complex that housed the offices for the District Attorney, Health Department, and various other county entities. He walked in, pleased to be recognized by several people and greeted with effusive warmth. If anything should happen, people would remember he was here.

He made his way to the office of Malcolm Hutto. The receptionist, Stacey, greeted Jason with a smile and informed him Hutto was gone for the day.

"Oh, that's okay," Jason said, striving to act cheerful even as panic gripped him. "I'm just here trying to find Zoe Calder. She was meeting with Mr. Hutto. Did you see her?"

"Oh, the cute lady with dark hair? Kinda tall?"

"That would be her."

"Oh yeah! She came in for a meeting right before I left for lunch. They were both gone by the time I got back though. Mr. Hutto was scheduled for a deposition this afternoon and cleared the rest of his calendar. I was just about to call it a day myself. You're lucky you caught me."

Jason fought the terror he felt, working to stay on his feet. Focus, damn it, he chastised himself as he tried to think of something. "Hey," he said as inspiration struck. "She isn't answering her phone. Is it possible she left it here and can't get to it because Mr. Hutto left? Do you think you could check his office?"

"Normally I would say no, but he is actually having some work done in the office tonight, painting and carpet cleaning, that kind of stuff. Which he does pretty often, but I usually have more notice than this. Sprung it on me this morning. There's been a couple of guys back and forth already. Hold on, I'll go take a peek for you. Try calling it while I check."

She left the desk, going into the office. Jason sat impatiently, calling Zoe and trying to clear his head.

Everything Stacey had said just seemed to make things darker and darker. Painting and cleaning with no notice? Workers back and forth already? If he had done something to her there in the office, the evidence would be gone by morning. Once again, the clock ticked in his head, seeming to speed up with every minute that passed. His calls to Zoe's number went straight to voicemail. Her phone was off.

After a moment, Stacey walked out of the office with an apologetic look. "Sorry, no phone. But, I did find an earring in the corner." She held it up to the light. "Is it possible she might have lost it?"

Zoe's earring. He recognized it immediately. She wore it to the funeral, picking it to complement the outfit she'd finally decided on. His heart stuttered, vision tunneling and going dark around the edges.

"Or I could take you to the lost and found." She had started talking again, but Jason was finding it hard to follow the thread. "I mean, I was going to say if the earring is hers, you could save me a trip, but if she's lost her phone—

"Oh, my gosh, sir. Are you okay? You've gone green!"

Jason sat on the couch staring at the earring, feeling his life unravel. He swallowed thickly, bile rising in his throat. "Ma'am, I think I need a restroom. I'm about to be sick."

"Here, here, use the restroom in the office. It's the closest."

He bolted for the bathroom, a small cubicle tiled in baby blue with off-white grouting. He sank to the commode. There for a moment, he caught a whiff of Zoe, so faint it could almost be confused for a memory.

Then he threw up in retching waves as terror washed over him.

RACHAEL HAD CALLED the cops.

Detective John Overstreet was still rumpled and his partner Roxanne Brandley was still mousy, but they were waiting for him in the lobby area when Jason left the restroom. They listened intently as Jason spelled out what they had found, and his fears for Zoe. They shared several private glances as he talked.

When Jason finished the tale, they sat quietly for several moments. Stacey, the receptionist looked dumbfounded.

"Well, hell," Overstreet said on a long exhale. "Right now, we have to find Ms. Calder. But, if there is any evidence in the office, yeah, we need to collect it before any cleaning or painting happens."

"We've been wondering about him for a while," Brandley chimed in. "Nothing concrete, but you hear things from the street. We've also had collars that should've been slam-dunks wriggle out of any meaningful jail time when he was the prosecutor. Still, this is a rather delicate area. We can't just accuse, or really even investigate an ADA, without some sort of legal reason, some probable cause."

"And if they did do anything to Ms. Calder here in the office, how did they get her out?" Overstreet pondered.

It was Stacey who spoke up. "Ah, guys, I can't believe I'm hearing this conversation about my boss. But, if this is true, I think I might know how they did it."

Her statement got everyone's undivided attention. The detectives gestured for her to continue. "Well, just after I got back from lunch, I saw one of the workers removing something. I figured he was preparing for the job tonight, the cleaning and painting. But he had rolled up the big Oriental rug that is usually on the floor in the office. It's a pretty large rug, he had to take it out on a dolly. Do you think she might have been maybe wrapped up in the rug? No, right?"

"Holy hell," Jason said. He felt his brain start working again, thoughts cascading on themselves. If he concentrated on following a trail, maybe it would keep the dread at bay. "They could've. What better way to get her past security and the cameras? Cameras! Can we check the videos? Shouldn't be too hard to find the rug guy, right?"

The security guard was not happy with their request, but the detectives pulled their badges, and he turned to the video feeds and dialed up the time in question. The camera in the corridor nearest Hutto's office showed the back of a tall person with coveralls and baseball cap pushing a dolly with the large Oriental rug secured with bungee straps to it.

"Damn, you're right," Overstreet muttered. "A person could fit in that rug, easy." Then to the security guy, he said, "Can you follow that guy?"

As the countdown ticked louder and faster in Jason's head, they worked with the video feed to follow the coveralls guy. The carpet went into a service elevator and down. From the basement of the offices, the rug progressed to the contractor parking underneath and into a van. It was a newer model Ford Transit van, most likely a rental. Coveralls put the obviously heavy rug into the back and pushed the dolly back toward a receiving area where a couple of others waited. As he parked the dolly, Coveralls happened to look up, the camera catching a split second of a three-quarters profile of his face.

"Freeze that!" Brandley shouted before Jason could. "Back it up to his face. My God, is that—?"

"Randall frickin' Bogen," Overstreet confirmed. "Alright, let's call the cavalry."

Jason watched as the pair swung into action. Overstreet called for forensic techs to go over Hutto's office. Brandley called in an alert for Hutto, Bogen, and the Transit van. She added the license plate information after the security guard found it on camera. It gave him cold comfort to watch them kick-start the search into life, because his heart knew the truth. They were too late.

This wasn't a search and rescue mission.

It was a recovery operation.

Chapter Twenty-Two

Zoe

I WOKE IN the dark, panic jolting me awake. My breathing was shallow and ragged, and something restrained my entire body, cocooning me like a fly just before the spider feasts. I jerked and twisted and fought, but it didn't change anything, didn't create any movement at all. I felt wetness on my cheek, and the smell of cold coffee hit my nose. Somehow, that anchored me to reality. The cold wet coffee. I held my breath, trying to calm myself and slow the hyperventilating. I had to think, damn it! Forcing myself to settle down took a while as I retraced my memories, trying to find where they went dark. I was going to meet with ADA Hutto, who had some evidence to show me. Now I was here. How had that happened? My breathing grew short and fast again. No! Stop that. Think. I had gone to the meeting…and then…?

I was in the chair and drinking coffee and got really tired and fell on the rug.

Coffee. Rug.

It rushed back to me in the space of an eye blink. Spilling the drugged coffee. Hutto's smug face as he grabbed my throat and pushed me over. Randall's entrance. Fade to black.

Now, I was wrapped up tight in that Oriental rug with the spilled coffee against my cheek.

I realized I was moving. Or rather, whatever I was traveling in was. The muffled *bunk kethunk, bunk kethunk* of the vehicle as it moved across an interstate or major highway was unmistakable.

What happens when we stop? I didn't want to think about that.

All I could do was breathe and wait.

Soon, I faintly heard gravel crunching under the tires, and I knew this trip was almost over. I fought the panic with everything in me. The rhythmic bumps of the interstate turned into the music of asphalt, and later, macadam. Apparently, I was being taken to a rural area, and I shuddered at what waited when the van stopped.

At some point during the trip, my bladder had let go, and now the wetness was cold against my legs. I thought of Jason, hating myself for the way I spoke to him and left things before going to meet with Hutto, but happy he wasn't involved. When would he realize I was gone? Would he blame himself? Would they ever find my body? Would he wonder if I ever truly loved him? Despair tinged with bitterness bled into the panic as I waited for the trip to end. *I'm sorry, Jason,* I thought in despair. *I loved you more than I knew I could love anyone. Mom, Jacob, I love you. Delphine, thank you for saving me.*

The truck moved slowly along the gravel, before coming to a stop. The engine shut off, and the sudden silence was horror incarnate. I had not managed so much as an inch of movement within that suffocating cocoon. The muffled sound of a door opening reached me and then another, and suddenly I was sliding backward, falling. I hit the ground outside with a heavy thump, jarred but unharmed due to the rug around me, padding my fall. Squeezing my eyes hard, I willed the tears away and waiting for the final bullet to end things. *At least I don't have to worry about being wrapped in this burrito anymore*, I thought darkly. Helpless, I waited. But the bullet didn't come.

Instead, I felt myself being dragged. First over gravel and then a smoother surface with less friction. Grass, probably. Then steps, and my head banged each one as Randall dragged me up to a level surface. Another small bump and I realized I had crossed a threshold from a porch of some type. The movement stopped, then started again as he shifted the position of the rug. Then all was still. Again, I waited for the inevitable.

After a couple of minutes that felt like hours, I felt myself spinning, tumbling, as my body lurched up and then down. I felt the layers of the cocoon growing lighter, and realized I was being unwrapped. A few moments later, I was free of the rug. I lay sprawled on the floor, eyes shut against the sudden brightness of the world. Jerking, I realized I was still restrained, wrists and ankles bound with duct tape, arms behind me.

I opened my eyes to see Randall towering over me, a side-cocked grin of amusement on his face as he studied me with flat, dead eyes. He had a gun in his right hand, loosely held straight down below his hip. When he was satisfied he had my full attention, he raised the gun, pointing it at my face. The barrel of the gun seemed to grow larger as he held it close to my eyes. Resignation and a flare of anger caused me to look away from the gun, back into those cold eyes. I said nothing, staring at Randall with all the hate and rage I felt for him. With my eyes, I dared him to shoot.

"BANG!" he yelled suddenly. I didn't flinch, and I saw a flicker of uncertainty in his eyes. He covered it up with a loud laugh. "Hah. Nope, not yet. There's someone else coming to the party. But we can have some fun before then, can't we? You remember the fun we had." He cocked his eyebrow in a grotesque parody of flirtation.

I let my eyes slide off Bogen, assessing the room I was in. The stench of the place, the mess—piles of newspapers and shoes and disassembled devices—confirmed where I was. My father's house.

Randall tittered at the confusion on my face. "Yep, dude, this is where it ends for you. Poetic, huh?" He squared his hands in a metaphorical frame. "Headline: 'Catfish tranny whore kills self at site of Daddy's deadly disappointment.' Ha! Probably not; hell, they probably won't even notice. The only reason they ever gave a shit about you and your story was because of me. Hell, faggot, I made you famous! Accusing a cop like that, shee-yit. That was irresistible click-bait to them. And don't lie; you ate it up and loved it. You loved the attention, and I know you loved what I gave you." He had started to strut back and forth in the small area. "But I'm dead now, wink, wink, so nobody is gonna give two farts from a gnat's ass if you felt pitiful and offed yourself at your daddy's place. I mean, everybody knows you fuckers are cuckoo, so it'll be 'Well, what do you expect from a crazy tranny?'"

The fear left me suddenly, and all I could think was *fuck this guy*. "Randall? Either shoot me or beat me, but shut. The fuck. Up! You goddamn shit-pimple on the asshole of—"

Blam! The kick was a casual flick of the ankle, but my head exploded with fireworks. I couldn't defend myself, and I knew there would be more pain soon, but I didn't care anymore. Until he pulled that fucking trigger, I would do anything I could to get under his skin.

He knelt and slapped me three times, quick and precise across both sides of my face, the blows sharp like rifle shots inside my head. "You hit like a girl," I taunted him after my vision cleared from the slaps.

"Fuck you!" he yelled as he balled his fists and rained blows on my face and body. I felt teeth come loose, heard the crunch of cartilage as my nose flattened. He stood and kicked, and I felt ribs crack. Finally, he stopped for breath, huffing at the exertion.

Carving my lips into a gruesome smile, I spit the blood in my mouth at him. "Pussy."

His foot moved, and the world blinked out.

I WOKE TO double vision and a world of hurt. My ears were ringing and every breath felt like a knife sliding into my side. Spitting more blood out of my mouth got Randall's attention. He turned back toward me, lifting the gun in alarm. I laughed out loud, even as my body begged me to stop taunting him. "Marshmallow. Terrified of a girl. Won't even untie me—too scared of li'l ol' me. 'Cause you know even I could take you, pansy little bi—"

He hit me again, and then I couldn't talk because it hurt too much. By this point, his punches and kicks had moved me up against the wall, piles of magazines crumpled and scattered underneath me, their spines digging into my back in odd places. Something more solid wedged in my back. Against my will, I groaned. I shifted position, trying to get comfortable, and also trying to get the solid thing closer to my bound hands.

"This beating is taking forever," I mumbled through swollen lips. "Can't you do anything right?"

He set the gun down and knelt over me, grabbing my shirt and propping my torso against the wall. He pulled me forward and hit me with an uppercut that bounced my head off the wall, then caught my head against his shoulder. He cocked his fist again, and I heard the *bam*, as my head bounced against the wall, and again he caught me against his shoulder. I turned my head slightly the second time as he caught me. The angle forced my face against his neck, and I opened my mouth as wide as I could and bit into him, trying for his throat.

His movements turned panicked, and he made an incoherent noise. He pounded his fists against my head as I felt muscle tear. He wrenched his body, and I felt him pull away from me. Blood poured from the bite as he scrambled for the gun, turning to point it at me, eyes wild as he took aim.

"Randall." The precise inflection came from the front door and stopped him cold. Hutto was here, still in his suit. He glided into the room, eyes darting as he assessed the scene. His face grew annoyed as he saw me, beaten to a pulp and spitting out flesh torn from Randall's neck.

"Jesus, MH," Randall said, clasping his hand over my bite. "Jesus, fucker bit me. Almost got my throat." He stood with his gun pointed at me, clamping his other hand against the wound as blood seeped between his fingers.

"You insufferable twat," Hutto replied. "Do you need a handkerchief?" He reached into the suit pocket on his right side and then smoothly drew a small gun and shot Randall slightly above his right eye. Randall shuddered and fell to his knees and then slumped and, with a wheeze, fell over on his left side, landing on top of my knees, further trapping me. Hutto held the gun on him until it was obvious Randall was dead.

Hutto reached into his inside pocket, and this time he did pull out a handkerchief. He mopped his face as he considered the scene. He shook his head.

"You have been quite the fly in the ointment, my dear. This should not have been the great big deal that it has been." He cocked his head at me. "You were just a job, a hit at the request of a valued customer, with the additional benefit of your old identity.

"He spent a lot of money with us, you know. Your father, I mean. Heroin and then meth. And with him being such an upstanding member of the community? Oh, we were happy to get our hooks in him. Do you have any idea how much money went through that fleabag church out there? Money that went into the books dirty and came back to us clean as, ha, well, clean as a preacher's sheets." Hutto shook his head, trying a sympathetic face.

I listened in horrified detachment to Hutto's monologue, my head throbbing. He probably didn't have many outlets to brag about his accomplishments, so I guessed it made sense he would take the opportunities when they arose. But I knew my fate was sealed. No way he would he be this open unless I would never be able to tell anyone. Thankfully, all the pain Randall had dished out to me would be over soon.

Waiting for the final bullet to come at any moment, my hands found the hard object from earlier and explored it. Large slots with metal inside them finally clued me in that it was a toaster. Well, most of one. I hid my movements with what I hoped looked like attempts to get comfortable.

"Now, one of Randall's little quirks is this weird thing for...the gender fluid, shall we say? Oh, he never let them live, a fact I'm sure is reflected in some of the names spoken during your particular community's Day Of Remembrance in November, but he had a thing all the same. Thus, when Jonathan offered up your identity, it seemed the perfect solution. Nothing wrong with getting paid for your hobby, right? It was your basic business-with-pleasure kind of deal."

There was a sharp edge, probably the gate on the bottom that opens to let the crispy bread crumbs out. Surreptitiously, I began to saw at the duct tape, covering the movements with gasping breaths that lanced hot pokers through me, thanks to my broken ribs. I felt a slight separation in the tape, hoping against all odds I would be able to free my hands before Hutto finished bragging and ended everything.

"That's fine, I guess." Hutto was saying when I tuned back in to his drone, "Everyone has their thing. So you were only supposed to be an amusement for Randall, a lagniappe, if you will, that he would get a new identity and a little folding money for. He set the dating site profile up after finding you on there. Said you were into all sorts of geeky stuff; thought he was so clever with the Arthur Dent thing. It worked, though, didn't it?" He smiled with teeth of a piranha and mopped his face again. I felt more separation in the duct tape around my wrists.

A sniff and he started talking again. "But you know what? I think he fell for you, in his own weird way. He told me what happened, later, after everything turned to shit. Decided not to pull the trigger, so to speak, when you were on your bike. Then, he spent hours talking with you. He never did that before. Told me he almost forgot why he was there. You must be quite the charmer."

"Thanks," I said dryly. "I try."

"Oh, I know sarcasm when I hear it, but it's true. He was my go-to guy before he met you. We spent years building a network, using our careers to muscle out any competition. And that boy was ruthless, I have to say. Just an unstoppable machine. But, as I said, everyone has their thing." He walked over to the window, nudging the slats of the blinds apart with his gun and looking outside. Then he checked his watch. I recognized it as a Patek Phillipe. A subtle reminder of the lucrative nature of his extracurricular activities.

"Would you like to know a secret?" he asked as he let the coat sleeve cover the watch after he was satisfied I had noticed it. "It was you who gave me the idea to kill Randall. I was impressed at how thoroughly you disappeared after his arraignment. I thought it might be best for everyone if he were dead. In a legal sense. It would close an investigation that was getting too close for comfort.

"When reporters and the like start digging around, you never know what might pop up and get them off on a tangent that leads to one's doorstep. That's why I composed and made him send that email the press salivated over. Misdirection, with the added bonus of implicating Randall and making disappearing slightly more palatable. As well, it was an attractive option for me: a phantom taking care of my accounts receivable. Simple. Beautiful. Perfect. So, we set up a plan where he would 'die' during the sheriff's attempt to serve a warrant that I swore out. It was damned annoying you cruised by as we were trying to set everything up. I had to scare you off, you understand?"

I coughed, the hurt covering my entire body. I spit blood on Randall.

He nodded, smiling almost approvingly. "Anyway," he continued, as calm as if we were in a coffee shop. "We booby-trapped the house, shoved an involuntarily deceased derelict from New Orleans in there who was a rough physical match for him, and let him ride everything out in a hole under the house in turnout gear. A little roll out from under the house in the excitement, spray a little water, then a quick walk across the road in the dark where a car came by to pick him up. Presto chango. A little paperwork chicanery so he's officially dead, and viola, I have a mirage doing my dirty work."

So there was never any witness protection. Only an unhinged prosecutor doing dirty business.

The tape separated, and my hands were somewhat free. Now, how to get to the gun just beyond Randall's body slumped over my legs? If I could ignore the pain, it'd all be fine. Far easier said than done. There was no way I could go after the gun, grab it, aim, and end this in a way that left me breathing tomorrow.

"But then he started to obsess about the job that screwed everything for him." Hutto said. "You should have heard him frothing at the mouth about you. *Fucking bitch* this and *cocksucker* that. He blamed you for getting him into the situation he found himself in. It's hard to be dead nowadays, you know? Have to go live in places where they don't know you, keep moving, can't make friends. It was his own fault, of course, but why waste a good hate? Once he made contact with you again, I knew he had to die for real."

Fuck this guy too. I'd had enough. If he didn't shoot me soon, I'd force the issue just to be fucking done with all this droning bullshit.

"We made plans for your demise, but he wanted to put a bow on it," he started pontificating *again,* the asshole, "so I gave him some leeway. I even put the rose in your glove compartment for him at the funeral. He wanted you utterly terrified of him before he got to you." He shook his head with amusement. "So theatrical. He brought up the idea of doing the job at this house because it's empty, isolated, and would give him time for *fun* with you. The thought of another toss with you with your new...ah...plumbing...obsessed him. I told him he could do whatever he wanted, with one caveat: I would be the one to do the wetwork. He thought I just wanted to get my hands a little dirty, or maybe, if he was honest with himself, he thought I didn't trust him to do the job right this time. He didn't realize I was planning my own little scenario. I don't imagine I can do the ADA thing any longer; it was always a matter of time before something fell through. So it seems I am in need of an identity." He gave an ugly chuckle, and angled his head as he considered Randall's body. "Guess I'll die in a housefire with you, and Noah gets away scot-free." He raised the gun to my head, and I knew this was the end of the line. I flung the toaster at him.

I missed.

My arms were numb and refused to cooperate properly. The toaster weakly sailed to the left of him, banging into the wall with an atonal *thong* as he flinched. It then hit a lamp as it rebounded off the wall, knocking it over and causing a mini-avalanche of newspapers and junk. The noise caused him to look over, buying me milliseconds as I scrabbled over Randall for the gun. He turned his attention back to me, firing as he saw what I was desperately reaching for.

He shot too quickly, the first bullet burying itself into Randall's body. The second bullet laid a line of red fire across the back of my left shoulder as it gouged me before hitting the wall. And then I had Randall's gun and was firing back. I fired without thought or aim, pulling the trigger long after the magazine was empty.

I watched Hutto slump to the floor as blue smoke hung hazily in the room, two innocuous holes in his chest oozing red. His bewildered gaze fixed on me for only a moment before glazing over. Slowly, laboriously, I ignored the pain from my ribs and face and the stinging of my back as I desperately worked to slide my still duct-taped legs free from under Randall's corpse. Before I could get free, the sound of tires on the gravel outside reached me through the ringing in my ears. What fresh hell was this? Hutto's gun was tantalizingly close but might as well have been on Mars, considering my ability to get to it in time.

Within seconds, the room was swarming with heavily armed men intent on protecting and serving. *Too late*, I thought hysterically. *I did it myself.*

They secured the room in moments, and one of the guys gingerly scooped me up and brought me outside. He gently laid me on the ground and cut the tape off my ankles as the ambulance arrived. The EMTs checked me over before putting me on the stretcher. Every part of me hurt, but I held back the tears as I answered questions from cops and EMTs in a monotone, still waiting for that final bullet to put an end to all of this nonsense.

Jason, riding hot with the two detectives I still disliked, screeched into the yard about ten minutes later, just as they were about to close the doors on the ambulance and take me to the hospital.

When he saw me, saw that I was alive, his face dissolved into pure relief, happiness, and unalloyed love. My heart melted. I was such an idiot.

He pushed the medics away and jumped into the ambulance. "Oh, thank Jesus! You're still alive," he said as he smothered me in a hug that brought a yelp from me. "Oh my god, baby. Look what he did to you."

"How? How are you here?" I said when the pain let me talk again.

Jason told the story quickly, starting from the texts from my phone to my father. "And when we realized the van had a LoJack tracker, we were able to figure out where he had taken you. Called the local guys as soon as we knew." He touched me in places that didn't hurt as he talked, as if to convince himself I was really still alive. "God, I was sure we were too late. I made Brandley and Overstreet drive like maniacs with lights and sirens to get me here." He made to kiss me but stopped himself when he remembered what kind of condition my lips were in.

Grabbing the back of his neck before he could retreat, I pulled him to me for a kiss, not caring that it made my face feel like it was on fire. I kissed him desperately, holding him like a drowning person holds a life ring. Jason kissed me back, just as desperately, and I never wanted this moment to end.

I had been through hell; everything hurt, and Randall had turned my face into high-end hamburger. But holding Jason in that moment, feeling his passion as he answered my own, I felt more powerful—and more beautiful—than ever before.

Epilogue

THE SOUND OF compressors humming and hammers pounding greeted us as we got out of the car. Delphine and I were stuffed full from mimosas and excessive amounts of eggs from brunch, having spent the last three hours indulging as we conspired. We decided afterward to see how our home was progressing, considering it was being rebuilt from scratch. Her home, I mean. It was the first place since I was kicked out at sixteen that truly felt like a home should, but it was Delphine's house, inherited from her grandfather. My home now was where Jason was.

New studs stood in a familiar design, skeletal, but enough to see what they were working toward. "You're rebuilding it exactly the same, aren't you?" I asked Del.

"Oui, cher. Is home I want, and what I will have again." She noted the approach of a sturdy man wearing a flannel shirt and Red Wing boots. "Thanks to our Captain Merone."

"Delphine," he said warmly, "please, call me Billy. It's these yahoos mangling the yellow pine over there gotta call me Captain." His chuckle was infectious as right on cue a "Fuck!" was roared and followed by a clattering sound of wood hitting the deck.

"Gentlemen!" He turned up his own volume, marching toward the work area. "We have ladies here."

"Sorry, Cap!" came the sheepish reply.

"Ooh, it's a lady," a voice said behind me, and the grin was automatic as I spun around to see Jason. He was wearing jeans with a nicely taut T-shirt and a tool belt slung low around his hips.

"Well, look at you," I said, making sure he knew that's exactly what I was doing. Trying to raise my eyebrow in place of a wolf whistle made the bandages on my nose itch. My face was healing from the recent reconstructive surgery to repair the damage, and sometimes all I wanted to do was yank the bandages off and just scratch the skin. Even for a second, it would be heaven. Jason read my frustration and gave me a sympathetic nod. He knew exactly what I was going through.

"Oh, there he is," Billy said with faux gruffness. "Son, don't you have half a job to do somewhere?" I heard a guffaw from one of the other workers. Yep, firefighters were firefighters, even at their other jobs.

On his days off, Billy ran a construction crew staffed to varying degrees by other firefighters. The fire here, and Jason's connections, ensured a full and rowdy group of Biloxi's bravest descended upon Delphine's home with gusto. Even with them going back to the firehouse every third day, Delphine would be back home sooner than expected.

She wandered off to take in the progress, and with a nod and a "ma'am" to me, Billy stepped away to lead her on a tour. That left me alone with Jason, and his insouciant lean against one of the studs had me thinking purely carnal thoughts. "Babe," he purred at me, and I knew he had the same idea. He waved his arm around at the bones of the house-to-be. "What do you think?"

"It's the same as the old house. Which I love and shouldn't be surprised at."

"It'll be the same from the slab to the gable. Delphine found the original plans archived at the Historic Commission."

"Oh my God. She didn't say a word to me about it. When it's done, it'll look just like when her grandfather first finished it." I stared at the foundation in wonder. It would be magnificent to see it restored.

"That's the plan. There are a lot of people hustling to make it happen."

"I see that," I said, then remembered why Delphine and I had stopped by in the first place. "Oh! We brought some refreshments for y'all. Everyone's over twenty-one, right?"

"Ah, you do know the quickest way to our hearts," he said, standing up straight. Considering the stud he had been leaning against, he knocked against it with the edge of his hand, rubbing it almost lovingly. "You know, this has me wondering... What if we... What about getting a house? You know, just for us? A place with a backyard where dogs could run around, maybe a swing set for ah...future additions."

My God, I loved this man. I loved *us*. My "yes, I'd love that" was muffled because my head was against his chest as I quickly stepped over and into his arms, smelling the sheen of sweat he'd worked up and liking that too. The hoots and hollers raised as we kissed reminded us we were, in fact, on a construction site, no matter how friendly the crew.

As we walked to the car to retrieve the cases of beer, I told him my news. The reason I wanted to meet with Delphine in the first place.

"Babe, that's great," he said as he grabbed a case. "But why didn't you tell me you were thinking about this?"

"I didn't want you trying to talk me out of it or helpfully interfering in that way you have. I wanted to do this on my own." Grabbing the other two cases, we walked back into the work zone where Delphine stood with Billy. The beer was soon spotted by the crew, their instant excitement contagious.

"Gather around, fellas," Billy had obviously been briefed by Delphine on their tour. "The lady of the house wants to express some well wishes."

They assembled together quickly, and Jason and I schlepped cans still chilled from their cold storage into grateful hands as Delphine spoke. "In April of 1966, a young carpenter by the name of Moses Roulet began building a house for his bride. It took him two years to fully complete, using the spare moments he had from his employment. He drove every nail and set every shingle with love and a determined wish for this place to be truly a home for his family.

"I see him now, reflected in each one of you: using spare time so that I might once again have the home I love. My heart is overwhelmed, and I claim you now as family. Thank you all." As she finished, raw emotion making her voice tremble at the end, the guys lifted their cans to her, cheering lustily.

"Guys, I have news," Jason said after a few moments and a couple of sips. "My girl told me just now. She's been accepted into the academy. She's gonna be a cop!" The cheers were every bit as enthusiastic as before, and I could only blush at the attention and congratulations. *I love you,* I mouthed at Jason, and his wink in return made me flutter.

"Well, in light of all this celebration," Billy said, "It's clear there won't be much more work accomplished today.

At Ms. Roulet's suggestion, we're gonna suspend operations for the day. With pay." The cheers at this were the loudest of all. Somewhere in a corner, a jobsite radio's volume was cranked up, and the impromptu party was on.

Delphine caught my eye, cocking her head toward Jason. I smiled, catching her meaning. "Hey, Jason, you big stud," I said as I bumped his hip, "take me to bed or lose me forever." It felt oddly appropriate to borrow lines from the favorite movie of the friend he had lost in the event that had somehow led to this happily ever after.

His faraway smile was bittersweet at Dave's memory, the quick tears in his eyes glinting in the sun. He raised his beer to the sky in salute to his fallen brother, then drained it and looked at me with so much love my heart couldn't hold it all.

"Show me the way home, honey."

Author's Note

Although many of the cities named in this novel are real Mississippi locales, this *is* a work of fiction and is not meant to reflect in any way on the wonderful people who live and work there.

Acknowledgements

Book writing is a team sport, and I wish you guys knew how amazing my team is. KT Hanna, Jami Nord, and Owen Littman from Chimera Editing really brought out the story, and BJ from NineStar Press made it shine. Thanks so much, y'all!

Huge thank-yous go out to A.B Ledger for her critique skills, and to Cliff and Valerie Frazee for letting me crash at their home while I finished this book over a long Thanksgiving Holiday.

And finally, my biggest thanks go out to Mel: you were the first reader of this story, and this would not have happened without you demanding more chapters. Thank you so much.

About the Author

Jessi Noelle was born in South Mississippi, where she worked as a lifeguard, a zookeeper, and a professional firefighter (although not at the same time). She is transgender with two sons, and currently lives in Nashville, TN, with her fiancé and a cat named Dingo.

Through the Inferno is her first novel. She is an alum of the inaugural #DVPit, a Twitter event where marginalized authors pitch their books to agents. She is currently working on another book set in the Inferno universe.

Twitter: @jessigibs

Other books by this author

Pulse of My Heart (Coming November 2019)

Also Available from NineStar Press

Connect with NineStar Press

www.ninestarpress.com

www.facebook.com/ninestarpress

www.facebook.com/groups/NineStarNiche

www.twitter.com/ninestarpress

www.tumblr.com/blog/ninestarpress